The Man Whose Dreams Came True

Tony Scott-Williams had dreams—after all, which of us doesn't dream sometimes, about winning the pools or inheriting a fortune from an unknown relative? But Tony (born Jones, a name which he had rejected) ran into trouble when he tried to put his dreams into practice There were three dreams. First, marrying a rich woman, who would give him a free hand with her money; second, winning a fortune at roulette; third, spending the rest of his life in a foreign country in the company of glamorous girls.

To make his dreams come true Tony gambled, forged, and was led finally to murder. Everything he did went slightly wrong, and to his astonishment he found himself in the dock. Yet in the end Tony's dreams did come true, although the results were far from those he would have chosen.

There is no more distinguished name in the whole field of crime fiction to-day than that of Julian Symons. Here is a novel, brilliantly plotted, cunningly told and often bitterly funny, that will bring pleasure to the legions who have acquired a taste for Mr. Symons's novels, among which *Progress of a Crime* and *The Man Who Killed Himself* will be well remembered.

JULIAN SYMONS

The Man Whose Dreams Came True

PUBLISHED FOR
The Crime Club
BY COLLINS, ST JAMES'S PLACE, LONDON
1968

Contents

PART ONE

Misfortunes of a Young Man

ONE

When the alarm bell rang Anthony Scott-Williams lay quite still and let the warm sun of Siena seep through his eyelids.

The day stretched out in front of him, an endless tape on which he would print the pleasures of eye and ear. He would rise and dress leisurely, leave the small hotel and go out into the whisky-coloured town not yet noisy with cars and scooters. Coffee and croissants on the pavement outside a small café and then the morning walk which would include perhaps the Duomo with its historical figures set in the marble that covered the whole floor of the church like an immense carpet. After the Duomo perhaps the Pinacoteca Nazionale, home of the Sienese painters, perhaps simply a random walk through the narrow streets, soaking up sun without bothering about churches or art galleries. In any case by midday he would be sitting in the Piazza del Campo, that wonderful shell-shaped open space, looking at the hard elegance of the Palazzo Pubblico, drinking the first apéritif of the day and letting the liquid Italian speech flow over him.

He yawned and opened his eyes. Siena disappeared, but he retained it for a few moments more by looking at the guidebook beside the bed. Had he placed the Palazzo Pubblico properly? Yes, here it was: "The Public Building, now used as Town Hall, is erected in the Piazza del Campo, a proud specimen of Middle Age architecture . . ." And so on. Would he really have visited the Duomo, might he have been bored? In any case he was not in Siena but in Kent, and it was time to get up.

A look round the bedroom usually gave him pleasure.

9

The Morris wallpaper—oh yes, he knew that it was Morris —with its great splashy purple flowers and delicate biscuit-coloured background, the dressing-table with silver hair brushes set out on it, the plain pile carpet, the comfortable bed in which he lay with its polished brass rails, and best of all the door leading to the green and black tiled elegance of the bathroom, really, what more could one want? And then to pad across the spongy carpet in bare feet as he did now, turn on the shower and adjust it so that the water was at just the right temperature, expose oneself to the hot water and end with the sharp ecstasy of the cold, all these were undeniably pleasures. He told himself so as he looked in the glass after shaving. "You're a clever boy," he said. "But you're lucky too." He stuck out a tongue which was revealed as perfectly pink. The glass showed him a leanly handsome face, yet one by no means cadaverous. Good teeth, a wide sensitive mouth, none of your nasty little rosebuds, a straight small nose, yes, he really congratulated himself on his face.

It was certainly a cushy billet. The drawn curtains revealed the long lawn, the pond beyond it and past the pond a glimpse of cattle grazing, the grass shining wetly under weak April sunlight, it was all quite perfect in its way even though it was just a tiny bit boring. He dressed with care—not that he ever dressed carelessly—in a light weight grey suit with just a hint of tweediness about it, and went down to breakfast. A dish over a hotplate revealed poached haddock when he lifted the lid, coffee bubbled faintly over another hotplate, the toast was crisp outside and soft within. Something was added to his pleasure by the knowledge that the fish knife and fork were Georgian silver.

Beside the plate lay the post, three envelopes addressed to the General. He slit the envelopes with a paper knife. An account from a builder for dealing with the dry rot in the attic, a request from the local branch of the British Legion for the General to give away the prizes at their yearly fête, and a letter from Colonel Hasty with whom he had been conducting a long correspondence on the General's behalf about the movement of tanks in the Western Desert in June 1941. He skimmed through the letter, which contained mostly military information. It ended: "Re my suggested visit, my dear old Bongo, nothing would give me greater pleasure than to see you again and have a natter. It so happens I shall be down your way Wednesday the 21st, will you let me know if this suits you and at what time." A twinge of uneasiness touched him like a momentary toothache, but he ignored it. Why shouldn't the old man have a natter with a friend? After breakfast he rang the little silver handbell on the table, and Doris came in.

She was one of two daily girls from the village who did the chores and lent a hand to Mrs. Causley, the cook-housekeeper. Both girls were on the plump side for his taste, but he felt sure that Doris was ready for anything he cared to suggest. This sensibility to a woman's feelings was one of the things upon which Tony prided himself. He couldn't have said exactly how he knew, by a glance, a laugh, even a smell, but he always did know when a woman was ripe for love. It would be a mistake to do anything about Doris, who had a clodhopping boy-friend in the village, but he couldn't resist a smile that brought a smile back, like a return of service at tennis.

"Well, Doris, what news?"

"Mrs. Causley's just taken up his tray."

Everything was as it should be, but that early morning glimpse of Siena had unsettled him. He was really not prepared to cope with one of the old man's moods, and he saw as soon as he entered the bedroom that the General was in a mood this morning. The breakfast tray had been pushed aside almost untouched and he was slumped in bed, his fine white hair unbrushed, the corners of his mouth turned down.

"How are we this morning?"

"Don't know what you mean, *we*. *I* am not very well, I had a bad night. My back." The glare from under his brows might have terrified once. Now it asked for sympathy.

The *we* had been a mistake, too much like a male nurse, but what an irritable old thing he was. For that matter, he thought as he patted the pillows and eased the thin body up on to them and held the glass while the General used the brush painfully with rheumaticky hands, and gently massaged the area between the shoulder blades where the old man said he felt pain, for that matter he was a bit of a male nurse at times.

"That woman will have to go. D'ye call that a three and a half minute egg?" Tony looked at the top of the offending egg and made a clucking sound. "Can't think why you don't see it. She drinks." The remark seemed to call for no reply. "Don't know why I have these pains. I know, I know, Moore says it's muscular rheumatism. Moore's a fool."

"What about getting up? Shall I help you?"

The old man looked up at him. "You've no idea what it's like to be awake all night. I think about Miriam. Things were different then, I sometimes think my own life ended when she died."

Miriam, the General's wife, had died five years ago, long before Tony had come on to the scene. A photograph of her, aristocratic and disdainful, stood beside the bed and the General kissed it each night before he went to sleep. He sometimes wondered whether he would have got on with Miriam. Certainly he admired her flair for interior decoration as shown in his bedroom, in the striped wallpaper and chairs of the drawing-room and even the peacock blue walls and very pale blue carpet of this bedroom. But would they have found each other sympathetic? Looking at the jutting jaw he thought not.

"Shall I give you a hand with dressing?"

"Not a bloody invalid yet. Sorry, didn't mean to snap." The knobbly hand touched his own for a moment. Filthy old devil, Tony thought, I know what you're like, Miriam or no Miriam, soldiers are all the same. "You're good to me." The chalky fingers touched his again.

"You might like to see this."

The General read Hasty's letter and began to snort like a horse. "The man's a lunatic, a bloody imbecile. Look at this. He's got the audacity to say here, 'I had the impression at the time that we were unprepared for the speed with which Jerry moved his armour. Anyway, it caught us on the hop.' I told you Hasty was an idiot, didn't I?"

"Do you want to see him? You see he's coming down this way to-morrow."

"See him? I should think I do. I'll rub his nose in it, I'll rub Ted Hasty's nose in it. Call him up and ask him to lunch."

"There are a couple of other letters, one asking you to open a British Legion fête."

The General had been bouncing up and down in the bed. He stopped suddenly. "Can't do it. Not well enough, no time anyway."

"And here's Clinker's account."

The General examined it through a pair of rimless pince-nez. "Hell of a lot of money, should have got an estimate."

"If you remember he said he couldn't give one, couldn't tell how much work there was until he opened up the timbers."

"It's robbery, but make out a cheque and I'll sign it. Later. And get out all the Western Desert papers, I want

13

to go through them. I shall have something to say to Ted Hasty about the use of armour. Don't forget to call him up."

Tony did so half an hour later. A surprisingly quiet and cool voice (surprisingly because "Ted Hasty" conjured up a choleric personality) said that he would be down at about twelve-thirty and sent kindest regards to Bongo.

TWO

Tony had been at Leathersley House for just over twelve months. He had answered an advertisement in *The Times*, come down by train and been engaged on the spot. The General had barely glanced at the letter from Sir Archibald Graveney, written from Throgmorton Hall, Glos. "Don't worry about that stuff. I judge by what I see, Scott-Williams. No relation of Scotty Scott-Williams, I suppose, in my class at Sandhurst?"

"I'm afraid not." He had been appealingly frank. "My father's name was Williams. He died when I was three, gold mining out in Australia, and my mother married a man named Scott. Then she left her husband and called herself Scott-Williams."

"Brought up among the Anzacs, were you? Can't say I hear the accent."

"We left when I was ten, came back to England. My mother inherited a little bit of money, just enough to keep us going but not to give me an education, if you know what I mean, sir." He had practised his smile in the mirror, and it did not fail him now.

"Play billiards?"

"A little."

There was a pause. "Job's yours if you want it," the

General said, and told him about it. He lived alone, looked after by a housekeeper. He was writing his memoirs and his secretary's prime task would be to work on them, but he would also deal with correspondence and help to look after affairs generally. Tony gathered that there had been a succession of secretaries who had been sacked because they were lazy or had left because they were bored. The pay was not high but the job seemed to have possibilities, and he took it.

Leathersley House was small as the Victorians counted size, but absurdly large for a single man. It had eight bedrooms, half of which were shut up, a billiards room and a library. The house had been constructed in the middle of the nineteenth century to solid Victorian ideas of space and seclusion. There were more than three hundred acres of land, most of them taken up by two farms which were let, and looking after affairs meant visiting the farmers once a week, talking to their wives and patting their children on the head. Most of the correspondence was from ex-servicemen's clubs and societies in which the General took only an intermittent interest, and Tony soon learned that he was expected to deal with most of it himself. He was expected also to check over the accounts that Mrs. Adams the housekeeper brought him every month. But the essence of the job—and this no doubt had been the downfall of other secretaries—lay in the General's billiards and his memoirs.

Like some motor cars the General was a slow starter in the morning, when his rheumatism was at its worst. He would soak some of the pain from his joints with a hot bath, be moving with comparative ease by midday, and in the afternoon was ready for work on his memoirs. These existed in various forms, housed in two large grey filing cabinets which stood in the gloomy library, a room untouched by Miriam's restorative hand. There was a typescript of the book's first half which was several years old, there were revisions of it made over the year, there were bits of many chapters in the second half of the book, there were several thousand notes which had been filed in boxes by other secretaries. Most of the book was concerned with the General's (he had been a Brigadier then) command of an armoured column in the Western Desert, and his replacement and relegation to a home command after the disastrous failure of Operation Battleaxe in June, 1941. What precisely had happened, why were both official and independent histories so inaccurate, where did responsibility really lie for errors wrongly attributed to the General? It was such questions that the memoirs set out to answer, and the secretary's task was that of blending all the notes into a harmonious whole. Or at least that was his nominal task for in fact, as Tony soon realised, the memoirs would never be completed. The General revised notes, elaborated incidents, re-read histories of the desert war and dictated furious refutations of passages that concerned him. These sessions gave him great emotional satisfaction. His blue eyes would blaze, his white hair become pleasingly disordered, he strode up and down the library thundering denunciations of G.H.Q. and individual commanders. The resultant typescript took its place among all the other notes and fragments of chapters.

In the evenings after dinner they played billiards. The flexibility of the General's fingers had by now greatly increased, so that he could make a bridge with comfort, and his movements which in the morning were jerky as a puppet's had become smooth and easy. He was a poor player, and Tony had to play with some care to make sure that he sometimes lost a game without seeming to throw it away. The General liked a close finish and when he won by only a few points would say : "Nerve, that's what you need. You're a good player, Tony, but in the last stretch you lose your nerve." They generally played three games, then spread the cloth carefully over the green baize, had a nightcap and went to bed. There was a companionship about it that delighted the old man. "I enjoyed that," he would say after a close finish. "A damned near run thing, as the Duke of Wellington would have said." It was during a game of billiards that he became Tony instead of Scott-Williams.

The life was boring, but the situation might have been designed for him. Mrs. Adams made it clear at once that she would tolerate no interference with her handling of the household accounts, and within a month he had persuaded the General to get rid of her. She had been followed by other cook-housekeepers, of whom Mrs. Causley was the most amenable. She took no interest in the household accounts, and indeed could hardly add up. After Mrs. Adams's departure Tony kept the ledger in which bills were entered with scrupulous accuracy and insisted on showing them to the General until one day the old man waved them irritably away and said he never wanted to see them again. After this Tony arranged what he thought of as his commission. He changed the butcher and came to an understanding with another local man, who put in bills for steaks and chickens that never appeared at Leathersley House, in exchange for a percentage of the proceeds. He was able to make a similar arrangement with the local garage who serviced the General's Jaguar, which turned out to need a good deal more attention than it had received in the past. The invoices were rendered, Tony drew the cheques and the General signed them. It proved impossible to do the same thing with the grocer, and Tony shopped personally for groceries, adding his commission to the cost. He was at times inclined to resent the pettiness of all this, but the builders' work had provided an opportunity of which he had taken full advantage.

The cheque signed by the General for Clinker included a hundred pounds for Tony. He would take the cheque to Clinker to-night and collect the money.

Yet there were periods of discontent, and this fine April morning was one of them. Retyping "Off to the Western Desert," which contained an account of the General's feelings on learning that his only son, a fighter pilot, had been shot down and killed, the vision of Siena—at other times it was Florence, Monte Carlo, the French Riviera— became increasingly strong. When would he get away? A few pounds here, a few pounds there, even the money from Clinker, what did it amount to? He had occasional fantasies of forging the General's name to a really size-able cheque. He had practised copying the signature, simply for the fun of it as he told himself, but of course had never done anything about it. On this morning he contemplated, as he had done before, the rich opportunity that lay under his hand if he dared to use it. One of the first jobs he had done after coming to Leathersley was clearing out the contents of a lumber room. The tin trunks and suitcases were mostly filled with ancient movement orders, menus of regimental dinners and copies of unin-telligible or uninteresting army memoranda. He turned it all over quickly, and then his attention was caught by some letters from Miriam which he put aside for possible use in the memoirs. Beneath them was a thick sealed envelope which he opened. It contained more letters ad-dressed to "My dearest G" or "My own darling G" (the General's name was Geoffrey). They were love letters, signed "Bobo," and he had read two of them through before he realised that they were addressed by one man to another. Some of them made the nature of G's rela-tionship with Bobo absolutely plain.

He had shown the General the letters from Miriam, thrown out the rest of the stuff, and kept the Bobo letters in their envelope, locked up in the chest of drawers in his room. He had a vision of himself confronting the General with them and asking for some really substantial sum, say a thousand pounds, which would be more money than he had possessed at any one time. With all that money in his wallet he would go to the south of France, stay in a good hotel, meet a rich woman older than himself who fell in love with his looks, marry her and live in luxury ever after.

But he knew all this to be a dream. It would be blackmail, and he had never blackmailed anybody. And the dream conflicted with another, entirely different, in which the General's obvious liking for him was translated into practical benefits. In this vision he took the place of the long dead son and a will was made in his favour. But this meant staying for some years, since the General was only in his early seventies and seemed healthy, apart from the arthritis. "You've got to do something about it," he would tell himself, and the fact that he did nothing increased his irritation. He found it hard to work on the dreary old memoirs that day, and when the General mentioned billiards gave a reminder that this was one of his free evenings.

"Shan't be having our game to-night, then." He would have been annoyed had the old man asked him to stay, but somehow it was almost equally annoying that he simply said, "Have a good time."

"Is it all right if I take the Jag?" There was another car, a rather ancient Morris, which he used for shopping. The General looked at him from under thick white brows, then nodded.

THREE

Gravel crunching under tyres on the drive, speed on the road moving up effortlessly to seventy at the touch of his foot—he felt exhilarated always behind the wheel of a car. "There goes a lucky one," people would say to each other as he passed. "Young, handsome, well-dressed, big car, yes, he's got it made." The sense of exhilaration grew, he wondered why he had been low-spirited. After all, he was about to profit from the Clinker coup, and surely it was not beyond his ingenuity to find some new ways of obtaining commissions? He felt extremely cheerful when he drew up at Clinker's yard which was on the edge of Landford, ten miles away.

The builder was in his office. He was a dark squat morose man with a powerful sweaty smell about him. He took the cheque, looked at it, then put it in a drawer.

"You'll send a receipt. Got to keep the books in order." He was aware that his jocosity sounded uneasy. He was slightly afraid of Clinker.

"I'll send it."

"Then there's just the question of settling up."

A pause. Was there going to be trouble? Clinker slowly lifted his black head, looked ruminatively at Tony, then went to a safe and unlocked it. A cash box inside was filled with notes. He counted, keeping his back to Tony, put the cash box back in the safe, relocked it, thrust the bundle of notes forward.

Tony counted. They were one pound notes and there were fifty of them. "This isn't right."

Clinker was at his desk, short powerful legs thrust out in front of him. "How's that?"

"It's not what we agreed. A hundred."

"That's right. Fifty each."

"No no." The injustice of it overcame him, his voice rose. "A hundred for *me*. You—I arranged it so that you didn't even have to give an estimate. You could put in any price you liked."

"It was steep enough. Couldn't make it any more."

"I want a hundred."

"That's all you get." The builder rose and came near him, measuring his own squatness against Tony's height. "Not bad for doing nothing."

"I'll see you're not employed again."

Clinker laughed in his face. He stuffed the notes awkwardly into his pocket and retreated. As he drove away he saw the man standing in his office doorway, grinning.

Landford was a town without many attractions. There were two cinemas, eight churches and twenty-seven pubs. It had once been a market town and there was still a Thursday market, but the town lived now on industries brought down from London, canning factories, bicycle manufacturers, a steel pressing firm. Londoners had come to live there and complained that there was nothing to do, the place was dead. It was designated as an overspill town, and the council after long discussion had permitted the opening of a ten pin bowling alley with a casino attached to it. He paused before the entrance to the Golden Sovereign, then walked quickly past. Farther down the High Street a fascia said *Allways Travel*. When he pushed open the door, still smarting from the Clinker humiliation, it was like putting salve on a burn.

A poster inside showed a gondola, a bridge, water, beneath them the word Venezia. The maps, France, Spain, Greece, Italy, made him glow inside as if he had been drinking. Two girls sat behind a horseshoe desk, deep in train times and air connections. He waited his turn impatiently. One of the girls looked at him with a mechanical smile. He had been in here before.

"I'm interested in Italy."

"Any particular area? What time of year?"

"I'd thought of Venice." She reached for a folder. "But Venice in September, that's when I'd be going, I mean, will the season be over?"

"Our last Venice holiday, 837 B, starts on the sixteenth."

"A package tour." He laughed easily. "I don't want that. An individual holiday is so much more—well, agreeable, isn't it? The thing is, is late September quite the time for Venice?"

"If you're going on an individual flight you can go any time."

"Yes, I know, but that's not quite what I meant. The canals are liquid history, but they do smell, don't they?" He gave her a confidential smile showing—he glimpsed the glass on the wall behind her—his beautiful teeth. The smile was boyish, it would always be boyish. "So I did wonder about Athens."

"Individual flight again?"

She was the dullest of girls. "I'd never think of anything else."

"Here's the folder."

"Thank you. What hotel would you recommend? I stayed at the George the Fifth last time, but perhaps I might make a change."

She goggled at him. "Hotel list inside. Did you want to make a booking?"

It was almost as if she did not take him seriously. He spun the conversation out for another couple of minutes and left when the man behind him began to mutter about people who couldn't make up their minds. It had not, after all, been very satisfactory.

Later, sitting in the American Bar of Landford's best hotel, he became convinced that Fiona Mallory would not turn up. She was something different from the usual run of his girls, the daughter of a business tycoon with a house outside the town and a flat in London (Tony had looked him up in *Who's Who*), and at their only other meeting she had seemed obviously keen on him. He had met her in the Golden Sovereign, where she had watched him playing on his final disastrous visit, and as she told him afterwards had admired the calmness with which he faced a losing streak. Later they had had a drink together and he had taken her back to Frankfort Manor in the Jag, dropping her in the drive. She represented an agreeable variation on the vision in which he married a rich woman, in the sense that she was younger than he and had the wealth of Mallory Textiles behind her. But obviously she was not going to turn up.

He was sipping his second Manhattan when she said, "Sorry I'm late. Daddy dropped me off on his way to London and he kept dithering about. I thought we'd never get away."

She was a tall slender girl with a good figure and a long, slightly horsy face. Dark glasses with jewelled frames concealed her eyes. Her blue dress had obviously cost a lot of money.

"I've kept you waiting *hours*. I hope you're not getting sloshed."

"Only been here a few minutes. Hell of a lot of traffic coming down."

"You've not driven down specially?"

"When I make a date with a beautiful girl I keep it." He smiled. "What are you hiding?"

"How do you mean?"

"The glasses."

"They're a thing I've got at the moment. You don't mind?"

"They add a touch of mystery," he said, although in fact it made him feel uncomfortable to talk to somebody whose eyes were invisible. "Anyway I had to come down to see my aged uncle."

"Oh yes, the General. You told me about him. How is he?"

"Just about the same, one foot in the grave and the other in the Western Desert. I shall stay there to-night, combining pleasure with duty. Shall we eat? The roast duck with orange is rather good, or they grill a steak quite decently." He had looked up the place in the *Good Food Guide*. "Of course it's not London."

"If you ask me this place is just about the end, I can't think why daddy likes being here. He's divorced, you know that?"

"Yes."

"The bore is he wants me down here too. I'm useful as a sort of hostess cum housekeeper."

"And you always do what he tells you?"

The dark glasses were enigmatic. "Almost always. I'm a dutiful daughter. But I hope he'll get married again soon, then I'll be free."

Throughout dinner he was bothered by the glasses, which made him feel as if he was naked while she remained fully clothed. But still he seemed to be keeping his end up. It was lucky that she went to London very little, and to theatres and cinemas hardly at all, so that he did not have to admit his own ignorance of current plays. He talked vaguely about the firm of stockbrokers in which he worked and in more detail about his clubs and the famous people to be met in them. These were stories he had told before, with a few variations, and they came easily enough. Her own life was humdrum, friends of her father's to dinner always at weekends and sometimes in the week, a few stuffy dances with dreary local escorts. She wanted to get a job in London but her father wouldn't hear of it, or not at the moment anyway. It would be different if he got married again.

She pushed aside the food, at which she had only picked although she said it was delicious, and said suddenly, "Would you like to come back for coffee?"

"Back?" For a moment he did not understand.

"Home. Where I live."

"It's those glasses. They confuse me, I wish you'd take them off."

"All right." Her eyes were a shallow blue. She put the glasses carefully into a case.

"That's better. I felt as though everything I said was bouncing back at me. Yes, I'd love that."

Driving back through the lonely country lanes, the situation became real to him. They were married and Mallory had given them the house as a wedding present. They had been driving round Europe on their honeymoon and now they were returning. Fiona was fully provided for, and there was no question of working or of having to worry about money ever again. He placed a hand on her knee.

She took it off. "I don't like one handed drivers."

Why did she have to spoil it? But five minutes later this annoyance was forgotten as they went past the entrance gates, up the long drive, skirted the servants' quarters and entered the house. How could he ever have thought Leathersley House impressive? This was the real thing, an entrance hall with big brown pictures on the walls and lots of furniture that was obviously old and valuable. A great staircase led out of the hall, of the kind he had only seen in films when the ambassador received at the top of it, and she led him into a drawing-room so big that if you put it jokingly you might say it was hard to see from one end to the other. This too was full of pictures and, yes, he could hardly believe it, but there was actually a marble statue at the other end of the room.

He nodded approvingly. "Is that your father?" He pointed to a big head and shoulders. The man who looked out of the frame was tight lipped, unsmiling.

"Yes. You are clever."

"I thought I recognised him."

"Everyone's gone to bed." For a moment she looked directly at him with her blue shallow eyes. "I'll make coffee."

"I don't want coffee." He took one step forward, held her in a powerful grip. She nibbled his ear and murmured something. "What's that?"

"My room's upstairs."

He would have liked to see the upper part of the house, but the thought of the magnificent staircase intimidated him. He led her towards a sofa that was bigger than most beds. "We'll stay here."

Mr. Mallory watched their later proceedings. At the climactic moment Tony felt a pleasure that was by no means wholly sexual. I am making love, he told himself as he ardently kissed the body writhing below his, to the daughter of a millionaire.

FOUR

On the following morning he woke feeling shagged, and more than shagged, depressed. He had got only fifty pounds instead of a hundred, had spent several on Fiona when no doubt he could have had her for nothing, and in addition—this crowned his depression when the post came—there was a letter from the Golden Sovereign phrased in what could only be called threatening terms. It mentioned taking further steps regarding settlement of his debt to them of nearly a hundred pounds, including "getting in touch with your employer, if this regrettable necessity should be forced on us." If they got in touch with the General they might not get their money, but he would almost certainly lose his job.

Gambling was his one weakness, or that was the way he sometimes thought of it. More often it seemed to him to be the way in which he would eventually make his fortune. The club, where he had played roulette with reasonable fortune until two unlucky sessions saw him nearly a hundred pounds down, had allowed him to give cheques for his chips because he had played there so often. After he had been cleaned out he had explained to the manager, a man named Armitage, that it was no use presenting his last two cheques because he was temporarily out of funds. Similar things had happened before in other gambling houses but then he had always moved on quickly, changing his job and his address. He took his usual line, that the amount was trivial and that he had no doubt they could accommodate him. Armitage had shaken his head and said that he would have to speak to Mr. Cotton.

"Who's Mr. Cotton?"

"He's Number One. Up in London." He asked a switchboard girl to see if Mr. Cotton was free and then shook his head again. "Mr. Cotton won't like it."

"You'll get your money," Tony said easily.

He was startled when a voice in the room said, "What is it, Armitage?"

The voice came from a box on the desk. When Armitage leaned forward to speak into it his voice was that of a supplicant.

"You should have known better." The voice was mild, but Armitage flinched. "But forget it. I told you, no trouble. What's the name again?"

"Scott-Williams."

"I don't want him in my clubs. Tell him that."

Tony had been greatly impressed by this casual demonstration of power. Impressed and relieved, so that the letter upset him more than it would otherwise have done. He telephoned the Golden Sovereign, but found only the cleaner there.

The morning did not recover from this unhappy beginning. At breakfast his bacon was underdone and the toast burnt, and when he spoke to Mrs. Causley she said insolently that perhaps he would like to cook it himself. The General was up early, in splendid spirits and eager to get back to the Western Desert. He began to comb through the mass of notes about his tank operations there, so that he could refute Ted Hasty. It was on the third mention of Hasty's name that the faint twinges Tony had felt on the previous day turned into the pain of realising the truth. He had met Colonel Hasty, and their meeting had had unhappy consequences. It was at a time when he had been working as a salesman for AtoZed Motors, a firm which specialised in buying cars written off after involvement in crashes and putting them back on the market when they had been resprayed and reconditioned. He had sold Hasty a ruined Peugeot which contained several parts grafted on from some quite different car. Within a month the semi-Peugeot's steering had got out of control and the Colonel had driven it into a brick wall. AtoZed had professed their good faith, the Colonel had got most of his money back, and the affair had ended short of the Law Courts, but he had been indignant about Tony's selling methods and was not likely to have forgotten him. It was in total despair that he helped the General to sort out papers.

"Tank training, where the devil are those statistics about tank training?" The General looked at him. "What's the matter, my boy, you're looking pale."

"I'm all right."

"You don't look it. Leave it to me, I'll sort through this stuff and we'll see what Ted Hasty's got to say."

He lay down in the bedroom, stared at the Morris wallpaper and felt no better. He could stay in his room, refuse lunch and avoid meeting Hasty but if, as had happened before when the General met old army friends, the discussion went on for hours and he stayed the night, a meeting was inevitable. And what was he to do about that letter? He walked gloomily round the room and then went into the little study where he kept the estate papers and accounts. On the desk lay the cheque book in which yesterday he had written out with pleasure the cheque for Clinker.

In ten ecstatic minutes he burnt his boats. After half a dozen trials on a sheet of paper that he tore up at once he produced the signature itself on the cheque, done with the bold characteristic flourish the General gave to the tail of the "y" in "Geoffrey." He made out the cheque for two hundred and fifty pounds. If the thing was to be done it might as well be done properly. The General saw his pass sheet only quarterly. By the time it arrived, no doubt he

29

would have paid back the money. And if he had not—well, he kept at the back of his mind like an insurance policy the thought of the Bobo letters. Later, when he drove in to town and presented the cheque across the counter a part of him admired his outward coolness. He felt a surge of self-congratulatory pleasure when the clerk cancelled the signature without question and asked how he would like the money. This was the first really criminal act he had ever committed. How simple it was, how calm he felt. The thick wad of money in his pocket gave him such a warm feeling that he decided to wait a day or two before paying the club.

He had forgotten all about Colonel Hasty, but as he drove the old Morris back into the garage he saw a car in the drive. He avoided the front door, but just as he was about to go up into his room the General's head popped out of the drawing-room.

"Feeling better?"

There was nothing for it but to say that he did.

"Come in, join the party. Ted, this is Tony Scott-Williams."

A sharp bird-like look at his face, a quick bird-like peck at his hand. He felt recklessly confident, even when the man said he thought they had met.

"I've got that feeling too, but I can't remember where."

"Too young for the war. Were you out in Kenya in the fifties?"

"I'm afraid not," he said truthfully. "I was secretary to Sir Archibald Graveney for some time. If you ever came to Throgmorton Hall——"

"Never did. Dead now."

The remark threw him for a moment. The *Who's Who* he had looked up was three years old. It was bad luck to have picked a man who had died since then. "Yes, of course. I left a few months before his death."

"Used to see him in London sometimes, at the club. Never knew he had a secretary."

"I hardly ever came down to London with him."

"Yes yes." The General had been waiting with obvious impatience for this exchange to end. "As I was saying, Ted, the whole question of preparation goes back to G.H.Q. More than that, it goes back to the Government. We were landed with these Crusaders straight out of the factory. If we'd had time to train——"

"It's a matter of logistics."

"If you mean they had more tanks than we had and better ones, you're damn well right."

The Colonel said something, but his mind did not seem to be on the argument. Throughout lunch, which was served by plumply attractive Doris, Tony was uneasily aware of the bird eye swivelling round to examine him. Occasionally Hasty seemed about to say something decisive. Suppose it was, "I remember you, you're the man who sold me that dud car," what would he say? Perhaps an outright denial would be the best thing. But lunch passed without the decisive word being spoken, and over coffee he saw a chance and took it. Hasty had been talking about spending some time in Edinburgh, and Tony repeated the name of the city.

"What's that?" The bird eye swivelled.

"It's where we met. You say you were up there on the Commonwealth Research Board. I was working with a group collecting funds and goods for the underdeveloped countries." It was true that he had worked in Scotland for eighteen months as local representative of an insurance company that had gone suddenly into liquidation.

"Maybe." Hasty did not sound enthusiastic. "Some of those crackpot committees did more harm than good. No use coddling these chaps. Got to tell 'em, not ask 'em."

31

"Just what I thought. That's why I gave it up."

"Finished your coffee?" The General was fretting. "Come on then, Ted. I've got something here that's going to shake your ideas up. Not logistics, just plain common sense. I've got some letters that will surprise you."

They went to the library. The General was exhilarated by such discussions, and to-day his back was straight and his manner commanding, as they must have been twenty-five years ago. Tony excused himself, saying that he wanted to go round the farms. Before doing so he rang the Golden Sovereign again, spoke to Armitage, and learned that the letter had been sent by mistake.

"You can tear it up, though I wouldn't say that if it had been left to me." Armitage sounded venomous. "Cotton makes us pay five per cent of bad debts."

"I didn't like the tone of it," Tony said boldly. "If I had a word with Mr. Cotton he might not like it either."

The telephone was slammed down without reply. He need not have drawn out the money, but there was no need to worry about that for some weeks. He drove round the farm and had a long talk with one of the farmers about repairs needed to one of his barns. Tony promised to look into it. Whatever builder was employed, it would not be Clinker.

When he got back Hasty's car had gone. He met Doris in the hall and asked her if anything had happened.

"Only one telephone call. For the master. He's in the study, asking for you. Soon as you came in, he said."

So Hasty had remembered. Well, he would simply deny it, that was all. It was one man's word against another's. He gave Doris a little pat on the bottom as she turned away.

In the library the General sat at the desk with some of the precious papers in front of him. His knotted hands rested on them. Against the light from the window his fine profile looked weary.

"Sit down." Tony sat. The General did not look at him, did not speak.

He felt it necessary to break the silence. "I don't know what Colonel Hasty has said——"

"Hasty?" Eyebrows were raised in surprise. "He thought you seemed a nice young chap."

Everything was all right. As a gambler he knew that if you played your luck you couldn't lose. But why was the old man so silent? "How did the discussion go?"

"I'm an old fool." Was that a reply to what he had said? "Should have known better."

What was he going on about? From the papers on the desk the knotted hand picked a piece of pink paper, held it out. He stared at it unbelievingly. It was the cheque he had cashed that morning.

"The bank called me up. Couldn't understand it. Then they sent this back." But why, he wanted to ask, but why? The knotted hand pointed to the signature. What was wrong with it? "Geoffrey," he read, admiring again the tail at the end of the "y." Then he looked again. "Geofrey" : he had missed out one "f."

"Well done but careless." The old voice spoke heavily. The piece of paper was torn across once, then again. The pieces fluttered on the floor. So he was not going to do anything about it. Tony tried to speak, found it impossible. The voice went inexorably on.

"If you were in debt, why not come to me? I would have given you money. But I suppose you've done this before, it's a usual thing. As I said it seems a good piece of work."

"I haven't done it before."

"And you won't do it again? But if you didn't cheat me like this you'd do it in some other way. Through the accounts perhaps. Maybe you do that already, I don't want to know. You can keep the money, but I can't have you here. You must go."

The face was still turned away from him, the voice was never raised a semi-tone above the even uninterested note in which you might talk about the weather. Suddenly all this was too much for him, the bloody condescension of the man saying he could keep the money, the refusal to look at him, the manner which implied that he was an inferior being. As if he hadn't earned every penny of that money and much more, as if any money could have compensated for the year he had spent listening to that interminable drivel about the war, pretending to take an interest in the attempt to cancel out mistakes by rewriting history, losing games of billiards which he could easily have won. You think you're giving me something, he wanted to say, but you aren't, I've given you one of the years of my life. He got up and almost ran out of the room, up the stairs to his bedroom. When he came back he had the Bobo letters with him. He tore open the envelope and put the letters on the desk right under the nose disdainfully turned away from him as if he were a bad smell.

"What about these, then?" he asked in the shrill tone that overcame him under any stress of emotion. It upset him to see that his own hands were shaking while those that took the letters and turned them over were perfectly steady.

Now the old man did turn and look at him. "Where did they come from? Miriam said she had destroyed them."

"They were in the lumber room."

"And you kept them?"

"Don't you understand? If I'd been what you think I am I could have asked for money, I could have made you give me money."

"Blackmail," the quiet voice said meditatively.

He shook his head violently. "I never asked, did I, never

34

said anything. There are your filthy letters, you can burn them, do what you like with them."

"They are not my letters. They were not sent to me."

That took him aback. He did not believe it, but he was taken aback. "My own darling G. Your name's Geoffrey. And some of them are to my darling Gee gee——"

"My son's name was Gordon. We called him Gee gee, and so did some of his friends."

"Your son," he repeated foolishly, and in a moment saw that he had been mistaken, that the letters had been written by one young man to another, not by a young man to a middle-aged one.

"These letters came back to us with the rest of my son's papers when he was killed. We had had no idea that he was homosexual. It came as a great shock. I don't know why Miriam did not destroy them, but I shall burn them as you suggest." He put the letters back into the envelope. "Your assumption was wrong, these letters would have been useless for blackmailing purposes. In a way I wish you had tried. You are a scoundrel, Scott-Williams. I want you out of here at once."

He could think of nothing to say except that he would have to pack. Now at last the General's voice was raised, raised in the kind of shout that must long ago have frightened subordinates.

"Get out, sir. Out of my sight." The voice dropped again to its contemptuous monotone, as though a brief gale had spent itself. "You may take a taxi to the station and charge it to my account."

When he left the room the old man had his hands on the envelope, and was staring at the wall.

35

FIVE

On that Wednesday night he stayed at a hotel off Shaftesbury Avenue. By midday on Thursday he had found several reasons for cheerfulness. After withdrawing the money he had more than three hundred pounds in his wallet. The possession of actual cash always gave him a sense of well-being which he never had when reading a credit balance on a pass sheet. He had got away from Leathersley House showing a profit, and he was rid for ever of that boring old General. Now that he had left, it seemed to him that he could not have stood it for another week. The feeling of freedom was delightful, the knowledge that he could do exactly what he liked, walk through the West End, have lunch and take as long as he wished over it, go to the cinema, without any need to look at his watch and think that he ought to get back to play billiards or do this, that or the other. Leathersley House had seemed a cushy billet at the time, but in retrospect his duties appeared intolerably onerous.

And there was another reason for cheerfulness. The Fiona prospect.

What was the prospect exactly? You were a good-looking young man and a millionaire's daughter had shown that she was powerfully attracted by you. Putting it crudely, how did you get your hands on some of the cash? The first thing would be to find out whether she had a private income settled on her, enough to maintain them both. If she had, marriage without Papa's consent would be indicated. If she had only an allowance that might be cut off, then he would have to meet Mallory. He imagined the scene,

Mallory saying that he was a fine young Englishman, offering him a job in the organisation, Fiona in ecstasies, marriage in church with half London society there. But this was unhappily not probable, tycoons were notoriously tough and suspicious, his background might be investigated. Look at it another way then. Mallory saying this man's a fortune hunter, Fiona in tears, I'm going to marry him anyway, Mallory threatening to cut off her allowance—but behind the scenes taking out his cheque book and saying "How much?" What would he settle for? Ten thousand pounds seemed a reasonable amount.

He rang up the house that evening, asked for Miss Mallory. A man's voice said, "Who is that speaking?"

"Tony Scott-Williams."

A pause. Then her voice, rather subdued. "Hallo."

"Fiona. Remember me?"

"Yes."

"Was that your father?"

"No, the butler."

The butler. Certainly some people knew how to live. "I want to see you."

"Yes."

"Fiona, I have to see you."

Her voice, guarded, low, said, "I want to see you too. Are you at your uncle's?"

"In London. Can you come up? This weekend."

"My father——"

With what he hoped was powerful urgency he said, "I *have* to see you."

There was a pause, so long that he thought the connection had been broken. Then her voice again. "All right. I'll manage somehow. But I can't come till Saturday."

Before she could ask the address of his flat he said quickly, "Let's meet in the Ritz Bar. Can you come up for lunch?"

"Not till the evening. About six."

"Six o'clock, the Ritz Bar, I'll be waiting."

"Yes."

"Darling, I long for it."

"I do too. I have to go now."

"Good-bye, darling."

"Good-bye."

She was well and truly hooked. Play your cards right, he told himself, and you've landed the fish.

He had no friend from whom he could borrow a flat, so he had to rent one. It cost him forty pounds to take a furnished flat for a week. It was high up in a modern block near Marble Arch, a marvellous position, and he regarded the money as an investment. He told the agents that he was staying over in London for only a few days and wanted to do some entertaining that couldn't be done in a hotel. Whether or not they believed him, they took the eight fivers he gave them and let him move in immediately. He got in a stock of drink—there was a cocktail cabinet, something that he'd always wanted—hung up his clothes and settled down with the feeling that he was there for ever.

When we're married, he told himself, we'll always live in places like this, places where every room is warm and you can pad about naked, and people live their own lives next door to each other without knowing the names of their neighbours, and you can get almost anything you want by lifting a telephone. He looked at London sparkling beneath him and thought, this is my world, it belongs to me and I'm going to have it. The temptation was strong to go out, find in a bar the kind of middle-aged woman who responded to his smile as if she was a fire waiting for a match, and bring her back here. But he resisted it. Anyway, the setting was wrong. Women of that sort liked to give you things, to feel that they owned you, and they would be disconcerted to find him installed in such style and at such an address. He stayed in the flat from Thursday evening until Saturday morning, having meals sent up to him.

Just after six o'clock she came into the Ritz Bar, looking slightly nervous, carrying a small suitcase, and wearing a rather unsuitable hat. He was pleased to see that she had abandoned the dark glasses. He commented on that. "I feel I'm seeing you properly."

She ordered gin and tonic and drank it in sips. "Was it a job to get away?"

"Not too bad. Daddy hadn't got anyone coming down this weekend. He wanted to know where I was going. I told him I was staying with a girl-friend. I fixed it with her too."

"Clever girl." He patted her hand. "For a minute on the phone I thought you didn't want to see me."

"Tracey was there—the butler. I had to be careful."

After a second drink her manner was perceptibly easier. "It's wonderful to get up to London. I feel so cooped up down there."

"I'm your good angel. I just wave my magic wand and say 'Come up to London', and it's done."

She looked round. "It's rather quiet here."

"Kind of traditional." He was worried that she might have preferred to meet somewhere else, Claridge's or Hatchetts which he knew only as names. "I often use this as a meeting place because it's so convenient."

"Of course." She fiddled with her handbag.

"But let's get out. Harry, my bill." He had taken the precaution of learning the waiter's name. It was time to be masterful. He steered her up the stairs, got a taxi and kissed her ardently as soon as they were inside.

"Are we going to your flat?"

"Where else? I'm repaying hospitality." He laughed.

She disengaged herself. "Tony, I don't want you to think I do this with everybody."

"Darling Fiona."

"It's because I like you. Very much. I don't just want an affair for a weekend."

What do you know, he thought, I believe *she's* going to propose to *me*. But the time wasn't right for anything of that sort. He took her hand and kissed it, which seemed to cover the case.

He watched when they crossed the entrance hall and went up in the lift to see if she was impressed, and there could be no doubt that she was although she tried not to show it. He was apologetic when he unlocked the door. "It's not much like home, I'm afraid, but then I'm not here all the time."

Inside she exclaimed with pleasure, particularly at the view. They were on the fourteenth floor and quite a lot of London was spread out beneath them.

"Yes, I do think it's something rather special myself," he said with perfect truthfulness. "But of course you've got your own flat in Chelsea."

"My father has. I'm hardly ever there. Anyway, it hasn't got a view like this."

He came up behind her, put his hands on her breasts. She turned round and her blue eyes questioned him. "I meant what I said, Tony. I'm playing for keeps."

Wonderful words. "So do I, darling. I'm playing for keeps too." In the bedroom later he asked with attempted casualness whether she had really meant it.

"You know I did."

"Then what about meeting your father?"

Silence. Her fingers traced a pattern on his thigh. "I don't think that would be a good idea. Not yet anyway. He doesn't want me to get married. I told you."

"That's just damned selfish."

40

"It would be no good talking to him. You don't know what he's like. I've got my own money, but he won't let me use it to take a flat in town or anything like that. Most of it just stays in the bank."

He wanted to say that she was over twenty-one and a free agent, but refrained.

"And when I do marry he wants it to be some ghastly local. There's a boy he keeps talking about, the son of one of his friends. Marriage to him would be good for business, might even mean a merger." She said it without irony and repeated, "I've got my own money."

Again he refrained from speaking, this time from asking how much. She went on, looking up at the ceiling, speaking in a sing-song voice.

"You don't understand about Daddy. I can't explain it myself, but if he told me I was to have nothing to do with you I should have to do what he said. Do you know what I dream sometimes? I dream I'm a princess and shut up in a castle where I've got everything anybody could want except freedom. People come and try to free me, to let me out because they're in love with me, but there's an invisible barrier round the castle and as soon as they pass over it their view of me changes and they see me as an old hag, toothless and dirty, so they go away. And in the dream nobody ever gets past the barrier and at the end of the dream I look in the glass and I've become what they believed me to be, filthy and dressed in rags and old."

"That's just a dream. There aren't any barriers. You can do what you like."

"Oh, but I can't. Someone else has to do it, someone has to help me." She turned and clung to him, pressed her naked body to his. "Help me, Tony."

With everything arranging itself better than he could have hoped, he knew the importance of not saying a wrong word. It seemed best to say the serious thing he had to say lightly. "Here's some news, Princess. Prince Charming's arrived, and guess how he got past that invisible barrier? With a special licence."

"A special licence," she echoed wonderingly.

"I'll get one on Monday. You come up to London and, hey presto, the deed's done, the princess is free." He bounced off the bed, went into the bathroom. Her voice followed him. He put his head round the door. "What's that?"

"It won't make any difference to you? I mean, to your job and all that."

"Everyone will be delighted."

"Shall we live here?"

"Or take a bigger flat," he said recklessly. "Come on, let's celebrate, go out on the town." He felt an overwhelming euphoria at having pulled it off, a debt of gratitude towards the girl who was going to provide him with a permanent income.

They went on the town. He told her that he hardly ever used the Jag in London, driving was such hell, so they took taxis. Over dinner he learned that fifteen hundred a year was settled on her through a trust, although she couldn't touch the capital. There was quite a bit of money in her bank account, she didn't know exactly how much. He confided a few vague details of his stockbroking job, saying that it paid well but he was bored with it and thought of striking out on his own, starting a gambling club perhaps, which was a surefire way of making money. It seemed premature to mention that she would be providing the capital. He suggested that it would be fun to take a look at a club and they ended up in the Here's Sport Club in Soho. Her eyes were wide as he bought a hundred pounds' worth of chips and gave half of them to her. She asked if he could afford it.

"This is celebration night, Princess." He had called her Princess the whole evening. "There's plenty more. Anyway, we're going to win. We're playing my system, and it works best with a partner."

"Was that why you lost down in Landford?"

"It could be," he said shortly. He did not care for jokes about roulette. He explained to her the Prudential system which they would be playing. You made two bets at each spin of the wheel, a ten pound bet on passe covering the high numbers, and a five pound bet on the numbers from one to six. If a high number came up you won ten pounds and lost five, if a number from one to six turned up you were paid at odds of five to one so that you won twenty-five pounds and lost ten.

"And if it's one of the other numbers?"

"If it's seven to eighteen or zero we lose, but the odds are two to one in our favour. We'll stop when we've won a hundred."

They very nearly did it, too. She sat on the opposite side of the table from him playing the six number transversal, and the first time she won she gave a small scream of pleasure. At one time they were seventy pounds up. Then the bank had a run in which the numbers between seven and eighteen came up half a dozen times running followed by zero. They were losing a little, Fiona was looking slightly bored, and to amuse her he committed a roulette player's cardinal sin. He changed systems, and began to play a modified version of the Capitalist's system, which involves covering every number on the board except zero and three. When zero turned up he bought another hundred pounds' worth of chips. They lost these when three came up twice in eight spins.

"Two hundred pounds," she said, and repeated it. "Just think, if we'd stopped when we were winning——"

"You make rules and you have to keep them," he said sharply, although he had failed to do so. The exhilaration of gambling was so great for him that it remained for an hour or two afterwards, like the effect of drink, and he had the true gambler's dislike of complaints about losing. "Better luck next time."

"Next time?"

"When we're on the other side of the fence, running the club."

"It was a lovely evening," she said when they were back at the flat. "But I wish we hadn't lost that money."

Euphoria had worn off and he now wished it too, but he controlled his irritation. "Part of the ceremony of freeing the princess. Let's have a nightcap. We're still celebrating."

The celebration ended abruptly on Sunday morning.

He woke at half past nine. The princess was still asleep. He went into the living-room, picked up the papers from the hall—he had ordered them with the feeling that the daily delivery of newspapers gave an air of permanency—and carried them into the kitchen to look at while he made breakfast. Turning the pages idly he saw a picture and a story in the gossip column of one paper, passed it by and returned to it, looking incredulously at picture and story.

The picture showed a girl wearing a mini-skirt and a sleeveless brocaded blouse with a hooded headdress through which part of her face was visible. The story was headed: "Millionaire's Daughter Starts Yashmak Fashion" and it began:

"Fiona, up-and-coming daughter of industrial merger-maker Jacob Mallory, is touring Europe in search of something new in the fashion line to rock the younger set. Fiona's landed up in Ismir, Turkey, where she's certainly shaken the natives. It's not the mini-skirt that shocks them, they've seen those before, or even the local dress turned into something so, so sophisticated in the form of the brocaded blouse. No, it's the way Fiona uses that traditionally concealing yashmak combined with

44

the rest of the outfit that produces an effect on males. Just imagine what a glance from under that hood will do to them over here. Fiona, a working girl fashion-spotting for Philippa Phillips Associates, is going on looking for that elusive new something in Greece and Yugoslavia before she comes home."

He went into the living-room and sat down. He felt as dazed as somebody involved in an accident. As he read the story again his lips moved like those of a man spelling out the words. Then he got up, went into the bedroom and opened her case. She had taken clothes out of it last night, and now it was empty. Her handbag was on a chair. He opened it and spilled out the contents. Lipstick, keys—and a letter. The envelope said : "Miss Mary Tracey, The Cottages, Frankfort Manor." Tracey—the butler's daughter. It was like some wretched stage farce. No doubt The Cottages were the servants' quarters.

"What are you doing?" The words were whispered. She was watching him from the bed.

He handed her the paper. There was a smell of burning. It was the toast in the kitchen. The smell pervaded the flat. Tears welled into her eyes. She did not speak.

"Well?" he said questioningly, although he knew the answer. "You're Mary Tracey. The butler's daughter."

"He's a handyman."

"I suppose you're a housemaid."

"I help in the house."

Another Doris. "That's why you took me back. Because you knew nobody would be there." She didn't contradict him. "And I believed you. What a fool."

She blew her nose. "Sometimes she gives me clothes and I wear them when I go into town."

"Your father's in it too? I spoke to him."

"I told him I would speak if a friend of Fiona's rang up. I thought——" She didn't say what she thought.

45

"What the hell were you doing in the Golden Sovereign?"

"I know Claude." Claude? "Armitage. He's—he used to be a boy-friend of mine. I worked there for a bit, in the cloakroom."

A hat check girl. How could he have failed to recognise her for what she was? She went on.

"But I do want to get away. And I do have that dream, I think of myself as a princess waiting for somebody. You've burned the toast. Shall I make some more?"

Did she think he was going to sit down to breakfast with her? The thought of all the money he had spent, the flat, the food and drink, the roulette last night, rose in his mouth like bile. "You can leave. Any time. Now."

"You don't want to go on with it? I suppose you wouldn't. Still, let's have breakfast."

She got out of bed and moved towards the kitchen. He took her by the shoulders. "I said you could leave now."

"I don't see why you're so het up. After all, you've had some fun out of it, and you've got plenty of money."

"Plenty of money," he said bitterly. A moment afterwards he regretted the tone in which he had spoken, but it was too late. She began to laugh.

"Don't tell me you haven't got any money. Oh, that's good, that's really good."

"I spent it on you."

" 'There's plenty more'," she mimicked him. "So you were after my allowance? And I only said it because I didn't want you to think I'd be too much of a burden. It really is funny." Her tone and accent changed so that he could not think how he had ever been deceived. "I suppose you fiddled this place too."

"It's rented."

She stopped laughing. "But you're clever. Why don't we do something together?"

"What?"

"I'm not staying at home, you know, I'm getting out. This is what I want, what we both want." She put a finger in her mouth, bit a nail. "Let's team up."

"Why don't you just go."

"After breakfast." While she was eating her toast she continued to talk. "I've got a thing for you. And I'm not a fool, you know. We'd make a good team."

"I want you to leave."

She packed her things into the little suitcase. "Better luck next time. You might wish me that too." He did not reply. "Trouble is you've got no sense of humour."

When she had gone he lay on the bed and smoked a cigarette. He had several days to run before his week's tenancy was out, but what use was the flat to him now? With less than fifty pounds of his money left he did what he had done before. He took refuge with Widgey.

PART TWO

A Dream of Loving Women

ONE

Widgey had not changed in the two years since he had last seen her. The ash was long on the cigarette that stuck out of the corner of her mouth, and she sat at one side of a table in her private parlour with cards in front of her and a woman on the other side of the table. The woman was perhaps fifty, certainly younger than Widgey, and her fingers were crusted with jewels. She nervously twisted a gold bracelet on her left arm.

"A black ace, a red ten, a black queen. Not the queen of spades, that's something," Widgey was saying as he opened the door. She said hallo to Tony without surprise, holding up her face so that he could kiss her cheek. Ash dropped on the table and she brushed it away. "That explains part of it."

"What does it explain?" The woman opposite panted like a Pekinese.

"Ace of clubs, ten of diamonds, queen of clubs. Means an unexpected visitor. I thought it would be for you, but it's for me. My nephew Tony. This is Mrs. Harrington."

"But it's *my* future you were reading."

"You just can't tell, dear. Come for a visit? You can have your old room, thirteen."

"You mean to say you don't mind?" Bulbous Pekinese eyes rolled at Tony.

"Course he doesn't, he's not superstitious any more than I am. He doesn't believe the cards and I don't really." Widgey reshuffled expertly, stubbed out her cigarette, rolled another with paper and tobacco from an old metal case. "Just they seem to come true, that's all."

"Why are you starting again?"

"He disturbed the flow, and anyway when one thing's happened you always want to shuffle again, gets confused otherwise. Let's see now, two of diamonds, eight of spades, jack of hearts, not very exciting. See you later," she called to Tony.

Room thirteen was an attic, from which across the roofs of houses you could glimpse the sea. As he looked round at the cracked wash basin, the rose-patterned paper which didn't quite cover the whole wall because Widgey had bought a discontinued line and there had not been enough of it, at the painted chest of drawers scarred by cigarette burns and the disproportionately large mahogany tallboy which she had bought with him at a sale for thirty shillings, he felt a sensation of relief. He threw himself on the bed, which was placed so that you were likely to strike your head on the coved ceiling if you got up from it hurriedly, then after a few minutes began to unpack his things. The painted chest was still uncertainly balanced because one leg was shorter than the other three and the little piece of cork under it became displaced as soon as anything was put inside. And, yes, the top drawer still contained "The Bible For Commercial Travellers," bound in red leather with the editorial injunction on the opening page : "*Read this book* and it will bring you comfort." He turned to the back flyleaf and saw that the old message was still there, written in a flowing commercial traveller's hand : "If no comfort obtained try ringing Anna," followed by what was presumably Anna's telephone number. He had come home.

He had first visited the Seven Seas Hotel when he was five years old, brought down by his father and mother to see "the place where Belle's set up to poison people," as his father put it. That was during the war. There was barbed wire along the sea front, they had to bring ration cards, and his father complained that they did not get enough food to fill a gnat's belly. Mrs. Widgeon—her name was Arabella and she was his mother's sister—was the wife of a heroic fighter pilot who had been wounded, discharged from the service, and was in the process of dying quietly. His father was of the opinion that Alec had opted for a quiet life and that there was not much wrong with him, and he did not really change this view even after Alec had proved his case by dying just after the war ended. For years they had taken their family holiday at the Seven Seas, but his father had never really liked it. It was, he contemptuously said, not a proper hotel but a boarding house, which served only breakfast and an evening meal. After his mother died and his father married again, Tony had come down alone. If room thirteen was free he always stayed in it.

He could never remember Widgey looking any different from the way she looked now, a small woman with grey untidy hair who rolled her own cigarettes and always had one in a corner of her mouth. She ran the Seven Seas with the accompaniment of a continually changing staff, and she must have been less haphazard than she seemed because people came back year after year. Or perhaps it was the haphazardness they liked. Certainly it had always delighted Tony. There was no regular time for the evening meal at the Seven Seas, or rather there was a time but it was most erratically observed. There were no rules about not taking girls, or bottles, or both up to your room. Widgey had never applied for a drinks licence but drink often appeared mysteriously on the tables. Evenings of sparse meals would alternate with occasions when the astonished guests would see a turkey or a goose brought into the dining-room, to be carved by Widgey and served with the appropriate trimmings, cranberry jelly, apple sauce, stuffing. There was no question of the door being locked at eleven. The sign in the hall "Last In Please Lock Up" sometimes led to a reveller returning at three in the morning and finding the door locked against him, but Widgey would wave aside apologies and complaints when she staggered down in her dressing gown to open it. *Never apologise, never explain* : she might have adopted the motto had she known it. Her charm for Tony was that she was never surprised, reproachful, or disappointed by the conduct of others. In adolescence the Seven Seas became increasingly for him a home from home.

Home was a semi-detached house in Eltham, one of London's more undistinguished outer suburbs. The house was one in a long group put up during the nineteen twenties in the worst period of between-the-wars jerry building, and it fronted on to a main road where the traffic roared past both night and day. His remembrances of childhood were patchy. Going to the local school, writing his name *Anthony Jones*, and being upset because a teacher said "Jones, that's the most *common* name there is," wishing he had a brother or a sister, a terrible time in the school lavatories one afternoon with some older boys, good reports changing to critical ones. ("His ability is clear, but doesn't try hard . . . Can do well enough but doesn't seem interested.") His father was away a lot during the week, because he was a traveller. Tony told this to other boys, and could never understand why they were not more impressed. In his mind he saw his father travelling from one place to another, going to strange cities where wonderful things happened to him. On Friday, or sometimes Thursday, evenings when Mr. Jones came home in the little car and brought a big battered brown case into the house and said that it had been a good week or a bad week and that now he must do his reports, Tony associated these reports with travel, something similar to the essays he was asked to write in school about the most exciting thing that had happened on your holidays. Not until he was eleven years old did he realise that his father's travelling was not done for pleasure but to sell things, at one time electrical equipment, at another a new kind of electric lamp, at another still a range of toys.

Mr. Jones was a short stout man with a thick moustache and an ebullient way of talking. When, on returning after the week's travelling, he exclaimed "Hallo hallo, what have we here?" and lifted Tony on to his shoulders, the boy was conscious of a pungent smell which he eventually recognised as a blend of cigarette smoke, beer and male sweat. Mr. Jones was a great sportsman or at least a great watcher of sport, and in the winter they always went together on Saturday afternoons to watch a professional football match. At the match he would shout criticism freely. "Pass, you fool," he would cry. "Don't fiddle faddle with the ball, man, get rid of it . . . what's happened to your eyesight, ref, go and get some glasses . . . dirty, send him off." Occasionally they would find themselves in a nest of opposition supporters and then a verbal altercation might go on throughout the match. When the exchange of insults seemed likely to reach the point of blows Mr. Jones would calm down suddenly. "What's up then, what's the matter, it's a game, isn't it?" he would say, adding afterwards to his son, "Just as well you were there, I almost lost my temper with that fellow, I might have done something I'd have been sorry for." On the way home they often fell in with a bunch of home supporters and the discussion, no longer an argument, would be continued.

On Sunday mornings they would kick a ball about in the small back garden or on the nearby common. Tony would stand between a cap and a scarf placed to represent goal posts and would dive to try to save his father's rather feeble shots. "That was great," Mr. Jones would say after these occasions, which ended with him panting hard from the reputedly weak heart which had kept him out of the armed forces. "You're going to be a smashing little goalkeeper, you'll be playing for the school in no time." The truth was, however, that Tony was no good at games, and didn't like them. Awareness of this was kept from his father until the day when Tony said he had been picked as goalkeeper and Mr. Jones turned up to the match on Saturday morning to find that his son was not even a spectator. There was no row afterwards, but the occasion marked the end of something in their relationship. Afterwards Tony went to no more professional matches, and before long Mr. Jones also stopped going.

At about the same time, when he was thirteen, Tony became aware of other things about his father. The smell that had seemed in childhood to be warm, comforting and safe, became extremely disagreeable. He learned to identify the evenings when his father came home more than usually cheerful as those on which beer could be smelt strongly on his breath, and indeed it seemed to him at times that his father's whole body reeked of beer and that the smell permeated his clothes. He associated this smell in some way with the incident in the school lavatories, which had never been repeated. And he wondered for the first time about his father's relationship with his mother. When Mr. Jones came home he would embrace his wife in a bear hug and say something like "Give us a buss, Sheila, me bonny lass. You're a sight for sore eyes and no mistake." His mother would accept this embrace rather as if she were a statue with movable arms, which she laced in a loose and formal manner behind her husband's back. After a moment she would move away and say that she must get supper. Her husband, duty done, then dropped into an arm-chair, put on his slippers, and asked how every little thing was going on at school. Was this the way all mothers and fathers went on, could it be said that they loved each other? This was a question to which he never found an answer. Certainly they never had rows, there was hardly ever an argument, although Mr. Jones was argumentative enough with the neighbours who came in sometimes for a drink or coffee. At any sign of family argument, however, his wife would say that she must get the lunch or the supper, or clean the bedrooms, or wash some clothes.

He saw much more of his mother than of his father, yet she was never so real a presence to him. Like her sister she was untidy and vague, but unlike Widgey she was shapelessly fat, with an indeterminate figure shrouded in sacking-like dresses of anonymous colour. Like her sister again she was interested in the unseen world, but where Widgey read the future in cards, and had once possessed a tarot pack before evolving her own system of interpreting ordinary playing cards, Mrs. Jones was interested in spiritualism. She took the *Psychic News* and similar periodicals and was a member of a Spirit Circle which held regular séances. Occasionally she went to meetings in central London, and at one of these she herself had fainted after receiving a spirit message from her brother Jack who had been killed in an air raid. Sometimes Tony would come home from school and find his mother, with three or four other ladies, sitting round an ouija board or conducting spirit rapping sessions at a table. He would go into the kitchen and eat his bread and butter and jam listening to the murmur of voices, raised occasionally to small screeches of pleasure or dismay, that came from next door. When the session was over Mrs. Jones would float in at the kitchen door, rather like a spirit herself, and ask whether he wanted anything more to eat. Then he did his homework, and after that in the summer went out to play with other boys on the common, in the winter stayed in and read books.

Television was not yet endemic, and they had no set in their home.

When he grew up he wondered often whether she had wanted a child, and concluded that upon the whole she hadn't. She never spoke harshly to him, saw that he was clean and that his clothes were neat, but as he looked back it seemed that she had shown him no sign of love. Sometimes the ladies who came to the table rapping sessions would say what a delightful boy he was, so good looking, so quiet, so well behaved. His mother would smile vaguely and agree with them, but did she really think so? "He's no *trouble*," they would cry as if this were some kind of miracle, and this was true until the time of the Creighton affair, when he was fourteen years old.

Creighton was a big, rather stupid boy who had a gang of which Tony became a member. His qualification was the possession of a roulette wheel. The wheel had been bought by his mother at a sale, in a lot together with a pair of Victorian vases, which were what she really wanted, and a number of books. Among the books was one called *The Winning Rules, Or Roulette Practically Considered* by Sperienza, a gentleman who had played the game for many years at Monte Carlo. From this book Tony learned that you may bet en plein or a cheval, on a transversal or a carré or on one of the even chances. He learned also of systems that practically guaranteed you against losing, the Infallible System, the Wrangler's System, the D'Alembert System, and many others. He discovered the meaning of martingales and anti-martingales, intermittences and permanences. Why was it necessary to work, he asked his father, when you could play the Infallible System instead? His father merely said that he shouldn't believe any of that rubbish.

Was it rubbish? Tony and the gang played roulette, but few of them used any sort of system, and he could not make up his mind. After a time the rest of them got bored, and turned to other things. The gang's exploits were not remarkable. They took girls up into the nearby woods where Tony was initiated into sex, and they also pilfered goods from shops in Lewisham. The usual technique was for three of them to go in and talk to the assistant while a fourth took something off the counter or stall. The things were not of much value. Sometimes Creighton sold them, at other times they threw them away. Then four of them, including Tony, were caught in Woolworth's and brought into Juvenile Court, where they were all put on probation. The effects of the affair reverberated through the Jones household. Mr. Jones came back specially from Gloucester to speak for his son in Court. Later, at home, he was almost incoherent with rage.

"That a son of mine should——" he began, and tried again. "I can't understand it when you come from a good home. You all come from good homes." Later he said, "I should have known. Look at this last report, doesn't try. Doesn't *try*. Why don't you try, eh? You'll come to a bad end. He'll come to a bad end, Sheila, I'll tell you that." A quick switch of attack. "And you know whose fault it'll be. Yours."

His wife put a hand to her wide bosom. "Mine?"

"Too much freedom. If you hadn't given him so much freedom——"

"I must see to the potatoes." She elevated slowly from the chair in which she had been sitting and floated out of the room.

The Creighton affair marked another turning point. In a way Tony had been terrified by the serious way in which everybody treated something so simple, something as you might say that everybody did, but what was chiefly borne in on him was the difference between practice and precept. He had often jumped off a bus with his father before the conductor had got round to collecting the fares. His father had winked and said, "Freeman's ride, Tony, that's the best." At Christmas time they had more than once gone to a brewery where one of the men would come out in a van and stop round a corner. Bottles of whisky would be exchanged for money, and after the van had driven away Mr. Jones would chortle. "Half price, less than half price. Makes it taste better." How was the man able to sell them whisky at less than half price? Another wink. "Don't ask, son. It fell off the back of the van." When he understood what this meant he wondered: what was the difference between whisky falling off the back of the van and things disappearing from a store counter?

At fifteen he got his first job, as an insurance company clerk. He had been working for three months when he came home one evening to find supper in the oven. There was no sign of his mother. He ate supper and waited for her to come home. At eleven o'clock he went upstairs and found her lying fully dressed on the bed, with an empty bottle that had contained sleeping tablets by her side. She must have taken them immediately after putting his supper into the oven. She left no message, but there were a number of letters on the dressing table, written to her husband by a woman who signed herself Nora. These letters, left carelessly in an old overcoat, were thought to provide the reason for her death. Tony wondered—but this was much later—whether the loss of love or of respectability had been the decisive stroke. Or had she simply wanted to move over into the spirit world about which she was so curious?

Three months after his wife's death Mr. Jones married Nora, a brawny peroxide blonde with a flat Midlands voice, and soon after that Tony left the insurance company and went down to Widgey. He never returned to Eltham and never wrote to his father. He had had many jobs since then, but had held none for more than a few months before going to Leathersley House. He had sold insurance, had acted as debt collector for some bookmakers, and had worked as a salesman on commission for several firms. In all of these occupations he had practised a little fiddle, something had dropped off the back of the van as it were. He had kept back some of the insurance premiums, put a percentage of the collected debts into his own pocket, and with the co-operation of somebody in the office of a firm of vacuum cleaner manufacturers had sold a number of cleaners which never passed through the company books.

Such activities meant that you could never stay in one place for long, and Tony would have accepted if he had known it the philosophical idea that life itself implies movement, a permanent flow. Every so often, when he was in the money, he would play roulette, but he had never possessed enough capital to give any system the financial backing it needed, and the result almost always showed itself on the losing side. After leaving Eltham he abandoned the undesirable Jones, and since then had called himself Scott-Williams, Lees-Partridge and Bain-Truscott. He usually placed his origin in the colonies, and said something deprecating about his name. For a short time he had cherished ideas of becoming a journalist, and had taken a course in shorthand and typing at evening classes. He had found it impossible to get a job on a paper, but these accomplishments had been useful when at times he had been compelled to do secretarial work for private employers. Most of these jobs bored him quickly. Others involved too much work, and in two cases he had been dismissed because the lady of the house made advances which were noticed by her husband. There was something hungry but yearning about Tony's looks that was especially attractive to women over forty. Such women, he slowly realised, wished to be a mother to him and at the same time wanted him to be a lover to them. There was something vaguely disagreeable about this, but the thought had crossed his mind that he might marry one of these ladies. The proposition, however, had never been a practical one because they always had husbands.

Easter was over and only half a dozen people were staying at the Seven Seas, a young couple who looked as if they were just married, a husband and wife in their seventies, he wearing a deaf aid and she tottery, a rabbit-faced clergyman whose lips moved ceaselessly perhaps in prayer, and Mrs. Harrington. Supper was tomato soup, thinly sliced cold meat and salad, and ice cream. Obviously this was one of the bad days. Widgey appeared only intermittently at meals, and was not present at this one. The food was eaten almost in silence. The young couple whispered to each other as though in church, the clergyman's lips moved, Mrs. Harrington viewed food and company with a fixed smile. Only the deaf old man said, "What's this, then, what's this?" as each course came up. "Tomato soup . . . it's cold meat, dear, mostly ham I think," his wife quavered and then powerfully repeated as he turned towards her the deaf aid which made a slight whistling sound.

Afterwards he signed the visitors' book firmly, "Anthony Bain-Truscott," with a fictitious address in London, and went to see Widgey. She sat in an arm-chair in the parlour reading a romance called *Love and Lady Hetty*. She put the book down, marking the place carefully.

"Just having my evening cupper. Want one?" She took the kettle off a small gas ring, got two unmatching cups from a cupboard, made tea, rolled a cigarette and said, "Well?"

The tea was very hot, thick and in some mysterious way very sweet, although she had put in no sugar. "How do you mean, Widgey?"

"What's up? Landing here without even a telegram. What name, by the way?"

"Bain-Truscott."

"Tony for me." She swilled tea round her mouth. False teeth clattered slightly. "No need to say anything. Any real trouble, I'd like to know."

"There's nothing." But he felt an urgent need to talk about the way in which he had been deceived. "It was a damned girl." He told her about the Fiona who had turned out to be Mary and was indignant when she laughed. The laugh turned into a cough, ash dropped from her cigarette. She drank some more tea, stopped coughing.

"Glad it's no worse. You ought to settle down." He did not answer this. "Broke, are you?"

"I've got some money."

"Your father wrote the other day, asked if I'd heard from you. Don't worry, I won't tell him you're here. He's had an accident, broken his leg, laid up."

"Let him rot."

"He's not my favourite man."

"He killed mother." He wondered why he spoke so fiercely when he had never been close to his mother as he had to his father.

"Sheila killed herself. She was a stupid cow. She should never have married." She did not amplify this statement.

The conversation made him uncomfortable. He said flirtatiously, "*You* ought to marry again, Widgey."

"Who'd have me? They'd be marrying the Seven Seas. But you should think about it, you're getting on. Sure you aren't in trouble?"

"Oh, Widgey."

"Just I've got a feeling. Hardly ever wrong, my feelings."

"They're wrong this time," he said a little snappishly. As he bent to kiss her he caught her characteristic smell of tobacco blended with something both sweet and sharp like eau-de-cologne. The past rolled over him in waves, the years of bucket and spade holidays, the years when he had come down alone and walked about looking for girls. One of the rolling waves was composed of pure affection. "I won't be any trouble."

"I don't mind a little trouble. I just wish you knew what you were doing, that's all."

"That's ridiculous." He made a gesture that embraced his well-cut clothes and his personality. "What's wrong?"

"Nothing," she said flatly. He went upstairs, and to bed.

TWO

He spent the next forty-eight hours recovering his poise, as others convalesce from influenza. There could be no doubt that the Fiona-Mary affair had been a fiasco. He recalled it continually like a man exploring a sore place with his tongue, feeling each time the shock that had run through him on reading the story in the paper. The thought that he had been deceived was hard to endure.

Southbourne had grown dramatically since the war, sprouting a holiday camp and glass cliffs of flats, but it was still a small resort, a lesser Hastings rather than a miniature Brighton. He walked up and down the promenade as he had when a youth, moving very slowly like a man recovering from illness. He wandered beside the sea, played the slot machines on the pier, and on a day of blustery rain listened to the concert party in the Pier Pavilion. The season had not begun, and there was only a sprinkling of people in the canvas seats. Afterwards he went into the café under the Pavilion's dome, ordered a pot of tea and toast and sat staring through the plate glass window at the sea.

"Mr. Bain-Truscott. I thought it was you." Mrs. Harrington stood beside his table. "Isn't this the most awful weather?" She hovered, twirling a damp umbrella. At his suggestion she sat down and drank a cup of tea. They laughed together when the waitress said that a pot for two would cost more than a pot for one.

"English seaside resorts." Tony shook his head. "Can you wonder more and more people go abroad for holidays."

"Are you a great traveller?"

"I know France pretty well. Mostly around Paris." One of his secretarial jobs had taken him to France for a week. It was the only time he had been out of England.

"Ah, Paris in the spring," Mrs. Harrington sighed.

He moved off this dangerous ground. "You're taking an early holiday."

"Not exactly a holiday. We used to live here and Alec Widgeon was a great friend of Harrington's. I still know several people here. And of course I visit his resting place." From a crocodile bag she drew a small lace handkerchief and delicately wiped not her eyes but her nose.

"I'm sorry."

"How could you know. It was a motor bus. Driven by a coloured person. I miss him greatly, although of course he is over there."

He was about to ask where, when he remembered her attention to the cards. Her brown Pekinese eyes looked into his. "Harrington was a very vital man."

He did not know what to say, and remained silent. "You're Widgey's nephew, aren't you? She's a remarkable woman. Such intensity of feeling. I really think she *knows* things. Was your mother her sister?"

"Yes." He started to explain about the colonial origins of the Bain-Truscotts. Mrs. Harrington waved a jewelled hand and said it added distinction. She was wearing a diamond clasp that must be worth a lot of money if it was real, and no doubt it *was* real. And that large emerald ring—he became aware that she had said something and asked her to repeat it.

"I wondered what *you* were doing here."

"I sometimes come down to stay with Widgey. And I've had rather a shock. I thought I was going to get married, but it was broken off."

"You'll think I'm a prying old woman." She gave a trill of falsetto laughter.

"You haven't been prying at all. And I think of you as just the same age as myself."

"That's very nice even if you don't mean it. Remember, there are just as good fish in the sea." Her hand, podgy and slightly wrinkled but ablaze with the stones she wore, touched his. As they walked back to the Seven Seas he asked her to call him Tony. He learned her name which, rather dismayingly, was Violet.

On the following day they were going out of the door at the same time, and he accompanied her on a tour of the town's jewellery shops. She was looking for a pearl choker and examined some that cost three and four hundred pounds, but she did not neglect rings and bracelets. He was impressed by the professional way in which she looked at the things and bargained with the jewellers. In the end she placed a diamond and ruby pendant round her ample neck and asked him if he liked it. He said truthfully that it was very pretty.

"You really think so?" She said to the jeweller, "I'll give you a hundred and fifty."

The price was a hundred and seventy-five. The man raised his hands in despair, but she got it at her price after some haggling.

"Will you take it off, Tony." He stood close behind

her, his fingers touched the back of her neck, warm and smooth. He was aware of a faint tremor in her body as he undid the clasp. In the glass her brown eyes, warm and ardent, looked into his.

"You'll think I waste money, but you're wrong," she said afterwards. "I may be a fool about a lot of things but I know what I'm looking at with stones. I don't keep them for ever. I sell them after a few years, and I almost always make a profit."

"I thought you were wonderful. I could never have got the price down like that."

"Nothing to it. He wouldn't have liked it if I'd just said yes to the asking price."

He decided to make his financial situation clear. "A hundred and fifty pounds. By my standards it's a fortune."

She patted his hand. "Dear Tony, you're so straightforward. That's one of the things I like about you."

That evening they had a séance, or rather a table rapping session. It was against Widgey's principles because she only approved of seeing the future in the cards, but it turned out that the deaf man and his tottery wife were interested in the world beyond, and the five of them sat at the round table in the parlour with the lights out. For some minutes nothing happened.

"What's that?" said Deaf aid. "I heard something."

They sat in silence. Tony repressed an inclination to giggle. Three sharp knocks were heard. Mrs. Deaf aid grunted something unintelligible. Widgey said, "Have you got a message? Is it for one of us? Two raps means you have." Two knocks sounded. "Is it for Mr. Bennett?" So that was Deaf aid's name. One knock only. "For Mrs. Bennett?" Again one knock. "For Mrs. Harrington?" Two knocks. "Is it a close relative?" Two knocks. "Her husband?" Two knocks.

Tony's right hand was gripped by Mrs. Harrington's left. She held it tightly, the rings pressed into his fingers. She continued to hold it as questions and answers continued, slowly because as always in table rapping the answers were confined to plain "yes" and "no." When she herself began to ask questions about life over there her hot fingers slithered over his palm. It appeared that Mr. Harrington was happy on the other side, although he missed Violet.

"You were always so busy down here. Are you—is there enough for you to do?" Two knocks, rather peremptory.

Falteringly Mrs. Harrington continued. "I have bought a pendant and I should like your opinion on it."

The response to this was an absolute fusillade of knocks, irregular ones which gradually became fainter.

"Don't be angry," Mrs. Harrington said pleadingly. "Don't go away, I have so many more questions." She asked some, and then Mrs. Bennett put a question or two, but the spirit refused to respond.

"We may as well call it a night," Widgey said. There was the sound of chairs being pushed back. Mrs. Harrington took away her hand. As often happens when lights are turned on after darkness, the blinking faces looked guilty. Mrs. Harrington was flushed. "It's strange that it becomes difficult when you reach a really interesting point."

Widgey rolled and lit a cigarette. "Why should they answer if they don't want to?"

Mrs. Bennett agreed. "They don't want to know about our lives. Why should we expect to know everything they think and do?"

The conversation continued in this vein. Widgey went out and made them all a cup of tea. They dispersed, the Bennetts first, then Mrs. Harrington and Tony. Her room was number eleven, on the floor below his. She opened the door, turned back to him, took his hand.

"I want you to know that I'm grateful."

"What for?"

"You were so sympathetic. I know you must think I'm foolish." Her hand still held his, she had moved inside the room and it followed that he was now standing inside the doorway.

"I don't think anything of the sort."

"Come in." The injunction was not necessary for now he was quite certainly in the room. He closed the door. Around Mrs. Harrington there hung always some curious scent, rather like low-lying mist clinging to the ground on a damp morning, but in the bedroom this heavy cloying smell was thick, as though he were in the lair of some powerful animal.

"Look." She extended her arm, pointing, and for a moment he was absorbed in the spectacle of the arm itself, revealed as the sleeve of her dress moved up, a fine thick object against which the gold bracelet gleamed. The arm appeared to be pointing at the bed, but now she moved away from him and returned with a framed photograph which she pushed into his hand. It showed the head and shoulders of a tight-faced man whose brow was corrugated by a frown. What was he worried about?

"Harrington." She spoke reverentially.

Tony returned the photograph to its place beside the bed. Beside it stood another, of a pleasant large house standing in considerable grounds. "Is that your home?"

"Yes. It's William and Mary. Very pretty, don't you think?"

It was more than pretty, it was tangible evidence of large sums of money, which he saw suddenly adhering to her.

"Harrington was a passionate man. I am a passionate woman."

He was overpoweringly conscious of her nearness. The scent of her somehow gave the ordinary bedroom the atmosphere of a hotel room used by dozens of men and women for sexual purposes.

"Oh, Tony, Tony."

"Violet." In the moment before being enclosed by those plump white arms he thought: I am lost. Then the arms clasped him firmly and bore him back on to the bed which creaked, and even swayed disturbingly, under their weight. Her mouth opened like a sea anemone and sucked him in.

He went quietly up the stairs to his own room at six o'clock the following morning. Violet had told the truth in saying that she was a passionate woman.

THREE

He spent much of the next two days in her company. They walked round the town together, went round the country in her solidly elegant Rover. Tony drove, and it was a pleasure to be behind the wheel of a car again, but at times he felt like a chauffeur.

"In this village there's a nice little antique shop as you go in on the left, just stop there will you," she would say, or "I don't think we'll have lunch at the Blue Peacock, it's no good, just take us on to the next village like a dear boy." Not simply a chauffeur, but a chauffeur-cum-gigolo, for her manner towards him had become distinctly proprietorial, expressed in the requests she made for him to perform small services like getting her scarf and cigarettes. He did not mind her giving him money to pay for things, nor did he really resent being ordered about, but somehow it put their relationship on a footing which he did not feel they had reached. In the night she moaned for him and asked again and again if he loved her, but in the daytime he behaved as though absolutely certain of his dependence on her. What was the end of the situation, what did he want to happen? He was not sure himself.

On Saturday morning he came down just after eleven, feeling weary but looking smart in a very pale sports jacket with dark blue trousers and elegant grey suède shoes. The honeymoon couple were going home and Widgey was at the entrance to tell them good-bye. There was no sign of Violet. Widgey beckoned him with a grimy forefinger and he followed her into the parlour, which was untidier than usual. Half a dozen small receptacles were brim-full of ash and stubs, playing cards were littered over the table as if a midnight poker game had been broken up by a police raid, small bits of orange peel were scattered on the sideboard. Widgey herself was wearing an old grey skirt fastened by safety pins and a dirty blue pullover. The contrast she presented to his own elegance was somehow uncomfortable.

"Sit down." He sat in one of the stiff rexine covered chairs at the table. She rolled around the cigarette in her mouth, perhaps a sign of embarrassment, then suddenly emitted a powerful stream of smoke from her nose, like steam coming from a horse's nostrils. "How long are you staying?"

The question took him aback. It was something she had never said to him before. But she did not wait for an answer.

"I'm fond of Violet, known her a long time. What about you?"

"How do you mean?"

She made an irritated gesture, cigarette in hand. Ash fell to the floor. "What are you going to do?"

He began to feel annoyed. Was he to be blamed because a woman fell in love with him? He moved his shoulders.

"Harrington had some sort of engineering firm. She still

71

owns it. She's got plenty of money, only stays here for old times' sake." What was she getting at? "You going to marry her?"

"I don't know. She might not want to."

"She'd eat you, boy, she'd eat you up alive. Don't do it."

"It's my business." He said it with a sharpness he did not intend.

Widgey did not answer but she turned round and he was startled to see tears in her eyes. In the next moment he felt the pricking behind his own eyes, lowered his head and moved towards her. Then she was in the old arm-chair that had always stood in this room, his face lay on the rough texture of the grey skirt, he was sobbing and she was stroking his hair. He had the common sensation of thinking that the whole incident had happened before, and then he remembered that this was so, that there had been a time in childhood when he had been lost for a couple of hours on the beach and had been brought back by a policeman and been scolded, and had then dirtied his pants. Rejected by his father and mother he had run into the parlour, flung himself weeping into Widgey's lap and pressed his face into the roughness of her skirt. It was as simple as that. He wiped his eyes, got up.

"You're right, it's your business," she said huskily. "I'm telling you, that's all. Have you got to get married?"

"I'm not pregnant."

"You know what I mean."

"I told you I'm not in any trouble."

"You will be one day. I was looking at the cards."

"Oh, the cards."

"Don't laugh at the cards." Her face as she said this, thin, small and malevolent, was witch-like. "And about Violet. Remember what I said."

"It might be nice to be eaten up." He giggled. "By all that money."

She shrugged. The effect of the conversation was to make him feel that he would marry Violet if she said yes to him. Widgey, he thought, has never been short of money. But he knew that this was unjust, that she would never have done anything simply to get it.

He made the approach that afternoon, in the car, on a headland overlooking the sea with rain pouring down outside. He had gone for a long walk—alone, because Violet did not appear until just before lunch—and had made up his mind to ignore Widgey. It was time he settled down, he needed to marry somebody with money, and Violet was everything he could reasonably expect. After all, hadn't he thought in relation to some of those Violetish ladies in the past that he could happily settle down with them if they weren't married already? And when he thought of himself as the master of that delightful house, three or four servants, no doubt the squire of the village—and of course a trip abroad every year or more often, with inevitably a flutter at the casino—why should he hesitate? And flutter was the wrong word, he would have money enough to play the Prudential or the Rational System, and with enough capital you couldn't lose. The money would bring him independence. Certainly Violet was not up to Fiona, but Fiona had not been real and Violet was unquestionably there in the flesh. You had to think about the future, and it was nonsense to talk about being eaten alive.

Afterwards he could not remember what words he had spoken in the desire to avoid the straight question, "Will you marry me?" but whatever the words may have been they were not misunderstood. The car had a bench seat and in a moment Violet was upon him, holding him in her arms so that his very slight recoil pushed the side of his body against the door. The door handle dug into his

73

ribs. Her mouth was on his, her warm strong scent overpowered him.

"Darling Tony, we're going to be so happy. You don't know how lonely I've been."

"Not any more."

"Not any more. A woman needs a man to look after her."

He found himself being desperately honest. "I haven't got any money."

"What does it matter? I've got enough for two."

He moved slightly, almost lolling back on the seat. The door handle stuck into his side just below the armpit, like a hard finger.

"We could travel abroad," he said interrogatively.

"Yes. You'd like that, wouldn't you?"

Yes, he would like that. The hot animal breath was on him, the pop eyes looked into his own. Outside the rain changed suddenly to hail. It rattled against the windows as though somebody was firing at them with a pea shooter.

"We're cosy," she said. They shifted positions so that both of them lay awkwardly along the bench seat. She breathed in little pants; her mouth nuzzled the side of his neck. He was incapable of making love to her. Her dress had ridden up to reveal a patch of thigh, slightly mottled. He felt terror, the sensation of being caught in a trap. A man eater, Widgey had said.

"What's the matter?"

"The door handle." He moved again.

"Is it that woman?"

"What woman?"

"The one you told me about, that you were going to marry. You think it's just on the rebound, is that it?"

"Perhaps."

"I don't mind. I shall understand."

74

He disentangled himself and sat up behind the steering wheel. He could not go through with it. "I think we should give ourselves time. To consider."

"What for? We're over twenty-one."

"You don't know anything about me." She looked at him. He repeated feebly, "We ought to wait."

She sat up too, pulled down her dress. "That's not what you were saying five minutes ago."

The hail stopped suddenly. He looked out at the greasy sea. She said, "Drive back. And put down the window, it's stuffy."

That's the way it would have been, he thought on the way back.

I should have been her lackey, it would have been a terrible mistake. After their return she held out her hand for the keys, got out of the car. He got out too. They faced each other, with the car between them.

"I usually get what I want." With these words—were they an expression of disappointment or somehow an implied threat?—she turned away from him and went into the hotel.

That night Widgey put on one of her roast turkey dinners, with an elaborate ice cream pudding afterwards. She carved the turkey herself, attacking it with frightening ferocity. Flash flash, pieces of breast fell off. Crunch—a leg had been severed and in a few moments was sliced to the bone. A spoon violated the carcass of the bird, emerging with greeny-brown stuffing. Some new guests had arrived, and the sight of the small woman making so furious an attack on the large bird stimulated them to an excited buzz of conversation. They glimpsed a series of gastronomic feasts ahead which would never be put before them. Violet did not come down to dinner, Widgey never glanced in his direction.

After dinner, the reckoning. He looked at his wallet and found that it contained only twenty pounds. He would have to get some sort of secretarial job, and get it soon.

Later in the evening he told Widgey. She was sitting in the parlour eating chocolates and reading a book called *Nancy and the Handsome Sailor*. Playing cards were spread on the table.

"I'm not going to marry her." She nodded. "You're right. She would have eaten me up."

Widgey bit into a chocolate, looked at the centre, ate the rest of it. "She's gone."

"Gone!"

"She was staying another week, but she packed and left."

He felt uneasiness, guilt, the need to explain. "I only did what you said."

"I didn't tell you to do it that way. I told you, she's a cow but I'm fond of her." She spread out the cards again, turned them over. "You're a Gemini."

"What? Oh, Gemini. My birthday's on the third of June."

"Gemini. And you're twenty-seven. Black queen after a red queen and a red king before that. It means trouble. And it means a chance."

"I'm going to look for a job, I shan't be here much longer."

"Stay as long as you like, it doesn't matter to me."

Affection for her welled up in him. "Have you got any paint? In the morning I'll paint that chest of drawers in my room."

"I believe there's some in the store. Not sure what it's like though. Do you know something?"

"What?"

"Maybe I was wrong. Perhaps it would be good for you to be eaten up alive."

Later, in room thirteen, he wept as he looked at the

scarred chest of drawers. Was he weeping for his youth, for the lost days of football matches and kindness, for Widgey, for his present situation? He did not know. It was after three in the morning when he fell asleep.

FOUR

What Widgey called the store was a kind of cupboard out-house which contained a lot of junk like old bicycles with flat tyres (he had ridden one of them when he was a child), electric hedge clippers covered with rust, dozens of empty bottles, dozens of unopened tins of tomato soup, four brass fenders, various pieces of old iron and, sure enough, some paint tins and stiff old brushes. Most of the tins were empty and the paint in the others was covered with a thick crust which had to be broken before penetrating to the liquid below. He used one of these tins to paint the chest of drawers but did not make a very good job of it because the colour, which started off as light blue, deepened steadily as he went on. The result was a parti-coloured chest, which would obviously need another coat. Widgey, however, expressed herself as delighted when she came up to see it. She looked vaguely round the room.

"Think I ought to get some new stuff in here?" She patted the tallboy. "That's a good piece."

"Some more wallpaper perhaps."

"I've had people who like it, think it's original. And what the hell, they can't expect the earth for what I charge." It was true that her charges were low. "Know that grey haired man with the young blonde wife, came yesterday. I believe she's his niece."

"Why?"

"She called him Uncle. Still, it's not my business."

"I suppose not."

"You've made a wonderful job of this." She absent-mindedly patted the chest of drawers and paint came off on her fingers.

Sunday was the only day on which Widgey served lunch and, as always in her periods of abstraction, the food was poor. The remainder of the turkey had mysteriously vanished and the guests got pork luncheon meat and salad, followed by cold jam covering leaden pastry. Grumbles moved like distant thunder round the tables. After lunch Tony went for a walk. He was approaching the pier when he heard a shout. "Jonesy. Hey there, Jonesy." He felt a thump between the shoulder blades and turned to see a red faced man smiling at him.

"Passed you just now and thought to myself 'I know that face,' and then I thought, 'Of course, it's old Jonesy.'" He shook Tony's hand vigorously.

"I think you're making a mistake."

"No, I'm not. I tell you what, I know your other name, it's Tony, right? I'm Bill Bradbury."

And then he did remember. Bradbury had been the leader of the boys in the lavatories, the big boy who had started it all. And here he was now, a big man bursting out of his tweed suit, with horn-rimmed glasses and thinning hair. Tony hesitated for a fatal moment and then had to say "Yes, I remember. It's been a long time."

"And I've changed, don't I know it. Putting on weight where I shouldn't. I'd have known you anywhere. Still at Eltham, are you?"

"No. I left there long ago."

"Same here. Shaking the old dust off the feet. Now I tell you what we'll do, you just come along with me." And as though to enforce this policeman-like injunction Bradbury took an uncomfortable grip on Tony's arm and walked along with him. "I've had to come in to collect a couple of things from the office, then you come back and have tea and meet the wife and family."

"I'm not sure that——"

"Come on now, I won't take no for an answer." They turned off down a side street. A brass plate said *South Eastern Export Company*. Bradbury unlocked the door and led the way to an office with "Manager. Please Knock" lettered on it in black. The room had that ghostly chilliness common to offices when they are not in use.

"Sit you down." Tony sat in the chair that was no doubt reserved for clients. Bradbury busied himself behind a big desk, then took papers from a filing cabinet and began to make notes. From time to time he would look up with an encouraging smile, and say that he wouldn't be a couple of minutes. Tony felt like a mouse being protectively watched by a cat. Suppose he started to walk out, would Bradbury pounce? Contemplating the bullet head behind the desk, pink scalp showing beneath the carefully brushed hair, he wondered also what would happen if he said, "Do you remember a day at school . . ." and went on to recall the details of that afternoon. Bradbury had been only two or three years older than he, but at the time he had seemed like a creature from another world. No doubt he would look up and say with genuine incomprehension that he did not know what Tony was talking about. Now he took two differently coloured pens from a small battery of them on his desk and began to make notes on the papers. He returned the file to the cabinet, snapped it shut. His movements were brisk, business man style.

"That's that. One of the boys made a real cock-up on some bills of lading. Can't trust anybody nowadays, have to check everything yourself. I'll have something to say to that young gentleman to-morrow. Now then, let's get moving. I left the bus in the garage round the corner."

79

"You don't live in town?"

"Not likely. I'm out in the country, good clean air, can't beat it."

The car was a Hillman. "What d'you drive yourself?"

"A Jaguar."

"Do you now?" He gave a whistle between the teeth that Tony remembered. "Things are all right, eh?"

"As a matter of fact I'm between cars at the moment."

"Oh yes." Bradbury gave him one quick glance and said nothing more, but Tony was suddenly conscious of the tweed-trousered leg close to his own in the car.

He said with attempted carelessness, "By the way, I've changed my name. Lots of family complications, remarriages you know, things got difficult. It's Bain-Truscott now."

"I see." Again that quick glance, then he was looking at the road again. "I'll remember. What's your line then?"

"I've just been helping a General with his memoirs. Rewriting them."

"A writer, are you?"

"Yes." He regretted more than ever the decision, although it had hardly been a decision, to accept Bradbury's invitation.

"Gathering material down here?"

"I'm staying with my aunt. A short holiday. What does your company do?"

The question shifted Bradbury into another gear. During the rest of the drive he talked about himself, and about his contacts with other European countries and the agencies he held. By the time they reached Beaver Close Tony had heard about Bradbury's wife Evelyn whose dad was well in with Rotary, and knew that they had decided not to have any kids for a year or two and since then had been trying without any luck. Mr. Granville, Evelyn's dad, was staying the weekend with his wife and some friend of Evelyn's was coming to tea.

Beaver Close was a complex of half a dozen identical mock-Georgian houses neatly placed round their own small square of green on the outskirts of a village. It was not Tony's idea of living in the country but after getting out of the car Bradbury inflated his chest, taking in and expelling great mouthfuls of air. Each of the houses had a differently-coloured front door and Bradbury pointed this out. "Gives that touch of originality. Come in."

Inside there were rugs on parquet floors, a pervasive smell of newness. Bradbury tapped the parquet with his foot. "Underfloor heating all through. Wonderful investment. Paid five thou for it three years ago, sell it for eight any day I wanted."

A door opened and a small harassed woman appeared. "Surprise surprise," Bradbury cried. "Evelyn, my dear, I ran into an old friend, brought him back to tea. This is Tony, Tony Bain-Truscott." There was a slight pause after the Christian name.

Three people were in the neat sitting-room. Mr. Granville was a larger, older image of his son-in-law, red faced and white haired. They might have been father and son. His wife had a blue rinse and a manner of pained aristocratic reserve. "And this is——" Bradbury looked round. His wife had vanished.

"Genevieve Foster. We haven't met."

"Charmed." Bradbury inclined his body, then said with tremendous formality, "May I present my old friend, Tony Bain-Truscott." Their how do you do's rang out at the same moment. Tony received an impression of whiteness and fragility. Evelyn wheeled in a trolley on which every article seemed to be gleaming silver, teapot, milk jug, strainer, hot water jug, sugar bowl. On a lower level there were elegant china plates, thin bread and butter, scones, jam.

"I'm afraid it's just pot luck, Mr. Bain-Truscott."

"Call him Tony," Bradbury boomed. "Too much of a mouthful, the other."

He found himself sipping pale tea from a cup so frail that he feared it might break in his hands, and talking to Mr. Granville. "So you were at school with Bill. I expect he was a live-wire even in those days."

"Yes, he was."

"I spotted that the first time I saw him. That boy's got ideas, I said, he'll go a long way. It so happens I play golf in a foursome every week with the English director of Hispano-American Construction." Could that be what he had said? Mr. Granville sucked in his breath, winked, and went on, "Wheels within wheels."

Surely he must be Bradbury's father? He bit into a scone and said nothing. He saw the school lavatories with terrible clarity, the doors that were always being banged, the group of boys round him, Bradbury's big red face. Somebody spoke. He replied to Mrs. Granville's blue rinse. "I'm sorry."

"Eldon Truscott in Shropshire. Is he——"

"My branch of the family came from Australia."

"Colonial." She lost interest.

"Writing, now, is there money in that?" That was her husband.

"I have an independent income." Behind the horn-rims Bradbury was studying him curiously. Tony rose, took a plate, handed round bread and butter. Mrs. Foster held out her teacup. It was refilled from the silver pot.

"I hear you're a writer. My husband writes too."

"I'm not a professional writer. I was helping an old soldier with his war memoirs."

"How interesting. My husband's an amateur. He is interested in topography, which is too much for me I'm afraid." The chair beside her was vacant, and he sat down. At least he had got away from the Granvilles. Seen more closely Mrs. Foster was attractive. Her face was neat and small, the features classical, the hair cut short like a boy's. Her eyes were a strange colour, a flinty grey. The first impression of fragility was confirmed, the hand that held the teacup was small, but he had a sense of something controlled and fierce behind this delicacy.

He was wondering about her age when she said, "You look too young to have been at school with Mr. Bradbury."

"I'm twenty-seven. He was one of the older boys."

"But you were friends." Something about her flinty grey gaze seemed to question it.

"Of course. We've not met for years." He gave a start as he felt pressure applied to his upper arm. Tea spilt into his saucer, some went on to the mushroom coloured carpet. Evelyn mewed with distress.

"Startled you, old man, sorry." It was Bradbury's hand, of course. Then Evelyn had rushed out for a cloth and he was on his knees helping her to wipe the carpet, although really only a few drops had been spilled. Evelyn kept repeating that it was perfectly all right, but her stare at the carpet said the reverse. The tea trolley was wheeled out, he was shown round the neat suburban garden, and then it was time to go.

Mrs. Foster was taking him back. Bradshaw accompanied them out to her car.

"It's been good to see you, but we never got a chance to talk over old times." His leg brushed against Tony's. "Have lunch with me one day."

"I'm going back to town in a day or two. I'll ring you when I'm free."

When they were out of sight of the house Mrs. Foster said, "Are you pleased to get away? I am. I'd only met Evelyn before, we're both members of the Women's Club. He was a bit of a shocker, I thought. But I forgot, you're a friend of his."

83

"Not so much of a friend as all that."

"Do you know, that's what I thought." She flashed him a smile of what might almost have been called complicity. "It's a pity."

"What is?"

"That you're going back so soon. Eversley, my husband, needs help badly with his book and you do that kind of thing. Or am I wrong?"

There was the most curious kind of tension in the car. She did not look at him, she stared ahead at the ribbon of road. Why did some kind of invitation seem to lie behind those innocuous words?

"Not exactly. I told you what I did for the General."

"Eversley would expect to pay. If you wouldn't be insulted."

He wanted to say, I am not sure, I have been much deceived in women, I am afraid of what they may do to me. Instead he said, "I really ought to go back to London."

"It's up to you. Where shall I drop you?" When he opened the door to get out she said, "Don't make any mistake. I asked you because I thought you'd get on with Eversley. He's not the easiest man in the world."

"I'm flattered."

"There's no need to be." She shrugged her slim shoulders. "If you want to ring you'll find me in the book."

He was walking away when she wound down the car window. "Eversley likes to see references. If you've got any."

References indeed! He tried not to show by the stiffness of his back that this really did insult him.

FIVE

He rang the following morning from the Seven Seas, with the daily whizzing a vacuum cleaner about under his nose. Her voice sounded cool, almost uninterested, as she asked him to come along at three o'clock. The address was Villa Majorca, Byron Avenue.

Byron Avenue was on the outskirts of Southbourne. In the bus on the way over he tried to analyse the reason for the excitement he felt. Why had he dressed with more than usual care, in a charcoal suit with a faint stripe, a plain white shirt with button down collar, a discreet blue tie? This was only a temporary job, or no job at all if Foster disliked him. He felt the tingling in his stomach which told him that Mrs. Foster found him attractive, yet if Foster suspected this he might not get the job. But as the bus rattled along the sea front and then turned off, away from the hotels into a residential area of wide roads in which red brick or whitewashed houses stood detached in well kept gardens, the sense of approaching some climacteric in his life increased.

The few houses in Byron Avenue were solidly opulent in the Edwardian manner favoured by builders in seaside resorts soon after the beginning of the century, when Southbourne had been a village and these the residences of rich Londoners. He passed a plot with a "For Sale" notice on it and then came to the Villa Majorca, which was smaller and more modern than most of its neighbours. A gravel drive led up to the front door. On the opposite side of the road were school playing fields. When he rang the bell she answered the door and took him into the drawing-room. She wore a pale dress—he was never to see her in

85

any but pastel colours—which almost matched the grey flint of her eyes.

The room was quite small and although there were nice things in it the effect was not one of order or elegance. On the mantelpiece he saw some bits of what he recognised as Battersea enamel, a corner cupboard contained some porcelain, perhaps Dresden or Meissen, or perhaps only imitations. There was a piano with photographs on it, there were little tables studded with mother-of-pearl. An incongruous note was struck by African masks, a fur-covered shield and a pair of assegais or spears grouped in one corner. She saw his glance.

"They're my husband's, he spent some time in Africa. You were thinking his taste is different from mine? Quite right."

"I was thinking that. At that very moment." Where was Foster? She answered this unspoken question.

"Eversley had to go up to London, looking up references in some museum. He is so keen about this book."

"Perhaps I should come back."

"He wants me to interview you. Eversley is a fool about people. You said you can type. Come and show me."

He followed her to a room at the back fitted up as a study, with a big mahogany desk, a swivel chair, a filing cabinet, books behind glass. A window looked on to the garden. There was a typewriter on the desk, paper beside it. He put the paper into the machine, typed a few lines. She nodded.

"Good. You'll think I'm being very careful, but Eversley's last secretary typed with two fingers."

Back in the sitting-room he produced the letter from Sir Archibald Graveney and another, which he had typed on a different machine at a different time, which purported to be from Chalmsley Baker of Redmers Hall in Cumberland. Both testified to his satisfactory service as a secretary. She touched the one from Baker with her fingertips and asked if he would mind if she followed it up. He made his stock reply.

"Of course, but you won't get a reply for a week or two. Baker's yachting on the Riviera, lucky chap. He sent me a card." He forestalled what might be her next question. "And Sir Archibald died last year. Though I believe his widow's still at Throgmorton."

She made no comment, but went on. "You mentioned that you'd been helping a General with his memoirs. Eversley was particularly interested by that."

He moved uneasily. The interview was much more businesslike than he had expected. Then he smiled. The smile was one that he had practised in the glass, and he considered it devastating. "I practically wrote half the book. But there's something I didn't tell you. We parted on bad terms, I'm afraid."

"I couldn't ask him for a reference?"

"He might explode if you did."

"So there's nobody I can write to at the moment."

This really was a little bit too much. Anybody would have thought he was applying for a job at the Bank of England. He started to get up from his chair. As he did so she folded the two letters carefully and smiled.

"I'm terribly sorry, I really am insulting you." He did not contradict her. "And I'm being stupid. It's just that I'm doing it for Eversley. If you'd like to take the job we should both be very pleased."

He sat down again and she started to talk about money. She suggested an arrangement that was fair, even generous, for a job that was five days a week, mornings only, from ten o'clock each morning. "When can you start? Will to-morrow morning be all right?"

"There's no need for an interview with your husband?"

"The problem is to keep him occupied. He's not very strong and doesn't work. He doesn't know what to do with his time." Her tongue came out and licked her pale lips. There was again a hint of complicity, of a shared secret, in her manner as she showed him to the door.

A classic situation, he thought on the way back in the bus. Elderly valetudinarian husband, young discontented wife playing while husband's away. Yet this analysis did not satisfy him. There was something forbidding about Mrs. Foster, and this was part of the attraction she held for him.

SIX

He presented himself at precisely ten o'clock on the following morning, met Foster and began work.

Foster was far from the elderly valetudinarian of Tony's imagination. Mrs. Foster—Jenny as he thought of her although the name was not appropriate—was about his own age, and Foster was perhaps three or fours years older. He was a small man, a head shorter than Tony, of a weak Byronic handsomeness. A single white streak marked his black hair. The three of them sat in the drawing-room for half an hour talking.

"Mr. Bain-Truscott really can type," she said. "I tested him. His fingers fairly flew over the keys. Not like the last one."

"That's good. He was not at all satisfactory." Foster seemed uncomfortable.

"And he has splendid references." Her tongue crept out, touched her lips, went in again. The quick glance she gave him held no visible sign of amusement or irony.

"I leave all that to you." Abruptly Foster said, "Are you interested in topography?"

"To be frank I don't know the first thing about it." The moment seemed right for his smile. "But I can learn."

"I rely on my wife. She doesn't often make mistakes."

They talked about the weather and about the town and then Jenny said, "Perhaps you should start Mr. Bain-Truscott off, darling."

Foster led him into the study, and took out several large quarto volumes from the glass-fronted case. "What I'm trying to do is to produce a complete topographical survey of this area, and not only topographical but historical, so that it compares each period shown in the more important maps with every period preceding it. I want to make the comparison fully detailed about every village."

"That sounds like quite an enterprise."

"It's a survey of a kind that has never been attempted before," Foster said solemnly. "Just now I'm still in the stage of accumulating comparison notes. I'd like them typed up on separate cards and then I shall analyse them in detail."

He proceeded to rattle off at considerable speed, so that Tony had to ask him to slow down, a variety of extracts from the volumes in front of him. They went into great detail about population details, boundary changes and physical features of each district. Then Foster showed him the form in which he wanted the notes typed up. While Tony was typing he caught the man looking at him in a way that was hard to define. It was as though he were—what? Afraid of Tony, jealous of him, assessing him as a rival? Something of all these, perhaps, with something else that he could not place.

At ten minutes to one Jenny put her head round the study door. "Have you almost finished, Eversley?"

"For to-day, yes."

"You have time for a drink before you go, Mr. Bain-Truscott?"

They drank sherry in the drawing-room from small, beautiful glasses. He asked them to call him Tony because his full name was such a mouthful.

Foster was drinking his sherry in an abstracted manner, head sunk in his shoulders. When she rather sharply called him to attention he said, of course, Tony by all means. There was no reciprocal suggestion that he should use their Christian names.

"How did it go this morning?"

"Very well." Foster gave a weak smile. "Mr.—Tony is an excellent typist."

It was she who showed him out. "I'm sorry not to invite you to lunch, but we have only a very light midday meal. In the afternoon Eversley often lies down for an hour. I told you he's not very strong." As she opened the door there was the sidelong cat-like look suggesting that they shared some secret.

Wednesday morning was a repetition of Tuesday, the dictation, the typing, the glass of sherry. It seemed to Tony that Foster was reading passages from books and he suggested that if they were suitably marked he could save time by copying them without the need for dictation. Foster pulled at his upper lip dubiously.

"Perhaps. I shall have to go up to the British Museum to-morrow, and I shall leave something for copy typing. But for most of this material that wouldn't do, it wouldn't do at all. I have to select passages that fit together. I don't think I could possibly mark them all up in advance."

He spoke with concern, almost with agitation, and Tony left it at that. If Foster liked to pay him for wasting time, why should he object? Foster continued on an apologetic note. "I've had secretaries before who've done things their way and got into a terrible muddle. Doing them like this may take longer, but I can make sure everything is in the right order."

"Yes, of course. How long have you been working on the book?"

"Nearly five years."

"Since you came back from Africa, I suppose?"

A pause. "That's right."

"Did you live there long?"

"Quite a time." He opened another book, started to dictate again.

Suppose Foster was thirty-five, and he certainly could not be older, had he married Jenny out there or since he returned? And did his money come from Africa? Certainly he must have money, to live here and occupy himself with a project like this. There seemed to him something odd about the marriage, but again he reflected that it was not his business. That afternoon he put a second coat of paint on the chest of drawers, and in the evening told Widgey that he had a job and would pay for his keep. She waved the suggestion aside.

"Don't want any money, I've got enough. What's the job?" She listened with a sceptical air when he told her.

"You want to look out for that Mrs. Foster. Sounds to me as if she's got her hooks into you."

"She's not like that." He rather regretted saying anything.

"He must be pretty wet." On this he made no comment. "Don't get mixed up with her the way you did with Violet. Have a cuppa?"

"It would never have done," he said as he drank the scalding liquid. "You were quite right." The thought of Violet's opulent flesh and of those nights in her room came back to him and he shuddered uncontrollably.

"Sometimes I think you don't like any women."

He was indignant. "I like them much better than men."

"I wonder."

"I like you. I think you're the most wonderful woman I've ever known." He kissed the straggly hair on the top of her head.

"Thanks very much. Just don't get mixed up with this

Foster female, she sounds like poison. I don't want him coming round with a shotgun."

"He's wet, you said so yourself."

"It's the wet ones who use guns." There was a thunderous noise in the hall. "Christ, it's that man O'Grady. He gets tight every night. Give me a hand."

O'Grady was on his knees in the hall, glassy eyed, trying to right a hat-stand he had knocked over. They got him up the stairs and into his room. Widgey managed it all without removing the cigarette that drooped from her mouth. An elderly couple watched their ascent with awe, and asked if Mr. O'Grady was ill.

"Drunk." They stared after her unbelievingly. She said to Tony, "Thanks. Don't know how I'd have managed."

"You'd have managed. Are you going to get rid of him?"

"What for? Man's got a right to drink as long as he doesn't bother anybody."

"The other guests won't like it."

The cigarette moved up and down in her mouth as she spoke emphatically. "Then they can bloody well lump it. There are too many people around who try to stop other people doing what they want." As he was going up to bed she told him again not to get mixed up with Mrs. Foster, then started to laugh, her whole body shaking. "You see, I'm one of them."

On Thursday he got mixed up.

It began like the other days. She opened the door to him wearing one of her pale dresses, her face colourless above it. She said simply that Eversley had left things to type. There were passages marked in books and he began work on them. Just after eleven she came in, bringing a cup of coffee. As she put it on the desk she leaned over and for a moment her slight body was close to his. There was no scent about it, no warmth. She turned away to the window and her back was towards him, slender and straight. Below the short dark hair her neck was white.

It was, or so he thought afterwards, the whiteness and vulnerability of this neck and something hopeless yet un-yielding in the set of her shoulders that made him rise, move to her and put his arms round her from behind, feeling the bones of the rib cage and the small breasts. She stayed for a moment quite still like some animal unsure of its captor's intentions, then turned so that she faced him and pressed her mouth to his. The mouth was cool and dry, the body pressed against him felt hard as a board. She said nothing as they separated, but took him by the hand as if they were children and led him upstairs. In the bedroom their bodies were pressed together on one bed while another stayed unused. A dark blue medallion set like an eye in the middle of the counterpane stared at what happened.

He was amazed by the vehemence with which she made love to him, so that he was a passive rather than a dominant partner in what they did. Yet although he was surprised and in a way shocked by the passion contained in that thin white body, the sensations he experienced were more pleasurable than any he had known. To be used in this way by a woman as the vehicle of her own intense sexual desire fulfilled some emotional need in himself that he had not known to exist. Afterwards, while they lay and smoked, he took in the luxury with which the bedroom was furnished, the lacquered furniture, the smoke blue wallpaper, the silky Chinese carpet on which there was a medallion in another tint of blue.

"I know what you're thinking," she said. "I'll tell you the answer. Eversley's no good."

"I understand."

"I doubt it. I mean no good in any way, to me or to himself. He's stinking rich, that's why I married him. And he's got what he wants, he'll do anything for me. A couple of years ago I said I'd like a fast car. Next week he bought me a Jensen. When I got bored he sold it and lost a thousand pounds on the deal. A year ago he got me a motor launch. I'm bored with that too. Do you like mucking about in boats?"

"I don't know."

"I'll show it to you one day. I'm honest, you know, I told him all this when I married him. Four years ago."

"Soon after he came back from Africa?"

"How did you know?"

"He told me."

"Oh yes. I was an actress in rep on and off, but it's a hell of a life, often you don't know where the next week's rent is coming from. I daresay I was no good. I can't express my feelings." He laughed and she dug nails into his arm. "On the stage, I mean. People say what fun it is, living in boarding houses, not having enough to eat, but I never thought so. That's why I married Eversley. I didn't know he had this heart trouble, or that he'd want to moulder away here. Topographical history." She spoke as if it were something indecent. "If we were married, would you want to work on topographical history?"

There was only one answer to that, and he made it. Later she stared at him with her flint grey eyes.

"It's always the wrong people who have the money. You haven't got any?"

"No."

"Tell me about yourself."

He gave her an edited version of his life. She listened attentively.

"I didn't think anybody could be called Bain-Truscott. What's your name?"

He said with an effort, "Jones."

"What's wrong with that." She got off the bed, began

94

to put on her clothes. "You'd better do some typing."

He was surprised. "Oh. All right."

"My woman comes in the afternoon. I don't want you here then. If you've done nothing Eversley will notice. He may be a fool but he's not stupid."

This alternation of passion and coldness fascinated him. He left in a ferment of pleasure with which some anxiety was blended. He knew that for the first time in his life he had met a woman with whom he was emotionally involved. At one o'clock she saw him out as though he were a stranger. When he moved to kiss her good-bye she said nothing, but stepped back and away from him.

SEVEN

On the following morning Foster opened the door to him and they went straight into the study. Jenny was nowhere to be seen. Foster had brought back new material from London, and began to dictate at once. At half past eleven he looked at his watch.

"Can you get along on your own for the rest of the morning? Some of these afforestation details are not very clear and I shall have to check on them at the local library."

"Shall I check them for you? This afternoon I mean."

"I prefer to do it myself." Tony looked up and intercepted a glance that startled him, because it appeared to be one of pure dislike. It must have been a trick of the light, however, for now Foster smiled. "You'll think I'm fussy, but this sort of thing involves checking twenty different accounts against each other, and I'd sooner make my own mistakes."

95

"Are you satisfied with my work? Tell me anything I'm doing that's wrong."

"It's fine. I'm getting along faster than I have done for a long time." Foster gestured at the pile of cards, then pulled out his wallet. "We'll make the payments weekly, unless you object."

Tony said he didn't object. When he heard the front door close he came out of the study, looked in the drawing-room and the kitchen, then started up the stairs. Jenny appeared at the top of them.

"He's gone round to the library." Why did he speak in a whisper?

She said nothing, but took his hand and led him to the bedroom. Later they came down and drank sherry from the elegant glasses. She was silent.

"What is it, Jenny? What's the matter?"

"Nothing."

"There is something. Tell me."

"We suit each other. Don't we?" He placed a hand on her arm. "I don't believe you've told me everything."

"I don't know what you mean."

"Those references. You forged them, didn't you?" He had quite forgotten this, but now his silence was a betrayal. "I don't mind. You're clever, they're good letters. I just wanted to know."

He said boldly, with a sense of trusting her as he had trusted nobody since he was a child, "Yes."

"What was the trouble with your General. Or didn't he exist?"

At this he rebelled. It seemed to him that she wanted to probe the details of everything in his life that was most painful. "We had an argument."

She moved off, as it seemed, at a tangent. "Eversley goes away on trips sometimes. On his own. For two or three

96

weeks. He goes abroad and just wanders around. I think he's building up to one now."

He said uncertainly, "You mean he wouldn't want me any more?"

"Oh, he'd leave work for you. The sacred task must go on. He doesn't leave an address, just sends cards."

What was she driving at? "I'd be able to see you more often?"

She said coldly, "It doesn't matter. You ought to go now."

"I shan't see you until Monday?"

"Of course not. For God's sake don't start hanging about or come paying social calls." The white intensity of her face could never be said to soften, but the cool lips touched his cheek. "Until Monday."

What was he to do with the hours until then? On the way back to the Seven Seas he bought some vividly striped wallpaper and announced to Widgey his intention of repapering his room. He started on Saturday morning, but wallpapering proved more difficult than he had expected. The paper showed a tendency to crease and even to tear, and after doing half the room he could not pretend that the result was satisfactory. He was sitting on the bed contemplating what he had done when Widgey came up and stood in the doorway, hands on hips.

"I'm afraid it's a mess." He had got paste on his trousers, and even though they were old this distressed him.

"You're not cut out for it," she agreed. "Something on your mind?"

"No. Why should there be?"

"I don't know. Phone call for you."

He almost ran down the stairs, thinking of Jenny. When he heard Bradbury's voice he was irritated, and it was only because the rest of the day yawned ahead like an endless cavern that he accepted the invitation to have a drink with a couple of fellows and spend an hour or two on the town.

They met in the cocktail bar of the Grand. Bradbury's companions were a South African named Pickett and a Dutchman who was apparently connected with the European side of South Eastern Export. Pickett was lean as a greyhound, the Dutchman was thick necked and square. Both wore horn-rimmed spectacles. They drank three cocktails quickly and then went into the grill room and ate steaks. Bradbury was in great form. He winked at mention of his wife.

"Saturday's my night off. Evelyn knows that. All in the way of business, mind."

"I like a woman who knows her place," Pickett said.

"I am going to see swinging England." That was the Dutchman.

"Let's hope it doesn't swing you off balance." Bradbury roared with laughter. "Evelyn knows a man needs a bit of relaxation. And you might not think so but you can relax in this little old town, if you know where to go." Blood oozed from the steak.

Pickett speared two chips and began to tell a story about a man who had thought he was getting a lift from Cape Town to Durban and had ended up in Pretoria. The whole thing was connected, in some way Tony did not understand, with arms that failed to reach the Congo. Then the Dutchman, whose name was Van something, told an interminable tale about a man suspected of smuggling diamonds into Holland, who had turned out to be smuggling blue films. He was heavily fined. The joke was that he really had been smuggling diamonds too, and the films were only a cover. Bradbury shook his head over this.

"I don't know if you ought to tell such tales in front of Tony." He smiled. Supposing he told them about the General and the cheque, would they be shocked?

Bradbury, sitting next to him, squeezed his knee. "Our

Tony's a dark horse. You know you made quite an impression on Evelyn, she thought you might be a good influence on me."

"What is your business?" Van something asked.

"I'm independent."

"One of the lucky boys." That was Pickett.

"Tony's my old school friend. He's always looked out for number one." Bradbury ordered large brandies. When they left the Grand they were all a little drunk. They got into Bradbury's car, drove half a mile, got out, and Bradbury rang the bell of a house next to a greengrocer's shop. There was a muttered conversation and then they all went up a flight of stairs and into a room where chairs were set out in rows as though for a lecture. Was it some kind of political meeting? Half a dozen other men were in the room, most of them middle-aged. He did not realise what was going to happen until the man who had let them in, tidy and precise as a bank clerk, unrolled a screen at one end of the room and began fiddling with a projector at the other. Then he turned out the light.

Tony had never seen blue films before and now found himself unmoved by the images that flickered shakily on the screen. The men and women entwined acrobatically. He thought of Jenny and himself and the blue medallion eye watching them. Had they looked as grotesque as these figures, was the involvement he felt merely a matter of these routine embraces and postures? The actions were the same, and they were those he had performed with other women. Why did he feel that in their case it was all entirely different?

Beside him Bradbury breathed noisily. Beyond him Pickett leaned forward, lips pressed tightly together. On the other side the Dutchman sat, brawny arms folded across his chest, head sunk in his shoulders almost as though he was asleep. Bradbury's thigh pressed warmly against

Tony's, and he moved his leg away. He thought of walking out, but was not sure if he could find the door. He sat through the four films, listening to the whirring of the projector and thinking about Jenny. At one point the projectionist said sharply to a man sitting in front of them, "None of that, please, you're watching a film show," rather as if they were in the local Odeon. Then the screen went dark, the whirring stopped, the lights were switched on again, the men filed out down the stairs.

The Dutchman said, "What about an introduction to some of these ladies?"

The bank clerk shook his head. "Just the film show."

In the street Van something was critical. "In Amsterdam we will have a house attached to such a place, a house with girls."

"Not here, old man." Bradbury was firm. "I can give you an address later if you want it. Just now we're going across to Pete's Place. It's new, only been open a week."

He disliked them all, why did he not say good-bye and go back to the Seven Seas? He could not have answered that question, but it seemed to him afterwards that if he had left at that point everything that happened later would have been different.

Had he known what Pete's Place would be? As he entered and saw the green tables under their cut-off pools of light, the counters being pushed back and forwards, the dice clattering against the sides of the board, the cards turned to show colour and picture, he blinked his eyes. Bradbury was signing them in. Tony tapped his shoulder.

"I've only got a couple of pounds with me."

The Dutchman was taking out a wad of notes. Bradbury did not answer Tony, but handed him a pile of chips. "Pay me back any time. Your credit's good."

"Thanks."

"How did you like the show? Really something, the way

they got down to it." The grinning face was close to his own. "Old Van's randy as a goat."

As always he played roulette. Once he was at the table he forgot Bradbury and the show and even Jenny. He had thirty pounds' worth of chips and that was not much to play with, it gave you little scope for manoeuvre, but he might make a small profit playing the Rational System. Or he could go in for a doubling-up game on the transversals. He decided on the Rational and played with some success for half an hour. The Dutchman and Pickett were playing blackjack, Bradbury was moving between two or three of the games. When Tony felt the hand on his shoulder he shrugged it off. The damned man would interfere with his game when he was trying to concentrate.

A voice whispered "Mr. Scott-Williams. Here."

The man had a boxer's bruised face and hands like pieces of raw meat. Tony had never seen him before. He was about to say so when he saw the croupier at the blackjack table watching with a malicious smile. The man was from the Golden Sovereign. He must have been reported.

"We don't want any trouble." The man was not whispering, he simply had a hoarse voice. He decided to make whatever apologies were necessary. They went upstairs. The boxer tapped on a door, opened it, pushed Tony inside and stood with his back to the door.

The room was large and dimly lighted. A monkey-faced man in a lounge suit sat watching a closed circuit television which showed the room below. Tony could see Bradbury talking to Pickett. Were they asking where he had gone? The monkey-faced man turned off the set and looked at Tony. "You can sit down."

He sat in an arm-chair and put his hands on his knees. "I can explain. I was with friends."

"I'll do the talking. I'm Carlos Cotton." A thin layer of gentility overlay the harsh Cockney voice.

Carlos Cotton? Then he remembered. This was the man Armitage had called Number One.

"I don't go looking for trouble, I was good to you. But I put a black on you, right?" In the monkey face two eyes like beads considered him.

"I told you, a friend brought me."

"It's a new place. Why I'm down here, see, I always come down to a new place. Just to see everything's right. How many of my places you been to since I put the black on?"

"None. I told you, it's an accident, a mistake."

"You owe me money."

"But you said it was cancelled."

"Now I'm saying different."

The boxer said in his whisper "He's got some chips."

"Let's have them, Lefty."

The boxer stepped forward, Tony gave the chips to him and he counted them. "Thirty-five."

Cotton nodded. "You still owe me ninety."

"But the money was only ninety——" He heard his voice becoming shrill.

"Interest."

There was another door in the room, a door behind Cotton. Now this opened. A tall girl in a green dress came in and hesitated. Cotton saw her in the glass in front of him and beckoned with a finger. She crossed the room, stood behind the chair, and began to stroke his forehead, then his neck.

"You've got till Wednesday for the rest."

"But I haven't got it."

"I said don't play. You asked for trouble, you got it." The girl's hands rhythmically stroked Cotton's neck. "How's the headache?"

For the first time Tony looked at the girl. She stared straight at him without recognition. It was Fiona Mallory, Mary Tracey.

In a voice of ludicrous mock-gentility Cotton said, "It's getting better all the time, honey."

He was still staring at the girl when Lefty half-pushed him out of the room. At the entrance to the gaming room the big man said, "You heard what the boss said. Wednesday."

"He had no right to take my money."

"What's that about money?" Bradbury, red faced and smiling, stood beside them.

The big man said in his hoarse whisper "I'll see you," and walked away.

"I've lost the money you gave me," Tony said. "I can let you have it in a few days."

"All right." Bradbury seemed unconcerned. "No trouble with King Kong there?"

"No."

"Good. We've all had enough, I'm collecting up our party."

Half an hour later the Dutchman had gone off to one of the addresses Bradbury knew, Pickett to another. Bradbury seemed disappointed that Tony refused an invitation to get himself fixed up, and drove him back to the Seven Seas.

"I don't fancy it myself as a matter of fact, but I wanted to show old Van the town." Tony thanked him for the evening, and repeated that he would pay back the money next week.

"Don't worry about it. It means a lot to me, talking to an old friend." He scrambled out of the car as Bradbury was saying "I'm not a happy man, Tony."

"Thank you for the evening," he said again from the pavement. It seemed a ludicrously inappropriate remark. Bradbury looked at him through the window, put the car into gear and suddenly accelerated away. Tony went up to room thirteen, took off his clothes, brushed his teeth, got into bed and was immediately asleep.

On Sunday he woke with a headache and a bad taste in his mouth. He resolved not to have anything more to do with Bradbury. In the evening he attended one of Widgey's table rapping sessions. The results were disappointing.

EIGHT

On Monday the weather changed. Rain spattered the pavements, a strong wind blew, people struggled along the front in plastic mackintoshes. He rode alone on the top of the bus until it turned off the promenade. Then he heard steps coming up the stairs. A body dropped into the seat beside him. He looked sideways and saw that the man was small, dark, nondescript in appearance. There was something vaguely familiar about him. What was it?

"Message for you. From Mr. Cotton." The man lighted a cigarette, blew a perfect smoke ring. "He wants his money."

Of course. The man had been standing at Tony's table watching the play. He must have followed Bradbury's car last night, but still he seemed harmless enough. Tony felt annoyed. "He'll get it but he'll have to wait."

"Till Wednesday. Just to remind you. Cheerio."

The man rose to leave the bus, pulled on his cigarette and then leaned over and pressed the burning stub on to the back of Tony's hand. He cried out. The shock was so sudden, the momentary pain so intense, that he did not rise from his seat. The man swung along the bus, clattered down the stairs, dropped off at a traffic light. Tony looked at the red mark on his hand and found it hard to believe that the incident had really taken place. Was this the shape of violence, something done casually with a "Cheerio" at the end of it? When he got off at the end of Byron Avenue he was still shaking slightly, and looking at the red and swollen hand he felt sick. Taking deep breaths, letting wind and rain blow in his face, he walked towards the Villa Majorca. When the door opened he received his second shock of the morning. The figure confronting him was neither Foster nor Jenny but a moustached female dragon, who barred the entrance.

"I'm doing some work here. For Mr. Foster."

The dragon sniffed disapproval, but now he heard Jenny's voice. She appeared, as cool as ever.

"Sarah, this is Mr. Bain-Truscott, who is doing some secretarial work." To him she said, "Eversley's up in London, but he's left some work for you." Her manner was brisk, but that was natural in front of the dragon. She led the way to the study, pointed to the work arranged there, and said she had to go out. He saw nothing more of her that morning. At eleven o'clock the dragon brought in a cup of coffee and a biscuit. When he left she was still there, and Jenny had not returned.

In the afternoon the wind dropped, the rain died away, and he went for a long walk beside the sea. He had put ointment on his hand but the mark, an intrusion on the natural health of his body, was a constant reminder that his problems were real and urgent. He shivered at the thought of the knife marking his cheek, the boot in his ribs. Could Fiona, as he still thought of her, help? The problem of how she had got to know Cotton might have absorbed him at another time, but it did not seem likely that she could be of use to him and he put her out of mind. The obvious thing to do—and he had done it before, although never in quite such difficult circumstances—was to run, to take a train and bury himself in London, where it is so easy to hide. He found that he could not do this. He was frightened by the effect that Jenny had on him. He had never taken drugs, but he felt that he could understand why those who did found it impossible to give them up. The emotion that he experienced in Jenny's presence was something he had never felt before in his life.

There was one approach he could make to his immediate problem, and he made it late that evening when he and Widgey sat companionably drinking tea in the parlour, after a visit from Conway, the grey-haired man suspected of sleeping with his niece, who said that their room was too noisy and asked if he could move to the back of the house. Before Widgey's meaningful question, "Does your *wife* find it too noisy then?" Conway faltered, and then said that the room would do and that he was sorry to have bothered her. After he had gone Widgey drank her tea noisily.

"It's none of my affair," she said as she had done before. "But I don't like that man. He *fawns*. I like people to have a bit of nerve. If you're going to sleep with your niece do it, but don't look as if you're apologising for it all the time."

Somehow it seemed to be his cue. "Widgey, can you lend me a hundred pounds?"

She swallowed tea and sniffed. "Yes." Before he could express gratitude she expanded on the monosyllable. "But I won't."

"Why not?"

She pointed the teaspoon at him. Drops fell off it on to the carpet. "First, I'd never see it back. And if I never saw the money I'd never see you again. You're not so much unlike old hot pants yourself, you'd feel too guilty to come and see me. And then I can't afford to lose a hundred pounds."

"Widgey, I'd pay it back."

She ignored this. "But the main thing is I don't like the smell of fish. There's something fishy about it."

He stood up and looked at himself in the fly-spotted glass over the mantelpiece. "I owe somebody money and they want it back."

"Tell 'em to wait."

"They won't."

She lighted a cigarette. "Then do a flit. Don't tell me you've never done one before."

"I can't. Not this time."

She puffed smoke and looked at him. "What have you done to your hand?"

"Grazed it. On a wall by the sea."

"It's to do with that woman, isn't it? I told you not to get mixed up with her."

"You've never met her." He laughed rather shakily.

"I don't need to."

"Did you read her character in the cards? If I don't find the money I shall get beaten up."

"Then clear out. It isn't her character I read in the cards, it's yours."

"Oh, go to hell," he said, and slammed out of the room.

On the next morning, as he turned into the drive that had become so familiar, he felt his heart thudding like a machine that operated quite independently of him. He knew that he was engaged in an affair which was essentially similar to others in the past, but the thudding machine said something different and passed on the message to his nerve ends so that every area of his body seemed unusually sensitive. When she opened the door he could have cried out with pleasure at sight of her pale face and dark hair, her eyes that in their very incommunicativeness seemed to conceal a depth of meaning that must be discovered. The questions he had meant to ask were forgotten when she led him upstairs into the bedroom where, with the beds unmade and the blue medallion eye hidden by the folded counterpane, they made love with feverish anxiety. Again he was conscious of the subordination of his passion to her own, again the feeling was pleasurable. Later he began to ask questions.

"Sarah? She usually comes in the afternoons but yesterday she couldn't, so it had to be the morning. You don't think I wanted that, do you?" She sunk her nails into his arm. "Eversley's up in London. He needn't have gone to-day, at least I don't think so, but I told him I should be here to look after you."

"And doesn't he——"

"What?"

"Suspect something?"

"I told you he was no good. He's a fool."

"He's a fool," he echoed happily. As they laughed together she pressed her mouth forcibly on his. The feeling of subjection overwhelmed him, he let her do what she wished.

Later he did some work and left it piled ready for Foster to see. He was aware of her presence while he typed, it seemed to him that his body reeked of her. Below the layers of clothes were spots touched by her fingers and lips, and these spots were sensitive as bruises. She did not cease to surprise him. At a quarter to one she put her head round the door and asked if he would like a glass of sherry. When they drank together she was as coolly impersonal as she had been on that first day. How could she do it? As though in answer to his question she said, "He would expect us to have a glass of sherry. I shall leave the glasses for him to see."

"You've done this before." He was aware of jealousy, and astonished by it. "Haven't you?"

"I don't like being questioned." She spoke calmly. He could not tell whether or not she was annoyed.

"What did you mean about him going away? You said something the other day."

"It doesn't matter."

"But I want to know."

"I said it doesn't matter." Her voice was not raised, but the tone was such that he said nothing more. He knew that in any conflict of wills he was not equal to her. As she looked at him now he thought he saw in her eyes something hard and implacable, but it seemed that he must have been mistaken for in the next moment she gave one of her rare smiles. "Turn round."

"What for?"

"And close your eyes." He closed them and felt paper pressed into his hand, paper with something hard inside it. "Open them now. It's a present."

Slowly, carefully, he unwrapped tissue paper. He kept his head down because he felt the smarting pricking sensation behind his eyes that was a prelude to tears, and he did not want her to see them. That she should have given him a present made him feel loving and grateful in a way that had nothing directly to do with sex. He remembered one year when he thought that his birthday had been forgotten and then it proved that his present, a bicycle, had been in the garden shed all day waiting for him to find it. The sensation he had felt when his father took him by the hand, led him outside and opened the door had been, like his feeling now, one of pure gratitude for being remembered.

"Open it."

The last wrapping came off to reveal black cuff links with what looked like single diamonds set in them, and a matching tiepin.

"Do you like them?"

He made sure that there would be no tears, looked up. "They're wonderful." He was speaking of the act of giving, not of the gift.

"I wanted to get you something, and I thought they were pretty. I have a little money of my own."

He moved forward to take her in his arms, but she evaded him. "It's a present, that's all, I wanted to give you something. Now I've done it. It's after one, you'd better go."

She was an extraordinary woman, and part of the fascination she held for him was these sudden changes from love to something like hostility. It was almost as though she wished she had not given him the present, or at least that she wanted little attention paid to it. On the way back to the Seven Seas he put the links into his cuffs. Back in his room he took them out, turned them over and looked at them. The truth, which he came to unwillingly, was that he did not like them very much. This stone that looked like a diamond set in something like an opal produced a rather vulgar effect, and when you added the tiepin it was far too flamboyant for his taste. They looked as if they might be quite old, and probably she had paid a fiver for them in some antique shop, perhaps twice that. Anyway, it was the idea of giving something that mattered.

He put them on to the painted chest of drawers and stared at them. Not for some minutes did it occur to him that the stones might be real. Once he had thought of the possibility it became important to be sure.

He was half-way to the jeweller from whom Violet had bought her diamond and ruby pendant when his conscious mind linked the possible value of the links and pin with the money he owed to Cotton. It was absurd to think that they could possibly be worth ninety pounds, but suppose they could be sold for fifty? He rejected the idea vehemently, but once contemplated it refused to be ignored, raising its head again in the form of pictures flicking through his mind like shots from old gangster films, pictures that showed him cowering at one end of a cul-de-sac while two men advanced on him with open razors, or tied up in a room at Pete's Place while lighted cigarettes were pressed into his palms, his cheeks, his testicles.

He had hardly noticed the jeweller on his previous visit. Now the man emerged as a distinct personality. He was small, with a big wart on one side of his nose which gave him an expression of cunning. He remembered Tony.

"The diamond and ruby pendant, a nice piece. Your aunt, was it?"

"A relative, yes."

"She knew what she was looking at." Tony suddenly noticed a larger wart, dark brown and sprouting hairs, on the man's neck just below his ear. He took the links and pin, looked at them casually, got out his glass for a colser examination, nodded. "So what do yau want, a valuation?"

"They're a kind of family heirloom. I might consider selling them."

It was uncomfortably warm in the shop. A bird's call startled him, and then he saw that it came from a cuckoo clock on the wall. He was aware that the man had said something. "What's that?"

"What figure did you have in mind?"

"A hundred pounds."

With horny thumb and forefinger the jeweller pulled at his lower lip, revealing crooked and discoloured teeth. "I could go to eighty."

He heard this offer disbelievingly. "They're real, then? I was never sure about it."

"Black opals, very nice. And the diamonds, one of them has a flaw in the cutting, but still." He looked at them again with the glass. "I won't try to fool you, Mr.——"

"Bain-Truscott."

"You've been fair with me, I'll be fair with you. It's a nice set. If I sell it I make a profit. But how many times do

I get asked for black opals, people don't like them, think they're unlucky. I could make it eighty-five."

"No. I couldn't possibly—anything less than a hundred would be no use." The thought of the money made him almost frantic. "As a matter of fact it's a temporary embarrassment. If you hadn't sold them I could buy them back in a few weeks."

"I don't do business that way. You sell them, I buy them." He pulled again at his lip. "All right."

"What?"

"I take a chance, I give you a hundred."

The jeweller's face across the counter was only a few inches distant, his breath smelled of cheese and beer. On the side of his neck three grey hairs grew like monstrous plants in the fertile dung-coloured ground of the mole. Tony swallowed violently.

"No. I've changed my mind." He gathered up the things into their tissue, pushed them into his pocket and backed away. The jeweller rounded the counter, advanced on him with menacing crab-like slowness. Tony turned, opened the door, hurried out of the shop.

Later he felt an extreme exhilaration. He had been tested, tested as severely as possible, and he had come through. He could have taken the money and given it to Cotton. It was a kind of proof for him that his love for Jenny was something real. And hers for him was sufficiently proved by the value of her gift. Not until the evening did it occur to him that since the man had offered a hundred pounds the links and pin must be worth much more than that.

NINE

Wednesday morning. He had known that Jenny would not be there, because she had said that she was going shopping, but it was still a disappointment when Foster opened the door. They went into the study and started dictation as usual. After an hour Foster said abruptly, "I shan't be here to-morrow. I may be going away."

It would be better not to reveal that he knew of this possibility. "And Mrs. Foster too?"

"I shall be going alone. I find it necessary sometimes to get away, there are too many pressures."

What a fool the man was, wanting to get away from Jenny. Contemplating Foster's feebly handsome face and nervously twisting hands Tony felt both sorry for and contemptuous of him. "Does that mean you won't want me any more."

"I didn't say that. I may be able to leave sufficient——" His voice died away.

"If you could show me what you wanted perhaps I could do some research."

"Perhaps, yes." His hands coiled and uncoiled. "I haven't made up my mind. I only know I must get away."

"Where are you going?"

"What's that to do with you?" Foster said angrily, then recovered himself. "I don't know. I think I shall go to South America. Peru, Chile. I should like to spend some time in the Andes."

At midday Tony heard the front door close, and at half past twelve Jenny came in. Her usual calm was ruffled. "Eversley, you never do a thing I ask you."

Foster smiled nervously. "What is it?"

She ignored him, spoke to Tony. "Can you knock a nail in a piece of wood?"

"Yes, of course." He looked uncertainly at Foster, who rose slowly from his chair.

Jenny still ignored him. "Then I'd be grateful for your help."

He followed her out into the kitchen, where she pointed to a shelf that lay on the floor and handed him a hammer and some nails. The job was simply that of nailing the shelf to wooden wall brackets, and it took no more than five minutes. She stood watching, hands on hips.

"Thanks. I've been trying to get him to do it for a couple of days." There was something almost flirtatious and out of character in the way that she whispered, "I told you he was useless, didn't I? Even for knocking in a nail."

Later they went through the sherry ritual in the drawing-room. Jenny had recovered her usual coolness. Foster was moodily silent. Tony, feeling the silence awkward, admired the little Battersea enamel snuff and trinket boxes that said in ornamental copperplate, "A gift to tell you of my love, O pray do not forget me," with other similar sentiments. More to maintain the conversation than because he was really interested he picked up one of the photographs on the piano. Jenny joined him.

"Family group, my family that is. There I am." She pointed to a pig-tailed girl standing meekly beside a large man with flourishing moustaches and a thin elegant woman. "With mother and father."

"I'd never have recognised you."

Foster got up and poured himself another glass of sherry. She handed him another photograph, showing a mild old gentleman with an angry-looking woman beside him who wore a large floppy hat. "Uncle William and Aunt Hilda."

He looked at the other pictures. "No wedding groups."

"Eversley and I did it all as quietly as possible. No photographers, no family, no friends even."

"Who's this?" He pointed to a portrait of an elderly erect figure with a small moustache.

"A cousin of mine. His name's Mortimer Lands."

When he turned round a moment later to put down his sherry glass Foster was staring straight in front of him, his face white as milk. What was the matter with the man?

TEN

That night he went to the theatre with Widgey and O'Grady. "*Murder in the Cathedral*," Widgey said. "Should be good."

"I like a thriller." O'Grady had close cropped grey hair and although not tall gave an impression of bulging strength.

"I believe it's poetry. A play in verse."

"If it's got a murder in it, that's good enough for me." O'Grady glared at Tony as though inviting him to make an issue out of this. His eyes had the slightly unfocused look of the heavy drinker.

When they got to the theatre the posters showed naked girls prancing with their legs up. "Fine goings on in a cathedral." O'Grady crossed himself. *Murder in the Cathedral* had been playing the previous week, and the current show was called *Guts and Garters*. There were as many almost naked girls on the stage as there had been on the posters, but the principal performers were a couple of comics who told jokes all of which ended in rude noises made by a pair of clapper boards. Widgey, wrapped in an old fur coat, watched intently. O'Grady muttered unintelligibly under his breath. Tony thought about Jenny and about the future. He felt that he ought to ask for an explanation, but what exactly did he want her to explain? "Do you love me, did you buy those links, would you have kept a present from me which had cost a lot of money as I have kept this one from you?" It was not merely that he wanted to be reassured about her feelings for him. When he was away from her he found it difficult to believe in her existence.

At the interval they went to the bar. "Filthy," O'Grady said as he downed a large whisky. "A desecration of the human body. In the old country we'd not permit it."

"You live in Ireland?" Tony asked.

O'Grady glared at him. "I live in Leeds. I cannot watch another moment of this filthy performance."

Widgey gathered mouldering fur around her. "There's a lot of tit if you like that. I'm a bit old for it myself."

They ate fish and chips and visited three pubs on the way back, then took a short cut through an alley. O'Grady had become melancholy in the last pub and was singing "The Minstrel Boy." At the end of the alley a man leaned against the wall. As they walked slowly and uncertainly along their footsteps sounded curiously speedy.

There were too many footsteps. Tony's hand touched the rough brick wall beside him and found no reassurance in it. He was afraid to turn round.

"And his harp he's left *behind* him," O'Grady wailed. Then two men were with them, standing between Tony and his companions. One of them spoke to Widgey in a low polite voice.

"You go on ahead. We just want a couple of words with our friend here."

Widgey was not alarmed. In the darkness of the alley her face was a white blur. She began to move away, and O'Grady with her. Tony felt one of the men pushing against him, pressing him back hard against the wall. He saw, or thought he saw, the gleam of steel. He cried out. O'Grady stopped singing.

He could not have said afterwards just what happened in the next minute. O'Grady's body was launched towards them, Widgey screamed, he cried out again himself, there was a frenzied flurrying and mixing of bodies like that of fish in a pool after bait. Then one of the men was on the ground and the other was running back down the alley. O'Grady was furiously kicking the man on the ground and cursing at him. He stopped when Widgey pulled at his arm. The man slowly got to his feet and limped away.

Tony haltingly thanked O'Grady, who was immensely cheerful.

"Think nothing of it, I enjoy a scrap. I bruised my knuckle on him." He showed a bloody fist.

"They didn't hurt you? They had knives."

"Knives? Not they. Ah, they were just a couple of toughs. We don't have that type in the old country, I can tell you that. I could do with a drink."

Tony bought them all double brandies in a pub. Widgey said nothing at the time, but after O'Grady had gone upstairs she took Tony into the parlour, rolled a cigarette, stuck it in her mouth and puffed smoke at him.

"I hate to say it but you'll have to go."

"All right."

"It's about the money, isn't it? The hundred pounds."

"Yes."

"You can have it. To-morrow. But you'll have to go. I've got this place to run, they'll be round here."

Something about the way she spoke, combined with her refusal to look at him, made him cry out, calling simply her name.

"What's up?"

"I'll go away. But I can come back, can't I?"

"If you want."

"Widgey, don't——" He could not say what he felt about the severance of this tie with the past and his childhood. "I can manage without the money, I've got enough."

"Don't be a fool."

"It's true."

"You wanted it yesterday."

"I can raise the money. If I have to. But I don't want to borrow from you."

"Please yourself. Let's have a cuppa." She moved to put the kettle on the gas ring. "I still want you out, though. By the weekend. It's best for you too."

ELEVEN

"It's finished," Jenny said. She was alone and she had taken him straight into the drawing-room.

"Finished?"

"Eversley's made up his mind to go away. On Saturday."

"Where to?"

"He's talking about South America, but he doesn't really tell me. I shall be lucky if I get a couple of cards."

"And he doesn't want me to go on? I told him yesterday, I could easily do some research."

"He doesn't like you, Tony. I think he knows."

"But then——" He wanted to say that if Foster suspected her of carrying on an affair it would be natural for him to take her with him, but he could not phrase the words. What she said next did something to answer this unasked question.

"I told you, he's a strange man. When something like this happens, seriously I mean, he has to go away. Alone.

He gives it time to burn itself out as he calls it. Then he sends me a card saying where he is, and if I want to I can join him. Otherwise he sends another card to say when he's coming back."

He seized on the single element that was important to him. "It's as I said, it's happened before."

"You don't think I could live with Eversley without there being someone else?" And again in response to the question he could not ask about why she stayed with him she went on coolly, "He has the money."

There was something remote about her, something unreal in the whole situation that frustrated and infuriated him. The barrier between them did not fall when he stepped forward and took her unyielding body into his arms, telling her that he loved her. The words also sounded unreal to him, although he knew that they were true. The next words came more easily. "I have to be with you, I can't leave you."

"I want that too."

"But the others. You felt that about the others."

"They were nothing." She moved out of his arms. "Don't make a scene, I hate them. Let's have some whisky." While she was pouring it she looked at him with the wariness of one animal watching another. "Eversley doesn't have to come back."

"What do you mean?"

"He doesn't have to go."

"I don't understand." He knew that something terrible was being proposed to him, but he did not know what it was, and he wanted her to tell him; she did not do this. Instead, sipping her whisky like a cat and looking at him over the rim of the glass, she told him things that taken by themselves did not seem significant, appeared almost to be said at random. She and Eversley had a joint account at the bank, did he know that (the question was rhetorical, for of course he didn't), but there was not a lot of money in it, not more than a few hundred pounds. But supposing, just supposing, that Eversley decided to settle in somewhere like—oh, say Venezuela or Costa Rica—and supposing he didn't come back, and that he liked South America so much that he decided to settle there for good, then naturally he'd have his securities transferred to a bank out there, wasn't that so? And Eversley was rich, his securities would last for a long time, you could say for ever.

The sun shone through the windows, yet he felt cold. The whisky tasted bitter. He had to say again that he didn't understand what she meant.

"Look." She went out of the room, returned with a sheet of writing paper headed *Villa Majorca*. "Don't touch," she said. The paper was blank except for the signature at the bottom, "Eversley Foster." "I asked him to sign it because I wanted to write to the telephone people about a new extension. But it could be used for typing a letter to the bank, he's signed it. I told you, he's a fool."

"But what can we do with it, how does it help?"

"First we copy this signature until we're perfect at writing it. I mean perfect. And don't forget we'd only have to convince a bank in Venezuela."

"I suppose that might be possible." He spoke cautiously, he did not want her to know of his previous experience with signatures. She gave him a smile that raised her upper lip off her teeth. "But we couldn't keep it up, we'd be found out. One day the bank would ask to see him."

"Of course. And they would see him. You'd be Eversley."

"But how would——"

She talked quickly, like somebody who has rehearsed an argument many times. "You go out there as yourself, right? You just fly abroad on a trip. Out in Caracas we get a passport that makes you Eversley."

He began to expostulate. "You can't get a passport just like that."

"I know somebody out there," she said so brusquely that he did not like to ask more questions. "And he has contacts. It's not difficult, just a matter of money. Either we buy a passport or we use Eversley's and get the picture and the description changed. And then you're Eversley. He doesn't have any near relatives or close friends, you see the sort of life he leads. And then there's something special about Venezuela—or Costa Rica or Honduras or Dominica, it doesn't matter which. They don't have any extradition treaty with Britain. I fancy Venezuela though, from what I've read about it Caracas is a lovely city."

"You've worked all this out. You've planned it. For a long time." She gave him again that feline smile. "You've talked about it to other people."

"One."

"He was your lover?"

"He was frightened." Her thin shoulders shrugged under her dress.

He felt a tremor beginning in his hands and legs, and put down his glass on a table. She got up and turned away from him. Her profile seemed to him so beautiful that it took away his breath. The tremor stopped.

"I'm not frightened. Nothing frightens me."

"I love you." He repeated the words almost angrily, as though they were some kind of insurance against disaster.

"It's not a word I use." The coldness and rigidity of her features frightened him. "I told you, I want to be with you."

"But supposing in a few months——" He could not complete the sentence.

"I didn't want to be with you. You'd be Eversley Foster, you'd be signing the cheques."

He closed his eyes and instantly had an image of his body

121

descending silently down an endless tunnel, twisting from side to side, bruised and torn by the speed of a descent which he was powerless to check. There was a roaring in his ears which might have been the sound of water. He thought that he was going to faint. He opened his eyes again and blinked to find himself still in the room. "I can't bear violence."

"There won't be any violence." She went on, again talking with compulsive eagerness. "I told you Eversley has a weak heart, he takes capsules to speed it up. If I slip three of them into a drink he won't wake up. I'll be responsible for all that. If it worries you. I won't need any help from you until afterwards."

"Afterwards?"

"I said he was going away. And I told you he bought me a motor launch."

"Yes."

"You'll have to help me get him into it."

"And then?"

"A sea burial. By the time he turns up he'll be unrecognisable. And anyway we shall be in Venezuela."

"I don't know.'

"You mean you don't trust me. We want the same thing, you must see that."

What he wanted—but how could he say this to her?—was the ideal Jenny, tender and loving, not the real woman who cloaked hard shrewdness behind an impassive beauty. As though she understood this she gave the ideal Jenny's quick gentle laugh. "I trust you, anyway. You've got a passport?"

"Yes."

"Why don't you fly out to Caracas on Saturday and wait for me there. I shan't be able to come for—oh, perhaps a couple of weeks. They couldn't extradite you, you'd be safe anyway." It seemed only proper to ask about her safety. She came close to him and gripped his arm. "I don't want to be safe, that's the difference between us. If you're going to buy a ticket you'll want some money. The single fare is a hundred and forty pounds." He watched in amazement as she opened her handbag, took out a thick envelope and handed it to him. He put it on the table between them.

"You feel very sure of me."

"I'm direct, you see," she said as if she were explaining a mathematical problem to a not very bright student. "I know what I want and what you want, and they both amount to the same thing. And I know what you're like."

"I wonder if you do."

"If something's made easy you'll do it as long as you feel you don't have the responsibility, isn't that right?" He could not answer. "I'm making it easy. Have you got money to live on until I fly out to join you?" He shook his head. "I'll draw another two hundred and fifty from the bank. You see, this trust is a one-way operation. But you don't get the rest of the money until you show me the air ticket."

Everything she said humiliated him. "I wouldn't steal money from you."

"But you *have* stolen money, isn't that right?"

"Whatever I've done——" He stopped, and began again. "Those links. I found out what they're worth, but I wouldn't sell them."

"Oh, my sweet Tony, you priced them, did you? Don't worry, I don't mind, I wouldn't mind if you'd sold them. Being with someone like you makes it more exciting. I knew what you were like, I could tell from the first." Her eyes sparkled as they did while making love.

"To-day is Thursday. There's no time." It was impossible, surely, that on Saturday night or Sunday morning he should be in Venezuela.

"Of course there is. You can go up to London this afternoon and buy the ticket."

"And he's going away on Saturday?"

"That's right."

"I can't come here to-morrow morning. To see him. I couldn't do it."

"No, I suppose you couldn't," she said with no hint of criticism. "He wouldn't want to see you anyway. I'll tell him I've paid you off. He'd be pleased about that. Then come on Friday night."

"Friday night?"

"Ten o'clock. I'll be ready by then." He did not ask what she meant. "Come to the back. I can't see it would matter much, but try to make sure you're not seen."

TWELVE

"Saturday," the girl in the travel agency said, and tapped her pad with a pencil. "B.O.A.C. flies Tuesdays and Thursdays, Air France on Sundays. Now, let me see." She delved into time tables and came up with a bright smile. "You can either fly Iberia or K.L.M., both from London Airport. Iberia leaves at eleven-fifty Saturday morning by Caravelle, arrive Madrid fifteen o five, then you have a long stop over in Madrid, leave there o one o five Sunday morning in a Boeing, reach Caracas o seven hundred hours. K.L.M. might suit you better. Depart London o eight one o hours Saturday morning in a D.C. 8, call at Amsterdam, Zurich, Lisbon, reach Caracas twenty-two twenty-five hours Saturday evening. Depends if you mind getting up early on Saturday morning or if you'd sooner stop over half a day in Madrid."

"I'll take the K.L.M." As Jenny had said, there should be

no danger, but the sooner he was out of the country on Saturday morning the better.

"You want to make a booking now? Single, not return? Single is a hundred and forty pounds, return can be a little cheaper. Single, right." She got busy on the telephone, returned smiling and began to fill in a form. "Business trip? Are you staying long?"

"Yes, it's business, and I'm not sure how long I'll be there. I may be coming back by boat."

"Smallpox inoculation is obligatory, yellow fever is not obligatory but advised. No visa necessary." He handed over the money, she counted it and gave him the ticket. "Have a good trip."

Sitting in a café afterwards, he looked at the ticket. He was going to Caracas. In less than seventy-two hours he would be in a city of which he had barely heard, and of which he knew nothing. It is so simple, then, to make your dreams come true. Yet even now he did not believe in what he was doing. It could not possibly be true that on Friday night he would go to the Villa Majorca and help Jenny to—he could not frame the words to describe it. And on the following morning was it really possible that he would walk across the tarmac at London Airport, step into the great mechanical bird, and in less than a day step out of it into a new life? He found that he was able to envisage the new life itself easily enough, the apartment in town with a villa in the hills for the hot season, scarlet bougainvillaea climbing round the terrace where they ate breakfast, orchids and jacaranda trees, continual lovemaking, the pleasure of possessing and being possessed. All this was much clearer to him than what was to happen on Friday and Saturday.

He spent most of the afternoon finding out about Caracas. "At 3,164 feet above sea level, Caracas has one of the world's best climates. Springlike the year around, the temperature averages 64 degrees with a high of 80 degrees during April, May, September and October . . . English is spoken everywhere . . . The city has recently undergone a tremendous transformation. In the eastern part, where peons drove cattle just ten years ago, sophisticated Caracas residents now sip coffee and cocktails in chic sidewalk cafés in the best continental manner . . . the population of one and a half millions is cosmopolitan, and the faces of Italians, Spanish, Portuguese and North Americans are a familiar sight in the streets." Not, he noted, English. As Jenny had said, the chances of recognition by anybody who knew Foster would be very small. And really, the place seemed idyllic. There was nothing about poisonous insects or snakes crawling out of bunches of bananas, only descriptions of the variety of flowering trees and the national birds, turpials, toucans and humming birds, "resplendent in every size, colour and variety." Photographs showed him great white skyscrapers, enormous hotels with curiously-shaped restaurants and swimming pools, eight lane highways leading out to the mountains. Altogether, Caracas seemed as dreamlike as everything else. Caracas, he read elsewhere, was one of the most expensive cities in the world, but was also "a city where, if you have money, you can live like a king." And he would have money, he would live like a king with the queen always by his side.

But before that happened he had to endure an eternity of waiting. He went to the cinema and saw a Western, ate a meal, deliberately lingered in the streets so that he should take a late train back. In the Seven Seas he almost tiptoed up the stairs to avoid seeing Widgey. On the following morning he came down late, but met her coming from the dining-room to the parlour, cigarette in mouth.

"What's up, not working?" When he said that he had given up she nodded. "Husband find out? I tell you, that woman's a fair bitch."

"How can you possibly say that when you haven't met her." It seemed important to defend Jenny, especially in face of attack by Widgey.

"Some women you don't have to meet. Come in, I can do with a bit of help." The parlour table was piled with old bills, receipts, sheets on which figures had been scribbled. "Trying to do the accounts for the year, can't make head or tail of 'em. From what I can see I made about three thousand quid last year, only I know I didn't. See if you can sort it out, there's a good boy."

He spent the next three hours putting the bills in order and totalling them, sustained by several cups of tea and a ham sandwich. Widgey expressed her appreciation. "Bloody marvellous, you've got a real head for figures."

"I'm going to-day."

He had spoken abruptly, but she simply nodded. "This chap, what's his name, Foster, kicked up?"

"Nothing like that. He's going away for a bit, so the job's finished for the time being."

"He's going alone?"

"Yes."

"And you're going too?" Without saying so Widgey implied clearly that she thought this strange. He said that it was best in every way for him to leave.

"You want to get away from those hard boys, that's a fact. But what I saw in the cards—you know? You don't want to take too much notice of that. Sometimes they work out, sometimes they don't." It was then, perhaps out of the need to convince himself that the dream had become reality, that he showed her the air ticket. A moment later he cursed his stupidity. Widgey was rarely surprised, but this was one of the rare occasions. "Venezuela. What the hell you going there for?"

"I've got a job there."

127

Ash dropped on to the butcher's bills. "It's to do with that woman. Isn't it?"

"You've got her on the brain. She's nothing to do with it."

"What do you want to go to this place, what's the name of it, Caracas—for? How much did the ticket cost, two hundred quid?"

"Nothing like so much."

"Over a hundred anyway. You've got no money, who paid for it?"

What a fool he had been to show it to her. "I told you, I've got a job. The man who engaged me paid the fare."

"What sort of job? You hadn't got one yesterday. That ticket means trouble, Tony, I can smell it."

Something seemed to snap in his mind, as though a piece of elastic had been frayed until it suddenly snapped, and he was shrieking at her, using obscene words that were hardly ever in his mouth, talking about her sexual frustrations and her jealousy of him, accusing her of being like the rest of his family, wanting to rule his life, saying that he would leave now, this minute, and would never come back.

She heard him out, then started to roll another cigarette. "Okay, you leave now if that's the way you feel."

Upstairs in room thirteen, however, packing his suitcases among the apparatus of the past, the oversize tallboy and the wallpaper and the chest of drawers he had painted, he flung himself on the bed and wept without being able to give a better reason for his tears than that he had wanted Widgey to help in convincing him that the dream was true and that she had failed to do so. When he went down half an hour later he hesitated in front of the parlour door, then went in. She was asleep in the arm-chair, a copy of her latest library book, *Bettina and the Princess*, on her lap. She looked small, worn, old. He put down the cases, went across and kissed her on the forehead. She opened her eyes.

"You're off, then."

"That's right."

"Give my love to Venezuela." Her eyes closed again. He moved from foot to foot like a schoolboy, then walked out of the hotel and down the street with a feeling that he was walking away from the past for ever. He took a taxi to the station and left his cases in the cloakroom. Three-thirty. Six and a half hours to go.

He was on his way to the nearest cinema—time appeared in the guise of a large hole that must be plugged—when a car horn sounded behind him. Bradbury's face grinned from his car.

"Tony, old boy, what a bit of luck. Come and have a noggin."

"At this time of day?"

"I know a place. Hop in." Listening to Bradbury would fill time as well as anything else. A few minutes later, when they were drinking whisky in a second floor establishment called the Eldorado, he was less sure about this. Curtains were drawn over the windows and the lights were dim. In one corner two young men sat with their heads together whispering, behind the bar an ebony figure stood impassive. Bradbury's body, near to his, exuded warmth.

"The question is, old boy, filthy lucre. That money now, I don't want to press you, but when could you let me have it back?"

"You said there was no hurry."

"That was last week. Things have changed."

"To-day's Friday. I can manage it next Monday."

"You're sure about that."

"No question. I said it was just a temporary loan." On Monday he would be in one of the best hotels in Caracas, perhaps in the oval swimming pool. Now that his future was settled he could look with tolerance even upon Bradbury. He would pay the money back, Venezuelan bolivars converted into pounds and posted from Caracas. Or would that be wise? He saw with surprise that Bradbury seemed slightly disappointed.

"I had the impression you weren't too flush."

"Next week I shall be." It was wonderful to be able to say that.

"But you wouldn't say no to making another hundred, I take it." Bradbury fiddled with his pony glass. A throaty giggle came from one of the young men. "I daresay you've wondered about me."

"Well, yes," he said untruthfully.

"And if you did, you're right. I've got a little something going on the side. You remember old Van."

He said that he remembered Van. Bradbury went on talking, a conversation full of half-hints, and suggestions that it would be better if he did not know too much. He did not really listen, until a word caught his attention.

"What was that?"

"A little trip abroad. On Saturday."

He almost burst out laughing. If he could only show Bradbury the air ticket to Caracas, that would make him sit up. "Amsterdam," Bradbury said. "I'll tell you the routine. Van won't meet you at the airport, but I'll give you an address to contact him. You spend a weekend there, he shows you the sights, and believe me old Van knows how to do that, Sunday evening you come back. Then we forget what you owe me and there's a hundred to come. What do you say?"

A second whisky stood in front of him. There was nothing to lose by agreement, but the drink made him feel truculent. "What is it, diamonds or drugs?"

"Quiet." Bradbury's hand squeezed his knee beneath the table.

"Anyway, the answer is no, thanks."

"You don't want it?" There could be no doubt of Bradbury's surprise.

"You wouldn't be making the offer if there weren't strings attached. When I'm caught they can't touch you. That's the way you were at school. Any trouble, you slid out of it, somebody else carried the can."

"What's up?" The mottled red face raised to his own wore an expression of injury. Tony could smell the lavatories. Should he mention them, would Bradbury know what he was talking about?

"You were a bully. At school. Don't think I've forgotten." He stood up and Bradbury got up too. His thick cheeks were puckered with distress. He looked bewildered, like a man who has been bitten by a pet rabbit. His hand moved as though in reflex action and took its hard grip on Tony's upper arm. With one decisive blow, a man slapping a mosquito, he knocked off the hand. Bradbury's face purpled, its expression changed.

"I can be a bad enemy."

"You just go to hell." The cry was brave, although somehow inadequate. The face beside him, full of bad blood and reminiscent for a moment of another face he could not remember, seemed the most hateful thing in the world. He took a swing at it and missed. The whisky glass fell from the table and clattered on the floor.

"I shall want my money back. Next Monday. Or look out for trouble."

He ignored the words, turned and, consciously bracing his shoulders, walked away. The ebony barman watched his going, the two young men raised heads for a moment and stared. Out in the street, after turning the corner he remembered whose face Bradbury had called to mind. It was that of his father, involved in argument at a football match.

He went into the nearest cinema, saw another Western, fell asleep and woke when nudged by the man in the next

seat, tried to eat a sandwich in a pub but got no further
than the first bite, walked about the town at random for
an hour, looked at his watch. Nine-thirty.

THIRTEEN

The last time, he thought as he walked up the wide sweep
of Byron Avenue in a light damp mist coming off the sea,
this is the last time. Even as he said this to himself it seemed
impossible. The road with its cracked pavements and wide
grass verge and dim street lamps now melting in mist was
so utterly familiar that he seemed to have been walking up
it for ever. This was where he had become a person, where
love had given him some object in life. Was love the right
word? "We want the same thing," she had said, and
what did that mean but love? In his wallet the air ticket
warmed him.

He passed the "For Sale" notice, only dimly visible to-
night. The Villa Majorca was completely dark. He was
suddenly certain that the whole thing had been some kind
of hoax. His knock at the back door would go unanswered,
he would be left with the ticket and an unanswerable
puzzle. A small gravel path wound away to the back of
the house and he walked down this, making as little noise
as possible, although what ears were there to hear? Somewhere inside the house, here at the back, a faint light
showed. He rapped lightly with his knuckles on the kitchen
door. Silence. He rapped again and the door opened.

The face she showed him was a white blur. As he stepped
inside he saw that she was wearing gloves, a raincoat, high
boots, a scarf round her head. They stood in a passage
which led on the right to the kitchen, on the left to the main
part of the house. The light came from a small scullery.

"All right?" She made a gesture and he saw the body, lying on the floor beside the kitchen door. It was wrapped in sacking and tied round with rope. He caught his breath in relief that he did not actually have to see the thing. Then the thought came to him that Foster might still be alive, that she had put him into the sack unconscious.

"The garage," she said. They each picked up one end of the body, which felt horribly soft and pliable. A covered way led straight from the kitchen door into the garage and they took their burden round to the back of the car. Foster was a small man but he did not go in comfortably. He had to turn aside while she doubled up the legs and pushed them in. She closed and locked the boot, then switched on the garage light. The illumination showed her face not truly white but grey as tobacco ash, the lips drawn tensely together. They spoke in whispers.

"Are you sure?"

"What?"

"Is he really dead?"

"Don't be stupid."

"Was it difficult? I mean to get him to take——"

"Shut up," she said quietly but viciously. A shudder which he was unable to control passed through him. She stared, then asked if he wanted a drink. He shook his head. She whispered, "You're not wearing gloves."

"I forgot."

"Do you want to leave your prints everywhere."

She turned off the light, went back to the house and returned with a pair of woollen gloves which he put on. Then she motioned to him to open the garage doors. He did so, got in the car, and they drove away down a back road that ran into Byron Avenue. She had been driving for five minutes through the mist when he exclaimed. She turned her head.

"You've forgotten something."

"What?"

"The weights."

"They're in the boot."

After that they did not speak. She drove carefully down back roads that were unknown to him. After twenty minutes she pulled the car into a natural lay-by, hidden among bushes. He looked round, bewildered.

"We can't get any nearer. The river's through the bushes."

It was no more than thirty yards away, but the mist was thicker here, and he stumbled once or twice. The boat lay under tarpaulin. Peeled off it revealed itself as dull blue or black in colour. When she said "Now," he knew it meant that they would have to carry the body.

"I don't know if I can do it."

She said without raising her voice, "You have to."

He could see them carrying the thing through the bushes. They slipped and the head came out of its covering, lolling free, the tongue showing. He turned and retched without vomiting. Without saying anything more she went back to the car. After a few moments he followed and helped her carry the thing. It was not as bad as he had feared, a mere inert bundle. Then he went back and got the weights, which had hooks on their ends. He cast off and began to row down the river while she sat in the stern attaching the weights to the rope round the sacking. The river bank moved past them slowly. Once he got too near to it and was brushed by the branches of a tree, which dropped moisture on to him. After that she took one of the oars. He asked how far they were from the sea.

"Less than a mile. I'll start the motor when the river broadens."

The rowing seemed endless. Everything was dripping, it seemed to him that he was soaked in moisture. Strangely the mist cleared as they approached the sea, and when she scrambled into the bows, knelt down and pulled on the starting cord for the engine he saw in front of him black sea, felt the plash of waves on the side. When she started the motor the chugging sounded loud in his ears. Wind blew through his thin coat, a little spray went over him. The pinpoints of coastal light receded. He asked her how much farther they were going.

"Do you want them to find him?" she asked sharply. Five minutes later she cut the engine and asked if he was able to do it. The very lack of passion in her voice shamed him into action. He picked up the thing, heavy now with its weights, half-threw and half-pushed it over the side. There was a splash. She took a torch from her pocket and shone it downwards. Nothing was visible but the black sea. She turned the boat and they headed back to the mouth of the river.

With that final act accomplished his spirits were lightened. He wanted to talk, but sensed that she would not like it. The row back up the river was longer and harder than that out to sea, and he would not have known where to tie up if she had not told him. After tying up he was in a feverish hurry to be away but he helped her as, calmly and methodically, she stowed the oars and fitted the tarpaulin into place.

Walking back to the car he said, "I'm sorry. You did everything."

"It doesn't matter."

"I wanted to help, it was just——" He did not finish the sentence. They reached the car. She unlocked the boot, shone the torch inside and nodded with satisfaction at its emptiness. Inside the car he produced the ticket. "You wanted to see it."

She took a wad of notes from her bag. "Ten tens, twenty fives, the rest in ones."

"Jenny."

"Yes?"

"How am I going to get the money out there? I mean, there are currency restrictions on how much I can take out."

"Put it in your wallet."

"But I might be searched."

"It's a ten thousand to one chance. If you don't want to carry it, parcel it up and post it to yourself in Venezuela. Then it's a million to one chance they won't open it."

"There must be some way that's completely safe."

"Not when we've got so little time. There's no risk really." She looked at him. "What's the matter? You've got an air ticket and two hundred and fifty pounds in your pocket. I'm the one who should worry. You could run out on me."

"You know I shan't do that."

"Yes." She started the car and drove away.

"How soon will you come? In a fortnight, you said."

"As soon as I can. I'll have to settle things here."

"Venezuela seems to be a marvellous country. The cities, anyway. Do you know Caracas has a perfect climate? I shall stay at the Grand, it has the most wonderful swimming pool. If that's full I shall stay at the Corona. Shall I let you know where I am, I'll write poste restante to Southbourne, is that a good idea?"

"Perfect."

He felt a need to cancel out what they had just done by speech. "We're going to be happy."

As they approached the town she drew in to the kerb, shut off the engine. "I'll put you off here, you can walk to the station."

She looked straight in front of her. He leaned forward and kissed the side of her face awkwardly, then got out of the car. She put in the clutch and moved away.

FOURTEEN

He spent the following hours in a state of dazed happiness, like a small boy who has swallowed several doses of nasty medicine as prelude to a promised treat and now, with the medicine consumed, sees unalloyed pleasure ahead. He spent the night at a hotel near London Airport, arranged for a six-thirty call—the ticket said he had to report at seven-fifteen—and tried to sleep, but found it impossible. In the end he took the travel pamphlets out of his case and spent an hour looking at them.

Caracas would be wonderful for a time, but no doubt they would get tired of it. And after that? Perhaps a journey to the hinterland which revealed, so the pamphlets said, the real history of the country. He was not much interested in ruins and monuments, but probably he would learn Spanish. He saw that there were ample opportunities for gambling. He would be careful about that. Perhaps it would be a good idea for Jenny to control the money, and to make him an allowance. At the airport he would buy a Spanish phrasebook. He did not think at all of Eversley Foster, who seemed to belong already to a past so distant that it might never have existed. Nor did he think of Jenny. Strangely enough, his mind turned to recollections of the General, the book of memoirs, his own behaviour. Those wretched little fiddles he had worked, and then the business with the cheque—he felt really ashamed of them now. Yet even these thoughts were not wholly painful, for they carried with them the consolation that there would be no need for him to do anything of that kind ever again. With that in his mind he fell asleep at three o'clock in the morning.

He woke at six, and by the time his six-thirty call came had washed and shaved. He dressed with care, allowing himself to consider whether it should be the charcoal grey suit or lightweight trousers and sports jacket. He knew perfectly well that the decision had already been made in favour of informality, for in thirteen hours of travelling the suit would get rather painfully creased, but still he laid out both sets of clothes on the bed and talked to himself aloud as he weighed the possibilities, wondering what the weather would be like in Caracas when he arrived at night. Were the nights chilly? "Even if they are I think this is going to be rather cosier, don't you?" he said to an imaginary companion before hanging up the charcoal grey again in his travelling wardrobe. As a gesture, purely as a gesture to Jenny because they were distinctly unsuitable, he put the orbicular links into the cuffs of his shirt. The money stayed in his wallet. He had decided to take Jenny's ten thousand to one chance, and not to bother with a parcel. His euphoria was such that it did not need support from food. He did no more than nibble at the toast and sip at the coffee brought to his room. Then into the car that he had ordered to take him the couple of miles to the airport. The car arrived on the dot, everything was going to plan.

"European, sir, or Oceanic?" the driver asked.

"Oceanic. I'm going to Caracas. Venezuela."

"Venezuela, eh. You want to be careful. Friend of mine, merchant seaman, unshipped a crate of bananas once, bloody snake crawled out of it, six foot long and thick as your arm."

"I'll take my chance," he said laughingly.

"Lot of prickly heat you get there too, they tell me."

It was annoying that the man kept on in this way, and he told the fellow rather sharply that Caracas had one of the best climates in the world, springtime the whole year round. The faint blemish on his pleasure was removed when they pulled up outside the airport building, a friendly porter took his baggage to be weighed, and he was swept up in the delightful process of having his ticket checked and obtaining his boarding card for the plane. His bags had disappeared.

"I don't suppose I shall see them again until I get to Caracas," he said to the girl behind the counter.

"That's right."

"They wouldn't take them off by mistake at Amsterdam or Zurich or Lisbon?" He said it archly, not because he really feared this would happen, but to make conversation and actually to roll the names on his tongue. The girl took him seriously.

"Oh no, sir. You don't change planes, they're just stopping points. You'll find they are still on board when you get to Caracas."

She smiled. How nice she was. He smiled back. "I'm sure I shall."

"Have a good trip." What a different world this was from the one in which people threatened him because of unpaid debts and borrowed money, the world in which distasteful things had to be done. But that was all behind him, unalloyed pleasure lay ahead. He strolled about, bought newspapers and magazines and the Spanish phrasebook, felt the comfortable wad of money, looked at the people sitting in the lounge and wondered which of them would be fellow passengers. Very soon the call came and he was ready for the names which followed each other like notes in music: ". . . Amsterdam, Zurich, Lisbon . . ." Oh yes, that's mine, he thought, those places are for me. As they moved through the final barrier two anonymous-looking men stood on either side glancing at passports and repeating the same words. 'Have a good trip, Mr. da Silva . . . Mr. Cournos . . . Mrs. Walsh . . . Mr. Kellett . . .

Mr. Medura . . ." He waited for "Mr. Jones," but instead one of the men looked at the passport, then at him, and asked him to step aside.

"Is something wrong with my passport? How long will it take?"

"Just in here. Shan't keep you more than a couple of minutes."

He was shown into a small office. Through the windows he could see the man pick up a telephone and hear his voice murmuring indistinguishable words. He could not sit down but paced the room, looking at the desk which had a white blotting pad and "In" and "Out" trays, both empty, then at a notice on the wall which listed all the articles that could not be brought into or taken out of the country, then again through the glass at the figures who were passing through the barrier. Was he being kept back deliberately so that he would miss the flight? After a space of time he could not have measured, although it was perhaps no more than the two minutes mentioned, he opened the door. The last passengers were passing through.

"Look, I've got my boarding ticket. I don't want to miss the plane."

The man turned, his expression placatory. "Very sorry, Mr. Jones. They'll be here in a moment."

"But who are they?" He did not like to be aggressive, because the man was so polite.

"Here they come." He nodded at a point behind Tony. An abrupt turn and he confronted them, two large men wearing hats, the leading one apologetically smiling.

"Mr. Jones. Sorry to have kept you."

"What do you want?" With dismay he heard his voice rising.

"Don't suppose this will take more than a couple of minutes." They ushered him back into the room. The first man sat in the chair behind the desk and the other stood beside the door. "Lovely morning. Perfect day for flying."

So there was no question of stopping him from leaving on the plane. The sense of relief he felt showed itself in a nervous laugh. He took the seat that was offered him, opposite the man.

"Mr. Anthony Jones," the man said reflectively. He was hairy, with a red, drinker's nose. "So you're going to Caracas. Venezuela. Never been myself. Why?"

The last word, barked out, surprised him. "What do you mean?"

"Why are you going? Business, pleasure, new job?"

"I've got a new job. But anyway, I've had enough of England," he said recklessly.

"Have you now?" Without emphasis the big man repeated, "Had enough of England, did you hear that?"

"I heard it," said the man by the door. He was big too, but where his companion had taken his hat off this man kept his on. They both began to laugh.

Tony stood up. There on the desk, two feet away from him, lay the blue-covered book that was his entrance card to the new world, the new life. Leaning forward he snatched up the book from the table, and moved towards the door. Both men stared at him in amazement, their laughter cut off as suddenly as a record from which the needle has been lifted.

"Now then," said Hatless, "no use going on like that, you know. That won't do you any good, interfering with the course of enquiries, Mr. Jones. If you want to know my authority, here it is." He produced from his wallet some kind of card and put it back again.

"Or Mr. Bain-Truscott," said Hat.

Their questions fell thick and fast as a sudden snowstorm.

"You've been working for Mr. Foster, Eversley Foster, right?"

"Staying with your aunt, a Mrs. Widgeon, at the Seven Seas Hotel."

"Quarrelled with her yesterday, right?"

"Helping Mr. Foster with a book he was writing, correct?"

"Packed your bags and left in a hurry."

"Quarrelled with Mr. Foster too, correct?"

"Then off to South America, funny place to go."

"Wouldn't go there without a reason, not South America."

"Not South America, no. Stole from him, didn't you?"

"Then when he found out, that was it. You meant it right from the start, had it in mind."

"Or why use Bain-Truscott?"

"Why use Bain-Truscott, right. When your name's Jones."

Silence again, and they were both looking at him. He found his voice. "I don't understand, I don't know what you mean. I was working for Mr. Foster, but the job had finished. And I—about calling myself Bain-Truscott—what's wrong about that, it's not illegal."

"No, it isn't," Hatless said. "I'm a Jones myself, I can understand how you feel. Perhaps this is all a mistake."

He felt that he must make it clear that he had not meant to insult this hairy red-nosed Jones. "I didn't mean there was anything wrong with Jones, it's just, I've called myself Bain-Truscott for a long time." The customs man could no longer be seen through the glass, something was being said over the speaker system, it must be the last call for the flight. "I have to go, I shall miss my plane."

"Don't worry about that, Mr. Jones. Plenty of time."

"But there isn't. The passengers have gone."

"You've got ten minutes yet, we'll make sure you don't miss the flight."

At these words from the now friendly Jones relief swept

over him, and with it a vivid picture of the thing being dropped from the motor launch with the weights attached to it. There was one chance in a million, or no chance at all, that the thing had been found, these two police officers must be here because of some misunderstanding. Realisation of this made him smile his own particular smile that had charmed so many women, and to speak with a serenity that could not fail to be impressive.

"That's very good of you. Tell me how I can help."

Turn out his pockets! There were many things that he might have expected to be asked of him, but this was not one of them. Light-heartedly he complied, putting everything on the desk, loose change, a key ring with the keys of his cases on it, wallet and fountain pen, ticket— he put these things down with a confident and confiding smile, and he smiled again as he took off his watch and put it beside the other things. He picked up his top-coat, delved into the pockets and came up with some odds and ends of used bus tickets. In a final dramatic gesture he pulled out the linings of his pockets to show that nothing had been concealed.

Hat had come over to the desk and stood looking down at the things lying on it. Neither he nor Jones moved to examine them. Then Jones spoke, and his voice was no longer friendly.

"Where did you get those links?"

He made an involuntary gesture towards his sleeve. The links were invisible now, but his movement revealed them again. "They were a present."

"Tiepin went with them." That was Hat. The words were a statement, not a question, and Tony did not reply. Now Hat leaned over, stretched his hand to the wallet, glanced inside and passed it to Jones who carefully took out the notes and sorted them into piles according to their denominations. Hat retreated to the door and when Jones spoke again it was in a heavy Bradbury voice, the voice of school, authority, doom.

"Where did this money come from?"

"I——" He shook his head, swallowed, started again. "I had to have money to go abroad. It's mine."

"I'll tell you then. Mr. Foster drew them out of the bank yesterday morning. The tenners are new, and the bank have a note of the numbers. They correspond."

Mr. Foster. He could only shake his head. "I don't understand."

"Don't kid me, son. These links were Foster's too, right?"

"I told you, they were a present."

"You stole them and Foster found out, you had a row and killed him, then pinched the money, right?"

"No no," he said again and then, because they were so completely wrong, he was led into indiscretion. "He's gone away, Foster, he said he was going away. Just because he's disappeared—you can't prove murder without a body."

Jones stared at him. "I said don't kid me, son, I don't like to be kidded. And what's the point, anyway? Show him."

Like some malign prestidigitator Hat produced from nowhere pictures, horrible and glossy, a body in a room lying in the crumpled awkward attitude of death, the head turned away, wrecked and bloody. There were several pictures, and he could not bear to look at them.

"You wouldn't know it was Foster from those," Jones said. "But try this one."

He looked at the picture and felt a roaring sound in his ears. Groping for the chair he fell rather than sat in it. He had seen the photograph before, on the piano. It showed the elderly erect figure with a small moustache who had been named by Jenny as her cousin Mortimer Lands.

PART THREE

Dreams and Realities

ONE

At first the situation had so strong a flavour of absurdity that he could not take the warning, the arrest, and immurement in the prison hospital seriously. A *hospital*, of all places, did they think he was ill? Not until he was remanded did realities begin to come home to him. Had he got a solicitor? No. Had he private means, or did he wish to apply for legal aid? Legal aid.

In the cell below the Court his jailer, an elderly cougher, said: "Clerk of the Court says would you like—cough—Washington, Maple and Hussick, they're next on the rota. Are they agreeable?"

"Agreeable?"

"Do you agree to accept their services?"

"I suppose so." Since he knew no other solicitor there was really no choice. He asked timidly, "Are they here?"

The man's laugh was punctuated by a cough. "Here, no, they're not here."

"How will they know?"

"They'll be told, don't worry."

He was taken away to another prison hospital, Brixton this time. Everybody was very nice to him, and the food was surprisingly good. He asked the old man in the next bed, who had a cough remarkably like the jailer's, why they were in the hospital.

" 'Cause it's bloody cushy, mate, that's why, and because of my lungs. They know my lungs, I've been here before."

"No, I meant why am I here. I'm not ill."

" 'Cause you're up for murder, they always put 'em in hospital. The doc's got his eye on you, don't worry. You're what they call under observation."

Tony looked round, but nobody seemed to be observing him. That evening one of the male nurses asked, "Everything all right, no complaints?" The enquiry might have been made of a visitor in a hotel.

"Yes, thank you. But I haven't seen my solicitor."

"Plenty of time," the man said. "Don't you worry."

That night, however, he did begin to worry. He felt like somebody emerging from an anaesthetic aware that something is terribly wrong with him, but ignorant of the precise nature of his illness. Reluctantly he acknowledged that in some way he had been betrayed, and that there was only one possible betrayer, but he found it impossible to dwell on the details of what might have happened. The image of Jenny's face came before him, the neat profile, delicately pallid cheek, firm mouth and chin. What had happened to her, what was she doing, what had she said to the police? When he determined resolutely to put this image away from him he could think of nothing but the ticket to Caracas. It had been taken away with the rest of his things when he went into hospital, but where was it now? Supposing he were let out in a week, would it still be possible to use the ticket? This was the first thing he mentioned when, on the following day, he was told that his solicitor Mr. Hussick had arrived. The interview took place in a small square room with flowered chintz curtains. No prison officer was present.

"Your ticket?" Mr. Hussick beamed. "I'm afraid I don't know anything about that, but I'm sure we don't need to bother about it for the moment."

"I don't want to lose the money. I shall go there as soon as this is cleared up."

"I'll make enquiries." Mr. Hussick wondered for a

148

moment whether his client was showing diminished responsibility. He looked sane enough, although of course *that* was nothing to go by. Mr. Hussick was a little sandy man with dancing eyebrows, and as he often said he liked to look on the bright side of things. "How are they treating you? Best porridge in London, they tell me. Haven't sampled it myself." Mr. Hussick laughed with sheer pleasure at the thought of his sampling the porridge, and his eyebrows danced up and down.

"This is all some awful mistake," Tony said tentatively, and was surprised by the solicitor's hearty agreement.

"I'm sure it is. That's what we've got to put right."

"I should like—I want to get out of here."

The eyebrows danced up and down. Mr. Hussick laughed heartily, and then became momentarily grave. "It's a serious charge, you know. The most serious charge in the book, that's what they've thrown at you." He shook his head as though any decent sporting police force would have made the charge a lesser one, then took out what looked uncommonly like a child's exercise book, and said in the tone of a doctor asking a patient to describe his symptoms, "If you'll just tell me exactly what happened. Take it quite easy, quite gently, there's no hurry at all. Don't leave anything out."

Don't leave anything out. "Has anybody else been arrested?"

"Not so far as I know." With more assurance he said, "Of course the police don't take me into their confidence but—nobody else at the moment, certainly."

So Jenny was still free. *Don't leave anything out.* But it was inevitable, for his sake and for Jenny's, that he should leave things out, for how could he tell the whole story without incriminating them both? He told the solicitor of the work he had been engaged to do, of the fact that the work had ended because Foster was going abroad, and of the revelation about Foster's identity when he saw the photograph. He said nothing about the car or about the body—whose had it been?—that they had thrown into the sea. Mr. Hussick made notes in a neat clerical hand. When Tony had finished he looked up, his eyebrows not dancing but apparently permanently raised.

"So you never met Foster?"

"I never met the man who was—whose photograph the police showed me." Hopefully he said, "There's no question that it *was* Foster?"

"None at all. Can you describe the man who was introduced to you as Foster?" Tony described him, up to the streak of white on the top of his head, and Mr. Hussick noted the details, asked if Tony had any idea of the man's identity, and then tapped the exercise book with his pen.

"What it comes to is this. You were deceived by Mrs. Foster from the start. Do you have any idea what might have been the object of this deception?" Tony shook his head. "Its effect has been that you are under arrest. Are you saying that this was her purpose? It would be a serious accusation."

"I can't believe——" What could he not believe? He started the sentence again. "I'm not accusing her of anything."

Mr. Hussick nodded in a neutral manner. "As you may have gathered, the body was found in the living-room. Death had been caused by head injuries. At the moment I'm rather in the dark about the police case. I shan't know what it is in detail until the Magistrate's Court hearing."

"I see."

"But there are two or three things we might try to clear up now. First of all have you any record, any criminal record? It wouldn't come out at the trial, but I should like to know. Nothing? That's good. Then, why Caracas?"

The words *prosecution, defence, trial,* had distracted him. "What?"

"It seems a long way to go, but I understand you had a job waiting out there."

"No, that isn't quite right. I'd saved the money and I'm fed up with England. I thought I could easily get a job there."

"I see." Hussick seemed about to say something more, but did not do so. He continued almost casually. "The police believe that the murder weapon was a hammer, and I understand it has your prints on it. Can you tell me how they might have got there?"

It was not Mr. Hussick's practice to make up his mind about any case in advance, and he regarded all his clients as innocent until they were found guilty, but he was disturbed by the look on Jones's face. He meant to wipe his prints off the hammer and then forgot, the solicitor thought, and then put the idea firmly away from him. He offered cheerful words about it being early days yet to think of counsel and said he would handle things himself in the Magistrate's Court. It would help if they could find the mysterious man with a white streak in his hair.

"You must be able to find him," Jones said earnestly. He was a handsome young man, Hussick thought, although a little on the willowy side. He ought to make a good impression in the witness box.

"We'll do our damnedest. And let me know if you think of anything else, I'm here to help." A wave of the hand and he was gone. The officer who had been waiting outside the door took Tony back to the ward.

TWO

Life in the prison hospital seemed to be based upon a wrong conception of what he was like, for he was persistently treated as though he were an invalid or a schoolboy. One day he went to see the Medical Officer, who gave him a careful physical examination and asked how he was getting on.

"What do you think of the others, the other patients? Get on with them?"

"They're all right. But we're not patients, we're prisoners."

"What about your general health? Ever have any serious illnesses? As a child perhaps?"

"Only the usual things, measles, mumps, chickenpox."

"Meningitis? Any form of rheumatic fever? Nothing serious at all, you've been lucky, haven't you." He made little ticks and crosses on a form. "You're eating well, I'm glad to hear that."

Back in the ward he asked the old man the reason for the examination. "Just routine. They always like to have a look at you." On the following day he shook hands earnestly before leaving. Tony had somehow not liked to ask what he was charged with, but after the old man had gone he spoke to the warder and learned that it was rape.

On the following day he had two visitors. When he entered the interview room a little round-shouldered man was looking out of the window into a courtyard, clinking coins in his pocket. When he turned, Tony recognised his father.

Mr. Jones came forward and shook his son by the hand. His moustache was grey and he had grown fatter, but otherwise he had changed little. His characteristic smell of beer, tobacco and sweat was as strong as ever.

"How are things then? You're pretty fit from the look of you. Take any exercise?"

"An hour a day."

"That's good. I'm keeping pretty well. Nora too, she sent her regards. I've retired now, you know. Taken to watching the Codgers again, makes something to do." The Codgers was the football team they had watched in Tony's childhood. "Not a patch on what they were, though, shouldn't be surprised if they go down. You follow them at all?"

"No." How could he have loved and later hated this foolish little man? "What did you come for?"

"Just wondered if there was anything you wanted. I brought these along." He snapped open his briefcase. The officer by the door moved forward but relaxed when Mr. Jones took out a bunch of grapes.

Tony felt suddenly very angry. He flung the grapes on the floor. "I don't want your bloody grapes." His father looked at him in astonishment.

"Now then," the officer said, "that's enough of that."

Mr. Jones snapped the briefcase shut and stood with lowered head. "That's how it is, then. You're no good, I always said it. No good and never been any good."

Tony stood up too. "Get out."

His father appealed to the prison officer. "What do you think of it, eh? You bring 'em up, you give 'em a good home, and see the way it turns out. Right from the time he was a boy I said to his mother, 'You're spoiling that kid.' I was away a lot, had to be you understand, business."

"Get out, get out." Tony advanced upon his father.

The officer stepped between them, and Mr. Jones went. The officer shook his head.

"You've fairly blotted your copybook, you have."

"If he comes again, I won't see him."

"Your own father, too. I don't know. Knock you about when you were a kid, did he? Might have been better if he had, at that." He offered the comment in a philosophical rather than a critical manner.

The second visitor—he had grown cautious, and asked the name in advance—was Widgey. She gave him a perfunctory kiss and said, "Looks as though the cards were right, eh? How the hell did you get into this mess?" He said truthfully that he didn't know. "The police have been on to me asking questions. I told them we had a bit of a spat that last day. Had to when they asked me, understand?"

"I understand. It doesn't matter."

"Don't suppose it does. Wanted to tell you though, because they're calling me as a witness. Can't really refuse." She offered a cigarette and he took it.

"Widgey, would you do something for me?"

"What is it?"

"There's someone I want very much to see. I don't like to write because—well, I don't know what to say. Will you get in touch with her, go and see her, ask her to come."

Widgey's thin mouth was clamped shut. She released smoke through her nostrils. "You're a fool."

"You've never met her, you don't know what she's like."

"I'll tell you what she's like. This is something the police let out when they saw me, though they didn't mean to. She's the chief witness against you, that's what she's like."

THREE

"Your name is Genevieve Foster, and you are the widow of the deceased, Eversley Foster."

"Yes."

"What was your husband's occupation?"

"He was a director of several companies. He had spent a good deal of his life in South Africa, that was before I met him, and he had an interest in a mining company out there. Most of his directorships were connected with South Africa."

"And he went up to London on business every weekday?"

"Yes."

"Will you tell the Court in what circumstances you made the acquaintance of the defendant."

"I met him one day at the house of Mr. Bradbury. I knew Mrs. Bradbury, and he came to tea. I brought him back to Southbourne and happened to mention that my husband wanted secretarial help on a book he was writing in his spare time. It was a book on local topography. Bain-Truscott, that was what he called himself, said he had secretarial experience. He produced references."

"Is it a fact that the references were forgeries?"

"I understand so. I did not take them up."

"And your husband engaged him."

"Yes. Eversley thought he would be suitable. He left work each day for the secretary to do. Bain-Truscott came in the morning and left before lunch."

"Was he an efficient worker?"

"I believe so. Eversley did not complain."

"But after a few days your husband did complain to you about something, I believe. Tell us about it."

"It was at the beginning of the second week. Eversley missed a valuable pair of cuff links and a matching tiepin."

Tony closed his eyes, but her image remained on his retina, pale and composed. He opened his eyes again to see the door of the Court open and a man enter silently and sit down on one of the benches. The weak handsomeness, the white streak in his hair—it was Foster! He wrote a note quickly on one of the bits of scrap paper provided for him: "Man with white streak in hair—three rows from back—he is man I knew as Foster," and passed it down to Mr. Hussick. The solicitor's brows rose skyward. He nodded and passed over the piece of paper to his clerk, who sat next to him. The clerk got up and went out, grinning. What was there to grin about?

It is one of the peculiarities of English law that a prosecution case must be presented in full in the Magistrate's Court, where it is decided whether or not the accused person should be sent for trial, while the defence may reserve its case. The advantage to the defence is more apparent than real, because the proceedings are reported fully so that the jury empanelled to hear the trial know a great deal about the case already, and what they know is likely to favour the prosecution. The proceedings lack the tenseness of a dress rehearsal because the principal actors, the counsel, are missing. On the prosecution side a bored and sometimes inaudible young barrister appeared on behalf of the Director of Public Prosecutions, and Mr. Hussick had told Tony that he proposed to handle the defence personally at this stage.

"Nothing to do really," he had said when he saw Tony just before the hearing began. "Hear what they've got to say, spot their weak points, bide our time, that's the way."

"But I thought——" Tony had been about to say, "—

that I should have a proper counsel," but changed this to "—that you were engaging counsel."

"So I shall, so I shall, and you'll have the best. But at this stage, what's the point? It's not as though we're fighting here."

"Aren't we?"

"Certainly not. Reserve our defence, save our big guns for the time when they're needed. You'll see." Mr. Hussick spoke as though his client might be involved in many such trials, from each of which he would learn something.

So the atmosphere was undramatic, the Court was not even quite full, everything seemed to be conducted *sotto voce*, but as one witness succeeded another and left the box unquestioned or only cursorily challenged by Mr. Hussick, Tony's spirits dropped. There was Carlos Cotton to tell about the money Tony owed him, and Bradbury to give an account of the loan that remained unrepaid. There was Widgey, obviously giving evidence under protest. Then came Mr. Penny, which turned out to be the name of the little jeweller he had asked to value the links and tiepin. A bank clerk named Podger came to say that Mr. Foster had drawn out two hundred and fifty pounds on Friday morning, and to confirm the numbers of the ten pound notes. Then there was Dr. Dailey, who was what they called a Home Office pathologist. He said that Foster had been killed at between eight and ten o'clock on Friday evening by several blows struck from behind. The hammer was produced in Court and he confirmed that it was stained with blood of Foster's group, and had one or two hairs from Foster's head adhering to it. And Dr. Dailey was succeeded by a stiff self-confident fingerprint man named Moreston who said that he had found two clear prints of Tony's fingers on the hammer, together with several other prints too smudged for identification. Hussick questioned none of these witnesses, but sat with a smile of apparent self-satisfaction on his face, taking an occasional note. And now here was Jenny, intolerably calm and beautiful. What was she saying?

"On Friday morning my husband drew out two hundred and fifty pounds from the bank."

"Was it unusual for him to draw so large an amount?"

"A little unusual. He had a foible for paying all the accounts in cash each month where this was possible, rather than by cheque. This month they were for rather large amounts."

"Can you remember anything else he said on that morning?"

"Yes. Before leaving for London he said that he would have it out with Bain-Truscott, that is about the links. He was convinced that Bain-Truscott had taken them."

"Anything else?"

"Yes. He asked me to tell Bain-Truscott that he would like to see him on Friday evening. I told him when he came that morning, and he said all right."

"Were you in on Friday evening?"

"No. Eversley knew that I hate scenes. I arranged to go out to dinner with my cousin at Redling, particularly so that I should not be there."

"After that, you knew nothing more of the matter until you returned home shortly before midnight and found your husband's body?"

"That is correct."

"And then you telephoned the police?"

"Yes."

During this recital she had not looked at him. Once her tongue came out and quickly licked her upper lip as it had done after they made love. Remembering this, and remembering the things they had planned but which she never meant to carry out, he gripped the side of the box in which he sat so tightly that a splinter of wood went into the middle finger of his left hand. He took a piece of paper, scrawled on it in trembling capitals ALL LIES and handed it down to Mr. Hussick. The solicitor looked at it and put it aside. His clerk came back, still grinning. Would Hussick attack her, say she was lying? The solicitor rose from his chair. "No questions," he said. Jenny made her way out of the box. The man with the white streak in his hair rose and followed as she left the Court.

He hardly listened to the rest of the evidence. On Hussick's application he was committed for trial at the Old Bailey instead of at the local Assize near Southbourne, on the ground that there might be some local prejudice against him.

FOUR

After these proceedings he realised for the first time that his acquittal was not inevitable. This was made clear by Mr. Hussick who came to see him and said, with no diminution of cheerfulness, that they mustn't let the other side have it all their own way.

"But you didn't challenge them. I told you, her story was all lies."

"Tactics, tactics." Mr. Hussick shot up his eyebrows. "Play your cards close to your chest. One thing, though. I've got to know what the cards are."

"How do you mean?"

"You've been a little bit naughty. You never told me about Mr. Penny now, did you? I'm not going to hide anything from you. They have a case, no doubt about it they have a case."

"Everything she said was a lie."

159

Mr. Hussick ignored this. "I'll tell you what I don't like. Taking those links for valuation, they'll make a lot of that. Ask how you got hold of them. Then there's the money. I mean, I don't think we can deny that it was Foster's money, can we? And of course the hammer, I don't care for the hammer. Then your appointment with Foster on Friday evening, you must have known it wouldn't be pleasant, what happened? If I could clear up those points I'd feel a lot happier." He opened the exercise book at a blank page.

"Suppose they can't be explained."

"Oh, but they must be," Mr. Hussick said happily. "It would be very unwise to offer no explanation."

"You mean I might be found guilty?"

"I mean you mustn't keep anything back. You must tell me the truth."

"What about my ticket?"

"Ticket? Oh yes. When the time comes I don't think you'll find there will be any problem."

"Who was the man I pointed out in Court?"

"He's Mrs. Foster's cousin, the one she had dinner with on that Friday night. His name is Mortimer Lands."

Mortimer Lands. He had been deceived, then, from the start he had been deliberately deceived. The body in the bedroom twisting like a fish above the blue eye of the medallion, the gifts, the plans for the promised land of Venezuela, all of these had been a dream. The deception was reality. This was what he had to endure and to accept.

"She planned it. She planned the whole thing."

"What's that?" For once Mr. Hussick appeared surprised.

"She gave me the cuff links, said she'd bought them for me, that they were a present." Beginning at that point he told the whole story, Jenny's plan for disposing of Foster, the money she had given him for the fare and later for living in Caracas, the drive on Friday night out to the motor launch, the passage down the river to the sea and the thing being dropped overboard, then his own departure to London and to the airport. To tell the whole story was a relief, and he felt himself to be absolved from any consequence in doing so, because this little man was on his side.

Mr. Hussick covered several pages of his notebook. When the narrative flow had stopped he rubbed his nose. He seemed for once hardly to know what to say, and when he did speak it was in a manner unusually tentative.

"If that's the complete story——"

"It is."

"You were on your own account prepared to be accessory to a crime. It doesn't put you in a good light." Tony made no reply to this. "Although in fact according to you no crime was committed. What was in the sack? The thing you threw over into the water."

"How do I know?"

"No, of course not. This line involves an outright attack on Mrs. Foster, you understand that?"

"Yes." He leaned forward. "Somebody may have seen the car as we drove to the launch, or on the way back. Someone may have seen the launch going down the river."

"Possibly."

"You could make enquiries."

"Naturally I'll do that. You must understand that while legal aid covers my costs and those of your counsel, it may be difficult to put in hand a full scale enquiry of this kind."

"She wasn't where she says at ten o'clock that night. She was in her own house, and afterwards she was with me."

"The police will have checked this, I'm sure. I'll have a word with them." Mr. Hussick closed the exercise book, and said with a return to his customary cheerfulness, "Let's consider who we should brief for you. What would you say to Franklin Russell? George Pooling? Magnus Newton?"

"I don't know any of them. But if it's a matter of money——"

"Oh no no, not so far as counsel are concerned. If they aren't too busy they will be happy to take it on. It's just that legal aid won't run to a great deal of money." He left the sentence rather hanging in air, for he had been about to add *being spent on a wild goose chase*, but refrained.

"I leave it to you."

"The best thing you could do. I'll let you know developments. Don't worry, keep smiling." With a pat on the shoulder he was gone.

That night Tony slept soundly. He felt that by telling the truth he had exorcised Jenny from his mind for ever.

On the following day he saw the psychiatrist, who gave him tests involving putting shapes in different relationships to each other, and then consulted some papers. He was an urbane balding man with a pleasant smile.

"Well, Anthony, you know why I'm seeing you. You've been examined by the doctor and you're in good physical condition. I have to report on you mentally."

"Whether I'm mad, you mean?"

"That isn't a word we use. It's a question of whether you are fully responsible for your actions, and that involves all sorts of things like how easy you find it to adjust to other people and so on." The smile said that there were no aces hidden in his sleeve. "They tell me you've been very co-operative. There's just one little thing, what was it now? Oh yes, when your father came to see you. You got rather upset. Why was that?"

"We don't get on."

"I see. What about your mother?"

"She's dead."

"I know that, but how did you get on with her. Did you love her?"

"I suppose so." The man was as comforting as a bed-warmer. "She committed suicide. Took sleeping tablets. I found her."

The psychiatrist, who had an account of the suicide on the paper in front of him, nodded. "That upset you a lot?"

"Yes."

"It was after her suicide that you hated your father?"

"It was his fault. He had a mistress, she found out. And then he married this woman, very soon afterwards."

"You felt it was a betrayal of your relationship with your mother?"

"I suppose so." Had he felt that? He didn't know. Had he ever loved his mother? Surely it had been his father who was loved. "It was because of him that she took the pills."

"That's what you feel."

"It's why she took them."

"It was a terrible experience for you," the psychiatrist said in his warm voice. "And soon after it you left home. Then you had several jobs, but you kept none of them for more than a short time. Tell me about those jobs . . ."

He emerged bewildered from this long session. It seemed to him that his involvement in what had happened at the Villa Majorca was being treated far too seriously. Why should it be a reason for digging into his childhood and youth, why should it be thought that they had anything to do with it? He tried to say something like this to the psychiatrist, who seemed to regard his attitude as novel and curious, and interesting chiefly because it was sugges-tive about Tony's state of mind. But surely it was a normal thing to think that a single incident in the present had nothing to do with the past? Lying in bed that night, fingering the coarse sheet that for some reason brought the image of Jenny before his eyes, he thought of all the things he might have said. "I am going to be charged with murdering a man named Eversley Foster so that I could take his money. Will you tell me how that can possibly be connected with the dislike I feel for my father or with my mother's death?" Let him try to answer that one. Staring into the blackness of the ward he thought of half a dozen other questions that would have dented the psychiatrist's shell of urbanity, but of course the man was not there to answer them.

FIVE

During the next few days there were several developments in connection with the case, some of them important.

Franklin Russell read the papers given to him by Mr. Hussick and then turned the brief down. He said that this was because he had a full plate, but Mr. Hussick suspected that it was because of the nature of the defence. George Pooling was taken ill with pneumonia after playing eighteen holes in a rainstorm, and had to be ruled out. Magnus Newton, however, said yes, and if he was not the subtlest cross-examiner or the most intelligent man in the world, there was no doubt that he had a flourishing criminal practice. Hussick left the papers with him and a couple of days later had a conference at Newton's chambers.

"Extraordinary story, does this fellow know what he's doing?" Newton was a little snuffy red-faced man. He had had a good lunch and was smoking a big cigar. Mr. Hussick did not care for the smell of cigar smoke.

"I've tried to show him the implications."

"There's this to be said, that if his story's true he committed no crime at all, you realise that." Mr. Hussick smiled to show that he had realised it. "He was prepared to commit one, but that isn't the same thing. Have you tried to check his story?"

"I've done my best. The police say that on Friday night Mrs. Foster arrived at Lands's house—he's some sort of farmer, a gentleman farmer I'd suppose you'd call it— at seven-thirty. That's confirmed by Lands himself and by two neighbours who came in for a drink. The housekeeper had left a cold meal and gone out for the evening to see a friend. She had to go and come back by train— Lands's place is about a mile from the local station. It was arranged that she should come back on the last train, which gets in at eleven-fifteen. Mrs. Foster met her, took her back and then left. It was a drive of about fifteen miles and she got back just before midnight. It all fits."

Newton blew out smoke. "Why didn't Lands go to the station to collect his own housekeeper?"

"I'm sorry. I should have said he did go with her. His car was in the garage, so they used hers."

"Of course, according to his story Lands is in the plot."

"Yes."

"Would she have had time to do the things Jones says she did and get back to, what's his name, Lands in time to meet the housekeeper?"

"Perhaps. But I don't see how we can prove it."

"If somebody saw her car——"

"I've made enquiries, but so far there are no results."

"It's important."

Mr. Hussick's eyebrows shot up. "I know."

Newton grunted, looked through the papers again, then pushed them aside. "What his story comes to is this. She's in it with Lands, she must be Lands's mistress, he came to this house Villa Minorca——"

"Majorca." Newton was bad about names.

"Somebody must have seen 'em together."

Patiently Mr. Hussick said, "Certainly they were seen together, and naturally he had been to the villa. Foster knew him quite well. After all he was a relative."

"This is the story and we have to use it." Newton tapped the papers. "Get somebody on to it, do some digging, what was she like before she married Foster, did she make trips to London and meet Lands there, look for a link."

"I am doing so. But we haven't all the money in the world."

"Yes, well, I leave it to you." Newton got up and stood in front of an empty fireplace, cigar ash all over his waistcoat. He expanded his chest suddenly, with the effect of a frog blowing himself up. "What's he like?"

"Jones? A good-looking young man, quiet, polite. Conceited, I daresay."

"A good witness?"

"I should think so." Mr. Hussick hesitated, qualified this. "Rather lacking in self-confidence. Do you want to talk to him?"

"Not unless I have to." Newton did not care for talking to his clients. In his experience such meetings were almost never useful, and they were sometimes embarrassing. "It's all down here. If that's his story, there it is. You'll keep in touch."

Mr. Hussick took his bowler hat and got up to leave. Newton shook hands, went back to the papers again and then put them aside. They both knew that it was an open and shut case.

A couple of days later another conference was held in the chambers of Eustace Hardy, who was taking the case for the Crown. Hardy was an elegant, fastidious man, with a silver voice that matched his abundant silver hair, and an awareness of his own intellectual superiority that sometimes irritated juries. Just now it was irritating Detective Superintendent Jones, who wished that Hardy didn't have such an air of regarding the whole thing as a tedious chore. When he murmured to the Director of Public Prosecution's representative that it all seemed quite straightforward, Jones couldn't help feeling that something might go wrong.

The D.P.P.'s man, whose name was Walker, nodded. Jones felt impelled to put in a word.

"I think their line is going to be that Mrs. Foster egged him on, maybe even that she took part in the murder. These things get round on the grapevine. They've been checking her movements that night—she went to dinner with a cousin, man named Lands."

"Is there anything in that?" Hardy's fingers moved to straighten a silver cigarette box on his desk.

"As far as I can see, nothing at all."

"What is Jones's mental condition?"

"You've got the report there, Mr. Hardy." Jones could hardly conceal his annoyance. Why didn't the bloody man look at his papers?

"Yes indeed." Hardy glanced at it. "Well integrated in relation to ordinary social contacts, possible inferiority complex, affected by mother's suicide, poor relationship with father, yes, well, this kind of thing doesn't mean very much. He doesn't have any doubt that the man's fit to stand trial, that's the important thing."

"That's the important thing," Walker echoed.

Hardy scratched a red spot on his neck. The Superintendent was not usually an uncharitable man, but he could not help thinking, you're not perfect you bastard, you have spots on your neck like anybody else. And scratch them too.

"He's got no form, although he was hard pressed for money," Walker went on. "But there's one thing you should know about, although we can't use it, nothing to do with this case. Just a few days before he took up residence with Old Mother Widgeon, Jones was working for a retired General, helping with his memoirs, that kind of thing. The General got rid of him after he'd forged a cheque for two hundred and fifty pounds."

"Just got rid of him. He didn't prefer charges?"

"*And* let him keep the money," Jones said in disgust. "Slapped charges on him, he'd be in prison and Foster would be alive to-day."

"What name was he using then, Bain-Truscott?"

"Scott-Williams."

"Any idea why he used that name?"

Hardy was scratching the spot. Jones watched it becoming angrier. "I think he used quite a few, mostly double-barrelled."

"Compensating, I suppose the psychiatrist would call it. Where did you get this story from?"

"The General wrote to us. Seemed to think it would prove he wasn't a murderer."

"Did he say why he didn't prosecute?"

"I gather he felt Jones deserved another chance, something stupid like that."

"Interesting. He must be a persuasive young man." Interesting, hell, the Superintendent thought, he's a villain and that's all there is to it. "However, all the ends seem to be neatly tied up."

"It's an open and shut case," Walker said. Hardy smiled faintly and thanked them both.

". . . I don't see how you could do what you did to me. You know I love you, doesn't that mean anything at all? I'm not surprised you couldn't look at me when you were giving evidence, you knew it was all lies. How could you be such a bitch, bitch, BITCH." He read the long repetitious scrawl, then tore the sheet across. What was the good of writing? He put his hands on his knees and stared at the bed opposite. Every move she made was meant to destroy me, he thought. And I can't feel anger against her, I don't feel anything at all. When the warder came across, said he had a visitor and stuck a card under his nose he was incredulous at the name written on it.

The General was bolt upright in the uncomfortable chair that the interview room provided for visitors. Tony sat opposite him, the table between them. The prison officer stood in the corner. It was like some curious game. The General spoke.

"So your name's Jones. Don't know why you didn't say so, nothing wrong with it, had an adjutant named Jones, good chap." Silence. "Feeling sorry for yourself?"

"Not particularly."

"I wrote to the police, told them about our little affair. I thought it might help you, show that you had money, had nothing to do with the other business. I suppose you got through the money in a few days. Still, I wished I hadn't written. That's why I'm here."

Silence. He looked at the chintz curtains.

"I'm putting you on your honour now. Did you have anything to do with the death of this man?"

How was it possible to answer such a question? He did not even try. The General's head was a fine one, handsome and perfectly proportioned, but he noticed now for the first time that it was very small, almost a model of a head carved in brown and white.

"I should like to help you. I feel a certain responsibility, I don't know why. But I must know the facts."

"You said I was a scoundrel."

"You behaved outrageously. However, I still don't believe you capable of anything like this. Is your defence being properly conducted?"

"Legal aid." He was bored with the whole thing. Why should he sit here and let himself be questioned by this old fool, what had his past history to do with the disastrous present? He felt a longing to be back in the ward and looked at the man beside the door. The General misinterpreted him.

"Leave us alone for five minutes." The officer shook his head and Tony warmed to him. "You can tell me anything, any way I can help."

"There's nothing." Tony stood up.

"If you refuse to accept my help——" The General stood up too, erect and neat. Again it was a shock to see that not only his head but his whole body was small, he was like a large toy soldier.

"I'd like to go back now," he said to the officer by the door.

Strange things are found on beaches. Some boys digging for bait on the beach a couple of miles away from the place where Tony had thrown his bundle into the sea found an old pillow, a plastic hand of the kind sold in joke shops, and a partly-inflated football bladder. They were loosely joined together, and obviously other things attached to them had come away in the sea. They trod on the hand and squashed it and played beach football with the bladder. Later one of the boys took it home and kicked it about in his backyard until it hit a nail sticking out of an old toolshed and burst.

Life in the prison hospital was enjoyable in its way. The officers were overworked and Tony made himself useful in doing little jobs about the place, taking in the tea trolley and helping with the washing up. It was pleasant to find that he was respected by some of the other prisoners awaiting trial. A Cockney named Mobey who was to be charged with attempting to poison his wife with arsenic was apologetic about his own inefficiency.

"I have this bird, you see, who's fallen for me, twenty years younger than I am, you wouldn't think it possible would you?" Mobey was in his forties, and a carpenter by trade. "When the wife got to hear of it she played up, gave me hell. Between her and Sandra, that's my bird, I didn't know whether I was coming or going. But I should never have used arsenic, that was my mistake, it happened to be handy that's all. Should have used something else."

"Are you pleading guilty?"

"What do you take me for? My mouthpiece's going to say it was a mistake, she did it herself, cooked it with the greens." Mobey gave Tony a wink. "She was never much of a cook and I don't eat greens. But you, now, I can see you really gave it some thought."

"I had nothing to do with that man being killed."

"That's right." Mobey winked again. "Mum's the word. I admire you for it. Got a picture of her?"

"Who?"

"Mrs. Foster, that the name? Here's Sandra." He produced a dog-eared snap of a girl in a bikini. "How's that for a piece of homework? And she's hot stuff. Look at this." Tony read a letter from Sandra in which she told Mobey in detail of the pleasures they were both missing. "Can't wait to get back to it. What's your piece like?"

He found it impossible to talk about Jenny, but Mobey was not annoyed or disconcerted, considering this rather as a further proof of Tony's superiority in sensibility as well as in the conduct of his affairs. He had an enviable certainty of his eventual release and talked continually about the splendid times he and Sandra would have when he got out.

Tony was also surprised to receive a number of letters

from women who had read details of the case in the Magistrate's Court. Some called him a murderer and breaker-up of homes, but most wanted to start a correspondence and two suggested marriage after the trial. "If your heart is still free—and I do not see how you can have any feeling for *that woman* after the way she has behaved— I want you to know that there are real loving women in the world who are keen to get something *exciting* out of life," wrote a woman from Bedford who described herself as thirty years old and fancy free. Two or three letters asked for a signed photograph and one woman enclosed a lock of hair with the request that he should send one of his in return. He answered some of the letters and was annoyed when, apparently satisfied to have heard from him, the women didn't keep up the correspondence. At the same time there was something undoubtedly agreeable in finding himself a celebrity.

Upon the whole the days passed pleasantly enough. He seemed to have drifted out of life and did not feel seriously disturbed even when Mr. Hussick came in and reported that their attempts to disprove Mrs. Foster's story had come to nothing. He looked forward to the trial with a mixture of excitement and distress. Distress because it would mean the end, one way or the other, of the hospital life that in some ways suited him very well, and also to the sessions with the psychiatrist which had continued and which he rather enjoyed. He did not allow himself to think what might happen after the trial ended if he were found guilty, and on the whole distress was submerged by excitement. It would be the first time in his life that he had ever really been given attention, and he felt the importance of doing his best in the witness box not only because (as Mr. Hussick had said over and over) it was vital for his case, but because it was a real chance to show his true personality in public.

One or two experienced prisoners, men with long records, had told him that you got a lot of fan mail during the trial, especially if you made a good impression. Perhaps among those letters there would be one from a beautiful young woman, sexually demanding in just Jenny's way— he was unable quite to forget her—but a woman who really wanted all the things about which Jenny had only pretended. He called this imaginary young woman Lucinda, and the half hour in the morning that elapsed between the time he woke and the time they were called belonged to her. The trial ended with his acquittal, and she was waiting as he left the Court by a side entrance to avoid the crowd of screaming women who wanted to kiss him and to touch and tear his clothing as if he were a pop star. She moved over to the passenger seat of the sports car as he came out, he gunned the motor and they were away, driving down country roads, away, zooming at a forbidden speed down the endless lanes of the motorway, away, on and on until they reached the hotel where in the bedroom she imposed her body and her needs upon his own, using him as a man is traditionally supposed to use a woman. "Lucinda, Lucinda," he would whisper as he held her pillow body at this early hour of the morning when light filtered through the window into the ward and the man next to him moved and cried out in sleep. The hotel was only a stopping off place, on the following day they took the car over to Europe. When he asked where they were going she smiled and said "Everywhere."

Three days before the trial began he received a letter of a different kind. He had read two pages in the sprawling hand before he looked at the signature : "Fiona."

This is just to wish you good luck. Don't know what it's all about but it can't be nice to be in jug, and I hope you get out. It was funny seeing you with Carlos that night. Claude Armitage introduced us and I took it

from there. I told you I'd never go back, didn't I? Do
you know what Carlos likes most about me? I told
him my father had a castle in Ayrshire but lost all his
money, and he thinks I'm a nice class of girl. I thought I'd
better not let on I knew you but I tried to stop Carlos
doing anything. He was mad at you, said you had to be
taught a lesson because you wouldn't take a warning.
I'd have tipped you off if I'd known where to find you.
They don't like it when people bilk and duck out, Carlos
says he'd like to cut their you know what off personally.
He's nice to me. He runs a whole group of clubs for
the syndicate and he's put me in a flat off Curzon Street,
just super. I sometimes go to the clubs but he won't let
me play, says he doesn't want me getting into bad habits.
He hardly lets me out of his sight, says he'd cut me up
if he found me with anybody. Do you know you were one
of my bad habits, or could have been. You can't say
I didn't offer. Best of luck. I think about you.

SIX

Dimmock dissected his grilled haddock with the care he
gave to everything, first easing the large central bone away
from the flesh, then meticulously attending to the smaller
bones, pulling out one or two obstinate ones with his
fingers, finally flaking away the succulent flesh from the
skin and putting it into his mouth. He liked fish for breakfast, and had it three times a week. It was one of his
few extravagances.

On this morning he ate his haddock unhurriedly, followed it with one piece of toast and two cups of tea and
then said to his wife, "If I sit here for ever I shan't get

to Timbuctoo for lunch, shall I?" He had a number of
such phrases, some of them nonsensical, like "Lovely bit
of haddock, brought up in a high class paddock," or "Every
healthy growing nipper should eat each day a nice grilled
kipper." The fact that on this morning he responded to
his wife's query about the haddock only by saying that it
was very nice showed him to be unusually preoccupied.

"You're all packed ready. I've put in an extra shirt and
socks."

"Thank you, my dear. I'd better be getting off."

Dimmock got up from the table, brushed his teeth,
brought down his shabby suitcase, got out the old but still
reliable little car, kissed his wife, and drove away from
the semi-detached house in Wembley where he had lived
for twenty years, ever since the war ended. He had gone in
for a teachers' training scheme after being demobbed, but
with a couple of small kids it just hadn't been possible to
make ends meet and he had never been sorry that he gave
it up to go into his present work, which wasn't exciting
but provided a steady living. Now the kids, a girl and a
boy, had grown up and married and Dimmock was getting
on, in his fifties, with his wife the same. In a way he hadn't
got much to show for his life, but then look at it another
way and why should you want anything more than a decent
comfortable house and a bit of garden, a couple of kids
who'd never been any trouble, nice neighbours who never
poked their noses into your affairs, and a good programme
to watch on the telly? How many people had as much,
especially in other countries? And when people had more—
here Dimmock would make the point forcibly to his wife
or to a neighbour if one happened to have come in for
a glass of beer—did it make them happy? "Not always,
not by any manner of means. And I know what I'm
talking about," he would say.

He knew what he was talking about because, as his wife

said, he was a detective. Or as Dimmock himself put it, he was an operative in a firm of enquiry agents.

Most of the work was humdrum, concerned with chasing up bad debts or trying to trace crooks who had been practising confidence tricks or long firm frauds. He had been taken off divorce work because some of the cases had shocked and disgusted him, and at the Second To None Agency he had long since been classified by Mr. Clarence Newhouse, who owned it and was known to Dimmock as the Chief, as a willing workhorse, a man who was not too bright but would never fiddle his expenses or produce an imaginary report about footslogging when he had been propping up a bar all day. Such virtues are rare in the lower ranks of detection. If Dimmock was asked to find a missing woman last seen in Birmingham he would go on doggedly looking until he found her or was called off the trail. The fact that almost all disappearances are voluntary never depressed him. He would say that human nature is a funny thing, and be ready to get on with the next job. In his twenty years as an operative he had suffered violence only three times, the most serious of them being at the hands of a woman who beat him over the head with an umbrella and then threw him downstairs when he suggested that she should return to her husband.

Dimmock was assigned to the Foster case only because an operative named Berryman had been suddenly taken ill. Berryman would have known all about the case, whereas the Chief had to explain most of the details to Dimmock. However, the assignment was straightforward enough. He was to check up on the movements of Mrs. Foster with the idea of disproving her story of what she had done and where she had been on the night of her husband's murder. He was also to see what he could find out about her relationship with her cousin, Mortimer Lands. As the Chief explained all this Dimmock nodded again and again.

"It's likely you'll find that the police and the defence solicitors have made enquiries already. Use your loaf when you ask questions."

"I see."

"It's something out of the way for us, a murder enquiry. Bit of excitement for you."

"That's right." Newhouse gave up in despair. He looked at the long lugubrious face with the two deep lines carved in it and thought, oh well, at least he'll go through the motions.

There is a kind of routine laid down in such cases, and Dimmock followed it. He booked in at the Commercial Hotel, drove to Byron Avenue and past the house, found the nearest shopping area and began to ask questions. He found the grocer and the butcher who delivered to the Villa Majorca, produced a photograph of Lands and asked if they had ever seen him when they called at the house. They had not. He drove round until he found the milkman, went to the Post Office and saw the postman who delivered mail at the Villa, and received similar negative replies. The postman thought he had seen a Triumph Vitesse parked in the drive, and Lands owned such a car, but the man could not be sure.

Dimmock went back to the hotel, had two drinks before dinner, bought one for the barman, and asked where he should take a young lady if he wanted a good meal and a real slap-up evening. In town? No, not in town, out in the country, some really nice place where you could have a little celebration, no expense spared. With accommodation, the barman asked slyly, and Dimmock admitted that that might be an advantage. He got the addresses of three country hotels and three restaurants. Then he went in to dinner, which was thick cornflour soup, roast lamb, and treacle pudding without very much treacle. During dinner he read the local paper and got a couple more names from that, one a restaurant and the other a country club. If Lands and Mrs. Foster had gone out together, there was a good chance that they had used one of these places.

After dinner he made out his report in the bedroom. There was no writing desk or table and he wrote in a chair with a pad on his knee, in the firm copperplate hand he had been taught at school. At the end of the report he detailed the day's expenses calculated at so much a mile for the car, and including the pub lunch for which he had obtained a bill. Then he undressed, considered having a bath and decided against it because he thought that two baths a week were enough for a man of his age, put on his pyjamas which were silk, another of his little extravagances like fish for breakfast, and went to bed. He was not depressed by his failure to find out anything. He was only doing a job.

SEVEN

Four women, Mr. Hussick had said, it was splendid that they had four women. "Majority verdicts nowadays, you know, used to be enough to have one, now we need three. Ten to two guilty, nine to three innocent."

"Do you mean women are less likely to find me guilty?"

"Depends on the case. Child cruelty, killing somebody at a road crossing, I'd want men. Men every time in a car case. But something like this I'd choose women. If we had eight women and four men——" Mr. Hussick raised his brows, clicked his tongue. Eight women and four men, he seemed to imply, would mean acquittal.

The four women did not look very promising. One sat bolt upright and stared straight in front of her all the time.

Another had a blue rinse and spent a good deal of time contemplating her nails. The third was pretty but fatuous, smiled often, and looked round the Court when counsel on either side made a point as though prepared to join in a round of applause. The fourth, older than the rest, an iron-haired woman in her sixties, produced a notebook and made so many notes that she might have been writing an article. At times she raised her head and looked hard at Tony for a period of seconds. He was uncomfortably aware of this gaze, which he found hard to meet. When he did stare back at her, his eyes dropped first. Would she take that as an indication of guilt?

Mr. Penny the jeweller was in the box. Where was the wart behind his ear? Surely it had been on the left side? How extraordinary that it seemed to have vanished.

"He told me that it was a family heirloom."

"A family heirloom." Hardy repeated the words slowly, so that they should sink in. "He said that these links and pin were a family heirloom. And then?"

"I asked if he wanted a valuation, and he said he might consider selling them. I offered eighty pounds. He said he wanted a hundred."

"A hundred, yes, did he say anything further?"

"He said he needed the money, temporarily embarrassed were the words he used I think, and that nothing less would be any use."

"And after that?"

"I'm not a hard man. He seemed to be a nice young fellow." Hardy waited, eyes cast down at the papers before him, foot tapping slightly. With a quick beam at Hardy, at the judge, the jury, Penny the benevolent said, "I said, I'll take a chance, give you a hundred."

"Did he accept the offer?"

"No. He said he'd changed his mind, put them in his pocket and went out. Couldn't get out fast enough."

Hardy looked at his papers again, sat down. Newton slowly shuffled to his feet, rocked on his heels. Penny turned his head and Tony saw the mole. There it was, on the left side as he had thought. He felt relieved, as though the existence of the mole proved something.

"Just one or two questions, Mr. Penny, I shan't keep you long. You say you are not a hard man. Would you say you were a charitable one?"

The jeweller bristled, then gave a cunning smile. "I give a pound for my poppy on Remembrance Day."

There was a tiny ripple of subdued mirth. Tony looked quickly at the jury. Pretty But Fatuous put her hand over her mouth, Blue Rinse looked up in surprise and down again, Iron Hair wrote in her notebook. One or two of the men shuffled their bottoms uneasily. Newton went on rocking.

"That isn't quite what I meant. Did you think you were being charitable in offering a hundred pounds for this jewellery?"

The smile vanished. "It was a business deal."

"Precisely. What would you think the links and pin were worth?"

"I shouldn't like to say."

"Perhaps I can help you. Would it surprise you to know that they had been valued at two hundred and fifty pounds?"

"What they're valued at——"

"Just answer my question, would it surprise you?"

"Black opals are unlucky, people don't like them."

"Yes or no, Mr. Penny."

The judge, lean and birdlike, looked over the top of half moon spectacles. "Answer counsel's question, Mr. Penny."

Mr. Penny's mouth turned down in a pout. "No."

"You wouldn't be surprised. So when Mr. Jones took the

things away he might have been hoping to get a better price?"

"I offered what he asked."

"Quite. So if he had been just concerned with money he would have accepted. Wouldn't you say that his behaviour was that of somebody who had discovered that an article he had thought worth five or ten pounds was in fact much more valuable?"

"If you say so."

"No no, Mr. Penny." Newton scratched his wig, pulled it slightly askew. "Do *you* say so, that is the question."

Sulkily, still pouting, Mr. Penny agreed. "He could have been."

"Supposing he had just been given these articles as a present and had named what he thought was an outrageous figure for them, that would explain his reactions, would it not?"

"It might have done." Flaring up suddenly he asked, "Then why did he say he had to have a hundred pounds?"

"I am not here to answer your questions, Mr. Penny, but if he really wanted a hundred pounds why did he not take it when it was offered?" And before Hardy could intervene to protest that this was a statement rather than a question, Newton sat down.

Later that day Newton saw the accused personally, for the first and only time. He did so only because Hussick had said that the position ought to be made perfectly clear. The solicitor was also present.

"I want to make sure that you fully understand the implications of this defence," Newton said. "Mr. Hussick has already told you that extensive enquiries have been made to check your story without result."

"Yes."

"We have not been able to find anybody to confirm

your story that Mrs. Foster drove you to the point where the launch was kept, known as Bensley Water——"

"Bromley Water," Hussick said.

"Bromley Water. Nor that she took you near to the station. Nor that she did anything but what she said, and spent the evening with Lands."

"I've told you what happened."

"Yes." Newton lighted a cigar, then as an afterthought offered the case to Hussick and Tony. Both refused. "You say you don't remember passing cars or people."

"We did, of course, at least I suppose so. But not near Bromley Water. We went on side roads."

"And you can't think of any other way in which this can be proved?"

"Only by making her tell the truth."

"I was coming to that. When Mrs. Foster goes into the box I shall cross-examine her on these lines. The questions will be severe. It is possible that she may break down under them. If not——" Newton pointed the cigar at Tony like a gun. "The effect on your case may not be favourable. When you go into the box yourself you will certainly be subjected to a long cross-examination from the other side. It will be said that you are simply trying to blacken her reputation to save your own skin. I want you to understand that."

He was walking across from the dock, those few momentous steps to the box, body erect and shoulders braced back. Courteous and calm he faced the inquisitor, parried the questions and slipped the sword of a decisive answer past his opponent's guard. I was stupid, I agreed to help her in a moment of madness. Slowly he turned to the judge. My lord, I was in love.

"I asked if you understood." Newton looked at him impatiently, tapped grey ash on the floor.

He transferred his attention to the puffy little man. "I've told you what happened."

God help us, Newton thought, I believe you have. He felt annoyed with Hussick. What point was there in a face to face confrontation with a man who told a preposterous story like this? What was a solicitor for but to act as a barrier against such embarrassing confrontations? Yet although even by his own account Jones was nothing more than a contemptible weakling, there was something ingenuous and even innocent about him that was in its way touching. To his own surprise Newton found himself moved by the fact that Jones's fate rested in his hands.

"We shall do everything we can for you." Inadequate words, no doubt, but he rarely said as much.

Moreston, the police fingerprint expert, took up most of the afternoon. The evidence really amounted to saying that Jones's prints had been found on the hammer and that it had certainly been used to kill Foster, but Moreston was aware of his own importance and his examination in chief took more than an hour. Newton noticed one or two jurors fidgeting, and made his own questioning brief.

"Let me say at once that the defence does not dispute that the prints on the hammer are those of the accused. What I want to ask is this. Supposing he had used the hammer for some domestic task like—oh, knocking a nail in a wall—would he not have left prints like these?"

"He might have done."

"And then there are other blurred prints, are there not?"

"Perfectly true."

"If the hammer had been used for this domestic task by my client and then used afterwards for the crime by somebody wearing gloves, wouldn't you expect such blurring to occur?"

Moreston considered this. "It would be possible."

"Whereas if the blows were simply struck by Jones, who then dropped the hammer, the prints might be expected to be much clearer?"

Moreston again took his time. "No, I don't think so. More than one blow was struck and as the grip possibly shifted some blurring would be likely."

"But not so much, surely, as actually took place?"

"Are you asking me that, Mr. Newton?"

The judge coughed. "It was a question, I think."

Moreston was determined to make no concession to Newton, whom he disliked. "I have already given my opinion, my lord, but I will repeat it. The blurring may easily have been caused by a shifting of grip on the hammer. In the purely hypothetical case that the hammer was later used by somebody else wearing gloves, that also would have caused blurring. I can go no further than that."

The judge looked over his half-lenses. "Does that satisfy you, Mr. Newton?"

No, Newton thought, but it's all I shall get. "Thank you, my lord. Now, the effect of these blows with the hammer was to cause a considerable amount of blood to be spilt on the sitting-room carpet and elsewhere. Is it not surprising that not a single bloodstain was found on Jones's clothing?"

"I can't give an opinion on that."

Newton knew this perfectly well, and he put the point later to the forensic expert when he was in the box. But still, it did no harm to ask the question of this stubborn finger-print man. Anything must be useful which helped to counteract the evidence of the prints on the hammer

EIGHT

There was no fish on the breakfast menu and Dimmock ate eggs and bacon while he read the morning paper with its report of the first day of the trial. In the outline of the case given him it had been suggested that he should try to trace the movements of Mrs. Foster's car, but he rejected this as hopeless. What facilities did he have for making such enquiries, what could he do that had not already been done by the police? Immediately after breakfast he started on the trail of restaurants and hotels and pursued it until just after lunch, showing the photographs of Mrs. Foster and Lands everywhere he went. It was after lunch when he finished. Nobody recognised either of the photographs. If the couple had spent evenings together they had not done so at any of the places on his list. It began to rain before lunch and by mid-afternoon, when he reached Beaver Close, the rain had been joined by a high wind against which he struggled in his slightly shabby coat, pushing his way up to the door with one hand clasped on his hat to prevent it from being blown away.

He's selling something, Evelyn Bradbury thought as she watched him coming up the drive, but little as she liked door to door salesmen she felt sorry for him. One of Dimmock's few advantages as an operative was that women often did feel sorry for him. He had a hangdog honesty that many women found sympathetic. When Mrs. Bradbury, after looking at his card, asked what he wanted to know he flapped his arms in a hopeless way.

"I'm not sure, Mrs. Bradbury. I've been asked to make enquiries, that's all."

"On behalf of Jones, you say. But who's employing you?"

"I'm not at liberty to reveal that." In fact Dimmock didn't know, nor was he interested.

"The police have been round, you know." Dimmock's resigned nod said that he would always arrive second or third, never first. "And of course my husband has had to give evidence. He was quite upset about it, you know they were at school together, but I mean you have a duty, isn't that right?"

"I would sooner talk to you," Dimmock said truthfully. He found women much more responsive than men.

Few people said that to Evelyn Bradbury. She offered a cup of tea and took away Dimmock's damp coat and hat. When she returned with the tea trolley and little sponge cakes she asked what he wanted to know. It seemed that he was not sure.

"Well, of course you know it was here that they met. Bill says he will never forgive himself for bringing Jones back here. But they were old school friends, you see. He seemed quite a nice young man, although he spilled his tea. On the carpet, it's almost new——"

"A beautiful carpet," Dimmock said reverently and sipped the China tea. He preferred Indian. "Do you know Mrs. Foster well?"

"There is a Women's Club in Southbourne, and we had met there. She was a new member, though she didn't seem very interested. When she became a member we were hoping that she might bring her husband along at some time, he was something in the City you know, and Bill wanted to meet him. But we never did see him."

"You didn't meet her cousin, Mr. Lands?"

"I'm afraid not," she said reluctantly. "Do have one of these cakes, I made them myself."

"She never mentioned to you——" Dimmock was at a loss to know what she might be able to tell him that was useful, and continued lamely, "—anything interesting. About her husband."

"We didn't talk about him. I am sure it was a very happy marriage." She looked away with an expression of distaste. Dimmock humbly transferred his gaze to the carpet. "Except that she was left alone a good deal. It may have been rather dull for her. But then I always say that if you keep busy you are never dull."

"That's very true."

"And she had her golf." Dimmock looked up. It was the first he had heard about golf. "She belonged to the Mendwich Golf Club. I have seen a bag in her car."

"A bag."

"Of clubs." She spoke as if they were implements used by a primitive tribe.

The secretary of Mendwich Golf Club was red-faced and stiffish, but in the end he was softened by Dimmock's hangdog persistence. Yes, Mrs. Foster had been a member of the club and came there occasionally in company with a friend of hers, or perhaps it was some sort of relative, named Lands. How often? At this point the secretary became restive and said that they did not keep a check on the presence or absence of members. Dimmock thanked him, withdrew, sat in his car and thought. There was a club within ten miles of the Villa Majorca, why hadn't she joined that instead of the Mendwich which was thirty miles away? Because her cousin belonged to the Mendwich was the obvious reply. Probably there was nothing in it, but it was the first thing he had discovered that was of any interest at all, and Mendwich was outside the area in which he had visited restaurants and hotels.

He spent the rest of the day calling on those near the golf club. At the Great South Motel the head waiter recognised the photographs as those of a couple who had come in sometimes for dinner. Had they stayed the night? About this he was emphatic. They had not. A pound note, which he contemplated with the indifference that others might show to a half-crown, changed hands. Would his story have been different if the note had been a fiver? Dimmock did not think so. At the end of a long afternoon and evening in the rain he had learned nothing of real value, yet he had the feeling that he was on the edge of some discovery. He looked at the material prepared for him by the office and read: "Check housekeeper. Mrs. Twining keeps house for Lands, lives in." Below this was: "Check Fosters' maid Sarah Russell." He telephoned and found that Lands was up in London, no doubt attending the trial. It was a good opportunity to call.

It was twilight when he drove up to Lands's house, a rambling building which stood a quarter of a mile off the road at the end of a squelchy drive. Heavy rain fell out of a leaden sky. He could feel it seeping through his thin coat. The house was in darkness and there was no answer to his knock. He walked round and saw a light in what must be the kitchen, heard sounds of voices raised in high-pitched argument. He knocked on a side door and knocked again. There was a click. The radio argument was extinguished. A voice from behind the door said: "Yes?"

"My name is Dimmock."

"Yes."

"If you'll open the door I can give you my card."

The door opened on a bolt and chain. A woman's body, tall and bulky, was outlined against the light. She held something in her right hand. Dimmock fumbled under his wet coat and found a card which said that he was an insurance investigator. The voice, harsh and sexually neutral, asked what he wanted.

"Could I come in for a moment and explain."

"Is it about this business of Mr. Foster?"

Subterfuge seemed useless. "As a matter of fact it is."

"You want Mr. Lands. He's not here."

"You're Mrs. Twining, aren't you? As a matter of fact it was you I wanted to talk to."

"I've said all I had to say. To the police."

Rain from the guttering above was dripping steadily on to Dimmock's hat, and from the hat downwards. He could feel a cold trickle on his neck. "It's a wet night, Mrs. Twining——"

"I know your voice." He was so disconcerted that he stopped talking. "On the telephone. Sneaking round when Mr. Lands is away."

The drip ran under his collar. In desperation he moved forward and—a rare mistake on his part, for he was a man who respected the privacy of others—put his hand on the chain, not really with any intention of opening the door because that would not have been possible, but simply as a plea, a claim on her attention. The thing in her hand swung, and although he did not feel the blow his arm was suddenly numb. The door slammed shut, the radio voices started to argue again.

It was only the third time that he had suffered violence. Back in the car he told himself that he deserved it. He should have left his call until the morning, he shouldn't have stretched out his arm. In spite of these reflections he was conscious of an unreasoning anger that lasted all the way back to the Commercial Hotel. Dinner was finished by the time he got back and he had to be content with a sandwich which was made for him with a bad grace, and a bottle of beer. When he asked for a hot water bottle in his bed the maid stared at him as though he had taken leave of his senses and said that there wasn't such a thing in the hotel. After all, she added, it was summer.

Up in his room he examined the arm, which showed a livid bruise between wrist and elbow. He wrote out his report in a hand less firm than usual, and went to bed. It was a long time before he slept. The day had been unrewarding, but that was not what kept him awake. He felt it to be monstrously unjust that a man making polite enquiries should be met with a blow on the arm.

NINE

Mobey had gone. His place was taken by an inarticulate lantern-jawed man with a permanent sniff, who was charged with arson. Tony tried to find out what had happened to Mobey, but the warders were evasive. In the end he found out from Hussick.

"Mobey? The man who tried to poison his wife. He got ten years." Mr. Hussick's eyebrows danced. "Straightforward case. Silly fellow."

Tony found that he was upset by this. "He told me it was a mistake."

"Naturally he'd say that. Not true, I'm afraid." Mobey was dismissed. "Mrs. Foster's giving evidence to-day. Then Mr. Newton will put your case to her."

"What does he think of the chances?"

"We did very well yesterday, I thought. Moreston's a tough nut, doesn't give an inch unless he's forced to, but he had to agree about the blurring. It sank in with the jury, oh yes, I'm sure it sank in." He seemed about to burst into laughter at thought of the way it had sunk in, but refrained. "When Mrs. Foster is giving evidence, keep calm. No display of temper, judge doesn't like that and the jury don't like it either. You've been very good so far." He might have been a dentist congratulating a patient on the way he was enduring a long session in the chair.

On the way to Court in the little van he thought about Mobey. How extraordinary it was that somebody could be in your company one day, talking cheerfully about getting rid of his wife so that he could live with his bird, and then on the next day a group of people chosen at random could decide that he was to be shut up in prison for years. Ten years—just think what it would be like to be shut up for ten years, or even seven which would allow for good conduct remission, shut up in one small room, let out only to do humiliating meaningless work, continually in the company of vulgar men, never seeing or touching a woman, your horizon bounded by the single cell, living in a world removed from bright light and colour. Would it be possible for him to endure such a world, and could it be right that anybody should be forced to suffer in that way? He saw the Morris wallpaper in his bedroom at Leathersley House, the colours brighter than they had been in actuality. When one of the two prison officers with him asked how it was going he said that he didn't know, and saw the man look at his mate as though to convey an unspoken warning: "He's been cheerful so far, but it's getting to him now, he's beginning to realise what he's in for." The man offered him a cigarette but he shook his head. When the two of them talked about a cricket match to be played next weekend he listened eagerly, although he was not interested in cricket.

He had been braced for Jenny's appearance, and was irritated when she did not appear in the witness box at once. Instead they had the girl from the travel agency where he had bought the ticket for Caracas. Then they had Bradbury to mention the thirty pounds he had promised to repay, and then Carlos Cotton talking about his unpaid debt to World Casino Enterprises. Newton's cross-examination was brisk.

"This debt was contracted at—ah—Landford, is that correct?"

"Yes."

"And you subsequently agreed to forgo it?"

"I said he needn't pay."

"But then you changed your mind, I understand."

"I found he was playing at Southbourne after I'd put the black on him." Cotton was wearing a tight black suit with very high lapels. His fingers played uneasily with a button.

"Put the black on. What does that mean?"

"I'd barred him from any of my gaming clubs."

"Your clubs. That is World Casino Enterprises, those are your clubs, are they not?"

"Correct."

"And what is your position in them, Mr. Cotton?"

"Director. And general manager."

"With some special responsibility for bad debts?"

"We don't like them. Who does?"

"Who does?" Newton echoed and continued smoothly. "You know that gambling debts can't be enforced by law?"

"Yes."

"So how did you propose to enforce payment?"

"I've told you. If he didn't pay up he'd be barred. I'd barred him already." Cotton seemed to shrink into himself. He cast quick glances at Newton, the judge, the body of the Court, like a malevolent insect.

"You didn't threaten him with physical violence in any way?"

"Of course not." Cotton turned his monkey face to the public gallery. Tony followed his gaze and saw Fiona, leaning forward in the front row.

"So there was no reason why he should be specially worried?"

The judge had been tapping gently with a pencil. Now

he said, "I don't want to interfere, Mr. Newton, but isn't this line of questioning going rather far afield?"

"I hope not, my lord. My learned friend's purpose in introducing this evidence was I presume to show that my client was hard pressed for money. I am trying to bring out the point that one of these debts was to a friend and the other was not legally enforceable."

"I think we have taken the point, Mr. Newton."

"Had threats been employed it would be a different matter. I am happy to have the assurance that there was no question of this."

The judge bowed his head. Newton sat down and there was no re-examination. Cotton looked from one to the other of them and left the box. Shortly afterwards Fiona's head disappeared from the gallery.

In a way Tony felt indignant about this. He would have liked to ask Cotton questions himself and to say "You threatened me, one of your thugs stubbed out his cigarette on my hand and two more tried to beat me up," but he understood that if there had been no threats it was a good thing for him, it meant that he had no reason to worry about the money. This meant also that it didn't always pay to bring out the truth. Would it be right to say that truth was one thing and justice another? He was thinking about this when Jenny entered the box.

She walked through the Court with the care of somebody moving along a private knife edge, one foot placed before the other, her face a white blank and her head held high. She was wearing a dress in some neutral completely washed out colour, and as always she looked slight and vulnerable. The stir of anger he had been prepared to feel never flickered. He found himself as dispassionate as though he were watching a play. Hussick, looking up at his client, saw that there was no reason to worry.

For a long time the play was a repeat performance

of what he had already heard, except that there were some details of her life before marriage. Most of what she had told him was true. She had been a not very successful actress, had met Foster when he returned to England from South Africa, and married him. She talked about this with a straightforwardness and simplicity that, as Tony felt, must impress the jury. Hardy led her like a dancing master through the tale she had told in the Magistrate's Court, of his engagement, her husband's discovery of the missing links, his determination to "have things out" on Friday evening, her departure for dinner and her return to find the body in the living-room. For the first time Tony found himself wondering what had really happened. Had Lands come over, helped her, and then gone back in his own car before Tony's arrival? Or had she done the whole thing herself? He could see Foster—but then he had never met Foster, he was thinking of Lands when he used the name—turning round in the sitting-room when she asked for a drink, the hammer in her gloved hand, the first blow that staggered him, and then the hammer coming down again and again. Was there sufficient strength in those thin hands? He had felt them gripping him, and knew that there was. And remembering the look he had seen sometimes on her face when they made love, the look that made it clear she did not regard him as another human being but only as an object to be used, he had no difficulty in seeing her striking Foster, unmoved by the blood that spurted out when the eggshell head cracked.

It was these thoughts, and recollection of what Moreston had said that made him scribble a note to Hussick: "She must have had blood on her clothes when she hit him." Hussick read the note, nodded, folded the paper into small pieces and smiled. Tony scribbled another note: "HAVE YOU CHECKED?" Hussick read this, nodded again, and then set his eyebrows dancing and turned down the corners of his mouth. What did that mean? At Tony's finger-beckoning the solicitor wrote a note of his own which his clerk passed up. When unfolded it read: "We checked with laundry, etc. Nothing."

So how had she killed him? Naked, as the Liverpool insurance agent Wallace was said to have killed his wife? That was surely not possible. He found that it was hard to concentrate on the examination.

It was after lunch when Hardy had finished and Newton rose. His tone was friendly, almost paternal.

"First of all, I wonder if you could tell me just a little more of what happened when you engaged Jones. You did engage him, isn't that so?"

"On my husband's behalf."

"Naturally. I find that a little unusual. Why didn't your husband interview him?"

"He trusted my judgment." She twisted her hands. "God forgive me."

That's a bit corny, Tony thought, a bit too actressy. He took a quick glance at his four jurywomen, but to his disgust they were behaving as usual, Blue Rinse looking at her nails, Pretty But Fatuous staring round the Court, Iron Hair waiting with pencil poised and Bolt Upright naturally bolt upright. What was Newton saying?

"He accepted your recommendation. And your impression was favourable, you engaged him on the spot."

"He seemed pleasant. He could type. And I had met him at a friend's house."

"You liked him?"

Thin shoulders shrugged under the colourless dress. "I had no feelings one way or the other."

"At least you didn't dislike him?"

Again the shrug. "True."

Newton looked at his notes for what seemed a long time and then spoke abruptly. "Were you happily married?"

"Yes."

"Your husband was twenty-five years older than you, but that made no difference?"

"None at all."

"It was one of those marriages where age doesn't matter because husband and wife have so much in common. Is that so, Mrs. Foster?"

As she repeated in a neutral voice "We were very happy," Tony looked again at the jury, the men as well as the women. They were all keenly attentive. There was a man who looked ominously like Clinker the builder, short and swart with hairy hands which rested on the ledge in front of him. What was he thinking, what would Tony himself think if he saw the slim woman and heard her low-voiced replies? Newton struggled on like a ship ploughing through an icefield. Tony ceased to listen. He saw instead of the courtroom the confines of a cell nine by six—was that the size?—which would be his home for years. *I shall die*, he thought, *if they shut me up in a place like that I shall die*.

Below him Newton, as he followed no particular line of questioning but probed with all the delicacy of which he was capable to find a chink in this bloodless woman's personality through which he could attack, was conscious of attempting to make bricks not only without straw but even without the basic clay. At the same time he had the feeling, which comes to all advocates at some time or another and which they know they can trust, that in some essential respects the witness was not telling the truth. The problem then is to induce the same feeling in the jury. "You did not take up his references?"

"No."

"We know that they were not genuine. Had you written, he would have been exposed at once."

"Believe me, I'm sorry I didn't," she said in a low voice.

"You engaged him after a short interview, you didn't trouble to check his references. And you still say you didn't find him attractive?"

"I had no feelings, one way or the other."

"And then you saw him every day. Alone, since your husband was up in London."

"Yes."

"This young attractive man was alone in the house with you each day, but you still had no feelings about him?"

She raised her voice a little. "He was there in the mornings. To do a job of work."

Hopeless, Newton thought, hopeless. He speeded up his questions and changed his tone altogether, using the bullying peremptory manner that came naturally to him. "I put it to you that you were bored with your elderly husband."

"That is not true."

"That you were bored with him, wanted to get rid of him and still enjoy his money. Isn't that the truth?"

"Certainly not."

"And you used my client as a tool for this purpose, a tool who was like putty in your hands."

"That is absolutely untrue," she said without emphasis.

There it goes, Mr. Hussick thought as he listened to Newton putting to her the points about the hammer, about the plan to kill Foster and about the drive to the motor launch, to be met in every case by passionless negatives and a denial that she had been to the launch for three weeks before the murder, there goes our case. You couldn't blame Newton, what could anybody do with a story that didn't have the least fragment of fact to support it.

Although Tony had felt no emotion when Genevieve Foster gave evidence, the very sight of Mortimer Lands as he walked into the box and stumbled slightly over taking the oath made him so angry that he had to grip the sides of the dock to control himself. The weak delicate features, the lock of white hair conspicuous as if it had been painted on the dark head, could this possibly be what Jenny had preferred to him? And sexual jealousy was not the only cause of his anger. The thought of those mornings when this wretched little man had dictated to him in the study and he had typed out all the meaningless details from books was really too much to be borne. The prison officers behind him exchanged meaningful glances as he leaned forward, and Mr. Hussick looked up with a smile which managed to be at once reassuring and reproving.

There was really very little substance to the evidence which Lands gave rapidly in a low voice, confirming that he was a second cousin of Mrs. Foster, that he had worked for a public relations firm and had become a farmer after his father's death, had sometimes visited the Fosters at the Villa Majorca, and had given Mrs. Foster dinner on the night of the murder. Hardy elicited facts and times and then sat down. When Newton rose he did so this time with a flourish. He had sensed, as a counsel can do, that Lands was easy meat.

"Was this visit of Mrs. Foster's an unusual occurrence?" Lands looked puzzled. "I don't quite understand."

"Was it the first time she had been to your farm for dinner?"

"Oh, I see. No, it wasn't."

"She'd been before. Alone?"

"Yes."

"How many times?" Lands, head down, did not reply. "Just once? Half a dozen times? Twenty times?"

Still with his head down Lands said, "Three or four."

"I can't hear you." That was the judge. Lands looked up, startled.

"I'm sorry, my lord. I said three or four times."

"Always alone," Newton said with relish.

"She came with Eversley once or twice I think." Lands waved his white ladylike fingers. "These other times, when she came alone, he was away."

"He was away," Newton repeated meaningfully. "And then she dined with you. Did you ever go to dinner with her, or with them both?"

"I—I don't think so."

"These were one way visits." Newton looked at the jury. "I am not implying anything wrong. It just seemed a little strange to me that she should telephone and invite herself to dinner on this Friday, but if she were a frequent visitor that explains it."

The judge looked at Newton. "Three or four times, the witness said, Mr. Newton."

Newton bowed his head. "Three or four times. She had been before at all events. So you were not surprised when she telephoned and said 'Can I come to dinner?'" Suddenly he snapped. "Did she telephone?"

Like a rabbit facing a wolf Lands stammered, "Yes, on—on Friday morning."

"And what did she say?"

"She said——" he gulped. "—there had been some unpleasantness about the man Eversley was employing, and he wanted to see the man alone that evening. Could she come over to me. Something like that."

"This wasn't very convenient. Your housekeeper, Mrs. Turner, was out for the evening."

Lands perked up for a moment. "Mrs. Twining."

The correction appeared to enrage Newton. He thundered: "Mrs. Twining was going out. Why not take Mrs. Foster out to dinner?"

Lands stared, dumbfounded. "I don't know."

"Surely that would have been easier?"

"I suppose so. It never occurred to me. Mrs. Twining left something, something cold."

"And then you had dinner, *tête-à-tête*. What did you talk about?"

Lands put a hand to his head, touched his white streak as though he were touching his forelock. "I don't remember."

"She arrived at seven-thirty and left not long before midnight and you can't remember anything you talked about?"

"Local things," Lands said weakly. "And this man, Bain-Truscott. Eversley wasn't sure whether he would charge the man or not."

"And what did Mrs. Foster want him to do?"

Lands gathered a little boldness. "I don't remember. I wasn't much interested."

It appeared to Mr. Hussick that Newton was pressing it a bit hard, and indeed this was Newton's own feeling. He went on asking questions about the times and about Mrs. Twining being fetched from the station, but the effect he had made at first faded a little. Still, he had given Lands a bad quarter of an hour, although it wasn't of great importance in the long run, and he had encouraged their client. Mr. Hussick raised his eyebrows and smiled at Tony, and Tony smiled shyly back.

TEN

Mortimer Lands and Genevieve Foster had not really talked to each other since the trial began. They were both staying up in London, she at a hotel, he at the flat of a friend named Jerry Milton. He telephoned her that night when Milton was out.

"My housekeeper's been on the phone. Somebody's been asking questions at the farm. She sent him away."

"Yes."

"It wasn't the police, it was somebody else."

"No doubt some enquiry agent for the defence."

"One's been round already. I don't like it, Jenny."

There was a pause. She said coldly, "I told you not to telephone."

"I'm worried, I have to see you." She said nothing. "I could come round. Now."

"Don't be a fool."

"I've got to see you. I can't go on if I don't."

"I don't know what you're talking about," she said sharply. "It's upsetting for everybody. You don't think I liked all those questions to-day, do you?"

Lands had drunk a quarter of a bottle of whisky. Now he half-filled his pony glass. "I've got to see you."

"Very well. To-morrow night you can take me out to dinner."

"I could meet you somewhere quiet, nobody would——"

"I won't have anything hole and corner. Call for me here at seven o'clock." She put down the receiver.

When Jerry Milton returned an hour later he found Mortie Lands half cut and lachrymose with it. They had been friends at Oxford and had seen a good deal of each other since then. Jerry, who was an executive in a statistical research company, disliked drunks, but he tried to be patient.

"It's ghastly the whole thing, I do see that, but after all you've given evidence now, it's over."

"You don't understand," Mortie said. His hair was mussed up, and he was sprawled all over the sofa. Jerry privately thought it was a bit much—the whisky glass had left marks on a pretty little rosewood table—but Mortie had always been a little on the hysterical side. Now he said, bleary eyed, "It's terrible. That poor young man."

"Jones? He's just a dirty crook. And a murderer. You're

201

too soft-hearted, Mortie, that's your trouble. Come on, you'd better get to bed."

With the help of his arm Mortie rose, then staggered and knocked over a Victorian glass table lamp which broke into a dozen pieces. It was really too much to be borne, and Jerry told him so pretty sharply. Mortie began to weep.

"You're all against me," he said through sobs. "She is too. I can't bear it, I can't go on."

There was only one thing to do, and Jerry did it. He hauled the insensible disgusting lump into the bedroom and deposited him on top of the bed.

In the morning Mortie was apologetic, and he looked so haunted, so much like death warmed up, that Jerry didn't have the heart to say anything more.

ELEVEN

Dimmock sneezed when he got out of bed and again while he was shaving. By the time he got downstairs there could be no doubt that he had a cold. He could not have faced fish if it had been offered to him, and his breakfast was one piece of toast and marmalade and two cups of watery coffee. "I could eat some bacon and eggs if I hadn't this pain in my pegs," he thought, and it was true that his teeth did ache. When he set out in the car it was still raining, heavy solid stuff that came steadily down. As he drove out of town he felt distinctly ill. He did not think that there was much point in going to see the motor launch or in visiting Sarah Russell, but it did not occur to him that he might say this to the Chief. He had never yet failed to carry out the assignments given to him in every detail.

The day had begun badly with his cold, and it con-

tinued badly. He was misdirected to the place where the
launch had been tied up, and when he found the place
the boat was no longer there. He called at a house nearby
and learned that the *Daisy Mae* had been removed by the
police to the yard of a local boat builder named Clynes. It
was eleven-thirty when he found the boatyard, most of
the morning gone. Clynes received Dimmock in his office.
He was a thin lugubrious man.

"Police have been over her," he said. "What you want to
look at her for?"

Why did he want to look at her? Dimmock had no idea.
"It's part of an investigation I'm carrying out for somebody
interested in the——" He stopped and sneezed. "—
defence."

Clynes was concerned. "That's a nasty cold you've got.
You could do with a cup of tea."

As he drank the scalding liquid Dimmock was conscious
of his wet disgusting clothes, which seemed to have lost
their shape. His trousers hung round his legs like pieces of
cardboard.

"Know anything about boats?" Dimmock shook his
head. "No more did they. Bought her from me, Foster did,
just because his wife wanted it. Like buying a kid a toy.
Not but what she learned a bit. How to start the engine."
He laughed, and Dimmock realised that this was a joke.
"Now she wants me to sell the boat for her."

"What sort of man was Foster?" He asked it to keep the
conversation going, not because he was interested.

"Thought the sun shone out of her backside. Bloody old
fool if you ask me. I've seen her sort before, out for what
they can get. Gold diggers, we used to call 'em." Clynes
finished his tea. "Interested in cricket?"

"I'm afraid not." Hopefully, like a man excusing himself, he said, "My son plays."

"Local cricket club. I'm the president. Like to take

some?" He pushed a book of raffle tickets across the table. Dimmock bought the whole book, twenty at a shilling each. He would charge them to expenses, but suppose he won a prize what would he do then?

Clynes did not show satisfaction, but Dimmock knew that he was pleased. "Right then, let's go and have a look at her, shall we?"

He put on an oilskin and they squelched across the yard with the rain pouring down. Dimmock quite distinctly felt mud surge up round his left sock.

The boat was just about what he had expected. Clynes jumped in and Dimmock followed him more circumspectly, stumbling a little so that Clynes's hand had to support him. The boat builder pointed out features. "Evinrude motor, pull starter on it easy to work. Steering wheel. Oars to use if the motor packs up. Nice little cabin, sleeps two if they're not over six foot, calor gas cooker, even a baby fridge. And that's it. She's a pleasure boat, not for serious sailors."

"If you were taking it away from the place where it was tied up and didn't want to make a noise, you'd use the oars."

"Of course."

Dimmock poked about. There was nothing to see. "I suppose the police searched it thoroughly."

Clynes stroked his chin. "They took a look. Not a long one. Didn't expect to find anything, you won't either."

Dimmock went into the cabin, got down on the floor, peered under the two bunks, even put his hand under, more for the sake of appearances than anything else. Nothing. Half a dozen paperback novels stood on a small ledge above the bunk, and he read the titles idly. A small kettle was on the cooker and in an access of idiocy, disturbed by the figure of Clynes in the doorway watching, he lifted the lid. Bits of kettle fur rattled about inside.

"What you looking for, poison?" Clynes guffawed slightly. Dimmock responded with a wan smile. He was reluctant to go out again into the rain, but it had to be done. Outside again he squatted down and heard the bones crack in his knees. I shall be lucky if I don't get pneumonia, he thought. There was a little water in the bottom of the boat but to take the ache out of his knees he knelt down.

Something was attached to one of the rowlocks, if that was what you called the things in which you put the oars. You could not see it when you knelt, but he could feel something at the bottom of the rowlock. He called to Clynes, who came and bent down beside him. Dimmock gently removed the thing, a tiny piece of fabric. It was about two inches one way by an inch the other. One side was check, the other a muddy brown. It was made from some rubberised material.

"You saw me find it. I didn't put it there."

Clynes nodded. "We haven't cleaned her out yet. If we had done we'd have found that bit of stuff. Thrown it away most like."

"I didn't put it there."

"Course you bloody didn't. Think it's important?"

The discovery seemed to have changed Clynes's view of Dimmock. His stare held something approaching respect. It was unlikely that the fabric was of any importance at all, but Dimmock shrugged. He felt the heavy dampness of his topcoat. They squelched away.

"Might be a bit of mackintosh. Just what you could do with." Clynes guffawed. "Come in. I'll give you a tot of rum."

They returned to the office. Dimmock drank the rum and wrote out a brief statement about the way in which he had found the bit of fabric. Clynes signed it as witness. Dimmock was a man who believed in the value of routine.

With the statement in his pocket he got into his car, removed his soaking hat and coat and drove away. It was good to have the wet things off, but there was no heater in the car and within five minutes he began to shiver.

TWELVE

"To-day's the big one then," one of the prison officers said to him in the van that morning. "You want to look all bright and shining, doesn't he, Bill?" The other man said that was right, get into that box and show 'em, good turn-out, bags of swank, rather as if he were going on parade in the army. One of them offered him a little pocket mirror so that he could adjust the knot of his tie. They were very friendly chaps. He had tried once or twice to tell them what his defence was, what had really happened, but they always cut him short and said that it was not their business.

He had expected to be nervous, but once he had taken the oath swearing to tell the truth (and after all he was going to do just that) and had begun to answer Newton's questions, he did not feel nervous at all. And a quick look at the jury—Bill the prison officer had told him that it was a good thing to look at them sometimes as long as you didn't overdo it—showed him that they were paying attention. Blue Rinse had abandoned her nails and was looking at him with her lips slightly parted, Pretty But Fatuous was evidently attentive, oh yes he had them on the alert as he rode the gentle swell of the questions, answering them rapidly and with firmness in a consciously clear voice. He was rather pleased with the way in which he disposed of the *name* business. Why had he called himself Bain-Truscott?

He hesitated just a moment, permitting himself just a hint of his smile. "Snobbery, I have to admit. I did it to impress people."

"There was no other reason?"

Firmness at this, smile vanishing. "None at all."

It had been raining most of the morning, but now suddenly for a quarter of an hour the sun shone through the window, casting a lean knife shadow across the Court which moved slowly in the direction of the man in the box, away from the barristers in their wigs and gowns. There were one or two moments of drama, like the one when Newton asked if he had ever met the dead man.

"Never." Very firm, head up showing the clean line of the chin. Sunlight was strong on his face.

"But you talked to a man who called himself by that name."

"I did."

"He was an impostor?"

"I understand that now."

"Do you know now who that man was?"

"It was Mortimer Lands."

Later he admitted that he had agreed to take part in disposing of what he believed to be Foster's body.

"Are you ashamed of your conduct?"

Low voiced, but still firm. "I am."

"Can you explain what made you do it?"

He would have liked to look at Jenny, to search her out with his eyes, but she was not in Court. He stared boldly at the jury instead. "I was infatuated with Mrs. Foster. I thought she was in love with me."

They went through the tale of the drive in the car, the burden dropped out of the motor launch. "At the time you believed this to be Foster's body."

"Yes."

"What do you think now?"

"It must have been some kind of dummy already prepared."

"I don't want there to be any mistake about this. You were prepared to play your part in this wretched enterprise?"

"I was."

"You are not trying to deny that?"

"No."

"Can you think of any word that would fit your conduct?" He said again that he was ashamed. "When did you first learn that you had been taking part in a masquerade, that the whole thing was a sham?"

"When the detective at the airport showed me a picture of the real Eversley Foster."

Newton repetitiously made the thing clear. "This was a man you had never seen in your life?"

"That is so."

"And you had no part whatever in his death?"

"Absolutely none."

After his evidence in chief was completed the Court adjourned for lunch. Tony felt that he had done well and had impressed the jury. He ate a good meal. The prison officer with him watched him with surprise.

At just about this time Dimmock, fifty miles away, discovered the piece of fabric.

The line of defence had been fairly clear after the cross-examination of Mrs. Foster, but still it seemed hardly credible, Hardy's junior Gordon Baker said to him over their chump chops and pints of bitter that such a line should be seriously advanced. Hardy smiled faintly, with the air of superiority that made him so irritating, and said that if his client insisted on the story then Newton was stuck with it.

"Yes, but I mean there are limits." Hardy looked at him interrogatively. "They must have given him a hint of what he was in for."

Hardy had eaten half of his chop. He looked at the rest of it and pushed away his plate. "And if they did?"

"Well then, surely——" Baker was at a loss how to go on.

Hardy delivered himself of one of those apothegms that made him very little loved. "A counsel is no better than his client. Especially," he added with the faintest gleam of a smile like sun on ice in winter, "When the counsel is Newton."

After Jerry Milton had gone to work Mortimer Lands felt terrible. He thought of ringing Jenny at her hotel, but he knew that she would not want to speak to him. He felt physically unable to go to Court again, although he was still worried about the man who had called at the farm. Just after midday he thought that it might do him good to go out. This proved to be a mistake. He went into a pub and felt impelled to start a discussion about the case in which he maintained that Jones might be innocent. Fortunately he did not reveal his identity, but when he left the pub he had had too much to drink and nothing to eat. He went back to the flat and fell asleep. On waking he still felt terrible.

Genevieve Foster woke early, had her usual breakfast of orange juice and Melba toast, and then went shopping. Or rather, she went into shops and looked at clothes. She did not buy anything because she thought that it was too soon after Eversley's death for that to be wise. She had already decided that when it was all over she would not marry

Mortimer. She was not worried about him, because after all he could say nothing about her which did not implicate himself, but he was a weak man and she found weakness unsympathetic. When the case was over she would tell Mortimer that what had been between them was over too and go away for a time, perhaps to one of those Greek islands that people talked about.

Looking at the round immature body of an assistant in one shop, and at the girl's equally round soft face she felt the stirrings of desire, and wondered if she were basically a Lesbian. Perhaps on the Greek island there would be a chance to find out. When she came out of the shop she took a taxi and had lunch in a salad bar. Then she took another taxi to the Old Bailey and was in Court when Hardy rose to begin his cross-examination. As Tony entered the box again she was struck by his good looks, as she had been when she first saw him. It was a pity that he was such a fool.

THIRTEEN

There was not much to do at the Villa Majorca, but Sarah Russell had said that she would go in that day and in she went, cleaning and dusting as usual. Mrs. Foster had told her that she might be leaving Southbourne after what had happened, but while she was there the place had to be kept clean. She put on a kettle for a cup of tea, looked at the rain shuttering down outside and thought about the Fosters. He had been a perfect gentleman, although rather old and pernickety and set in his ways, but Mrs. Foster now . . . There was something that she had never quite liked about Mrs. Foster, although she couldn't have said what it was, except that she never had a chat with you as in Sarah's view an employer should chat with her daily help.

As the kettle boiled the bell rang. A little man—medium-sized really, but somehow he looked small—was outside the door, and he was obviously very wet. His hat and raincoat were thoroughly sodden. "Miss Sarah Russell," he said, and raised the sodden hat.

The gesture touched her. Very few men had ever raised their hats to her, and he looked pathetic in his wet clothes. She had no doubt of his respectability, somehow the age of the car standing outside certified that, and Dimmock did not even have to produce one of his cards to get into the house. She sat him down in the kitchen, hung his wet coat in front of the electric fire and put his hat beside it. She made him take off his shoes, commented on the wetness of his trousers. Dimmock felt that she would have been quite prepared for him to take them off as well. He put them close to the fire and they steamed.

"Thank you very much." The words came out as a crow-like croak, but the hot tea soothed his throat. "I hope I shan't infect you. I've got a cold coming on."

"You ought to be in bed." She spoke angrily. She seemed a formidable old battleaxe.

"To-morrow I shall be. Home in Wembley. And I can tell you I shan't be sorry."

"Wembley," she cried. Her brother and his wife lived there. Friendship was cemented, and it was not until he had had a second cup of tea and eaten a biscuit that she said, "You're not a reporter, are you? I've had some of *them* round." He shook his head and sneezed. "Bless *you*," said Sarah Russell.

He produced his card and told her that he was gathering information for the defence. She stared.

"You're too late, aren't you? The trial's half-way through. And there's been someone here already."

"Did you tell him anything?"

"There was nothing to tell."

Dimmock said that she knew how it was, he had been given this job to do. What use they made of any information he found—he lifted his shoulders.

"Funny the way they go on," Sarah said, and added sharply: "Something's burning. Your socks."

His feet certainly were near the fire, and he withdrew them.

"My husband used to burn his socks." In fact it came to her now that this little man reminded her of the husband who had been dead for twenty years. He too had always raised his hat to ladies. "Do you do this all the time? Going round and talking to people, it seems a funny way to make a living."

"I suppose it is. I don't always get so wet." It might have been her husband John sitting in the chair opposite. And because John too had sometimes made incomprehensible jokes she was not disconcerted when he said, "When my feet are very wet I sometimes get into a pet." He looked at her and said, "But not to-day. You've been very kind."

"What do you want to know?"

"Well, anything—anything odd. Out of the way, you know."

"I'll tell you something that *is* funny, something I've remembered." At another time and in other circumstances, perhaps even if the sun had been shining, she might have sent him away with a flea in his ear. As it was she told him the something funny she had remembered and then looked with interest at the bit of material he produced, which she recognised at once as resembling Mrs. Foster's raincoat. She looked for the raincoat but it wasn't where she would have expected it to be, in the hall cupboard.

When they found it eventually, tucked away with some old bedding in a tiny junk room, Dimmock knew that for the first time in his life as an operative he had discovered something of importance.

FOURTEEN

When Tony returned to Court after lunch he saw Jenny immediately. She sat in the row reserved for witnesses, pale and calm. He knew that in her presence it was more than ever important that he should do well.

Hardy opened quietly, almost amiably. "Would you call yourself a truthful man?"

"On the whole, yes."

"As truthful as most people?"

"I think so."

"Let us see." He consulted or pretended to consult his notes, looked up. "You called yourself Bain-Truscott when working for Mr. Foster, but that is not your real name."

"No."

"Have you also used the name of Scott-Williams?"

"Yes."

"And other names too?"

"I've explained, I did it to impress people. I didn't like the name of Jones." Just a hint of his smile there and a glance at the jury. One of them looked angry. Perhaps his name was Jones?

"Very well. Now, when you produced your references for this job, were they true or false?"

"I'd written them myself. Again, it was just to impress people."

"The references were false?"

213

"They weren't genuine."

"They weren't genuine. Very well again, since that is the phrase you prefer. Now, you will remember when you took the cuff links and pin to Mr. Penny. What did you say to him?"

"I asked what they were worth."

Hardy raised his hand into the air, then lowered it in a wearily patient manner. "But how did you describe them? Let me remind you. Did you say they were a family heirloom?"

"Something like that."

"True or false?" As Tony hesitated Hardy's voice rang out for a moment, clear and beautiful as a rapier blade. "True or false, Jones?"

"It wasn't true," he said sullenly. All this was not what he had expected, and it seemed to him unfair.

"It was not true," Hardy repeated. "Now, turn your mind for a moment to the time when you were interrogated at London Airport. You said you had a job in Caracas. True or false?"

He looked appealingly at the judge, who must surely understand that nobody could be expected to tell the exact truth in such circumstances, but found no help there. And Hardy was going on without waiting for his answer.

"And then you told the police that you had saved the money in your possession. True or false?"

This time the judge did speak, quietly, as Tony remained silent. His tone was kind, but the words brought no comfort.

"Just answer the question."

"I've already explained——" he began desperately, but now the judge's voice was hard as a headmaster's.

"Answer the question."

"I didn't tell the truth."

"False," Hardy said, triumphant as a man who has filled

214

in the last clue of a crossword puzzle. "You lied again
and again. And now do you ask us to accept you as a
truthful witness?"

Mr. Hussick leaned back just a little, as nearly as it
was possible to lean back in his hard chair. The boy was
standing up for himself quite reasonably, but how long
would he be able to do it when he was stuck with this
hopeless story? And for the next hour Hardy, rarely raising
his voice above his usual monotone, showed how hopeless
that story was, going through it detail by detail, demonstrating that everything the accused man said depended
on his unsupported word. He was particularly scathing
about the hammer and the cuff links.

"When as you say Mrs. Foster asked you to use the
hammer to knock in a nail, didn't you think it odd?"

"No. She'd told me that her husband was useless about
the house."

"Did you regard knocking in nails as part of your duties
as secretary?"

"Of course not."

"So it would have been possible for you to have refused?"

There was something hateful about Hardy. The thin
long-nosed patrician face, the wearily contemptuous manner, the voice enunciating its syllables with perfect clarity
and style, all of them represented an attitude to life which
Tony would have liked to think of as his own. He had to
restrain himself from shouting his reply, but he said calmly,
"I couldn't have refused without being rude."

"And I'm sure you are never rude." Newton stirred
uneasily at this comment, but Hardy continued swiftly.
"Supposing you had refused, one of the strongest points
in the case against you would not have existed?"

With a sense of self-congratulation at his own calmness
he said : "I can only tell you what happened."

"If you had refused Mrs. Foster would have had to find

some other—lethal implement—and asked you to handle that. Is that what you are asking us to believe?"

Doggedly he repeated "I can only say what happened."

"Just follow me for a moment. Since she was determined to incriminate you, if you had refused to handle the hammer she might have tried to get your prints on to a sharp knife—or a revolver—or a tin of weedkiller, which she would then have used as the murder instrument." Without raising his voice Hardy managed to infuse into it a note of scorn as he said, "Is that what you are asking the jury to believe?"

He made some kind of answer, but as he looked round the Court and found no help anywhere, in judge or jury, in his counsel or his solicitor, and as he finally found himself staring across into the pale unmoved face and the eyes that considered him indifferently, his grasp of what was being said to him vanished in a surge of hatred. He had lost the battle of wills with Hardy and his breaking point was only a question of time. The time came a quarter of an hour later when Hardy, showing the distaste of a man handling excreta with tongs, was questioning him about the sexual relations he claimed to have had with Mrs. Foster.

"You have heard Mrs. Foster say that hers was a happy marriage. Nobody has come here to say otherwise. But you maintain that this woman of good reputation, against whom there is no breath of suspicion, seduced you?"

"I thought she was in love with me."

"Within a few days of your entering the house she took you to her bed, that is what you are saying?"

The sneering voice insisted, the questions came at him in endless waves, what had she said to him, when had they first done it, how many times, what precisely had she said to him about killing her husband? It seemed to him that there were now only two faces in the Court, that of his tormentor and the white beautiful face that remained like a mask while the questions were asked that destroyed his self-respect and made him seem less than a man, so that at last he shook the witness box with the thump of his fists and cried out in a high woman's voice that she had done it, she was the bitch who had got him into this, and went on to use filthy words about her, words that had hardly been in his mouth for years.

When it was over he felt spent, as he did after the sexual act. He did not hear the reproving words of the judge or take in what it was that Mr. Hussick was saying to him so earnestly. Instead he looked at the jury, saw the expressions on their faces, and knew that he was lost.

FIFTEEN

Mortimer Lands insisted that he must get out of London for an hour or two. He drove Jenny out to a dinner and dance place on the Great West Road. He had been drinking whisky before he picked her up and went on drinking it throughout dinner. He talked incoherently about the trial.

"That poor bastard," he said. "From what I read they crucified him to-day, really crucified him."

"I was there." He looked at her almost with terror.

"He loved you, the poor bastard."

She had drunk a good deal herself and was less patient than usual. "What are you trying to say to me?"

"We're going to get caught. I know we are." She ate a green bean and looked at him enquiringly. "Somebody's certain to have seen the car."

"Nobody saw it. I told you I was careful. And I smeared mud all over the number plates."

"Somebody will——"

"I still don't know what you're trying to say."

"I must get out of London. I hate London."

"Then get out. Go back to-morrow. I don't know why you stayed in town anyway."

"I thought you wanted me to."

"It made no difference to me."

He leaned across the table. "Jenny, we can't do it, he'll go to prison for life."

The waiter came to take their plates and she did not speak until he had gone. "He was prepared to help in killing you, that's what he thought he was doing."

"I know. But he hasn't done anything."

"And you did help, Mortimer. You wanted to help." Before the intensity of her gaze he lowered his eye, mumbled something. "To-morrow there'll be the verdict, in a week it will all be forgotten, in three months we can be together."

"Three months!"

"That's what we agreed."

He looked up at her, then down again at the tablecloth. "Are you saying you want to call it off?"

"That's what you'd like, isn't it? You've got what you wanted, now you——" She told him to lower his voice, hushing him as if he were a dog, and he finished the sentence in a ludicrous murmur. "—don't love me at all."

"I'm trying to find out what you want. But I'll tell you this. If you come up with some different story now nobody will believe it. And if they did, then it would be as bad for you as for me. I'm ready to go." She picked up her bag.

He stared at her drunkenly. "I want to dance. And I want another drink." She paused, for once uncertain. "I want to hold you in my arms once more. The last time, I know that."

"Oh, for God's sake, Mortimer."

"It's my car. Shan't go home unless you dance with me."

She thought, not for the first time, that she would have

been better off with Jones. She was a reasonable, logical woman and total lack of logic was something she found it hard to deal with or understand. It was obviously not safe to leave him alone. She said that she would dance with him. He immediately called the waiter.

"A bottle of champagne. A celebration."

They did not leave until two in the morning, and by then Jenny herself was slightly drunk.

SIXTEEN

At first Mr. Hussick was sceptical about the telephone call from an enquiry agency he had never heard of, and one with a ridiculous name at that, but the excitement at the other end of the line communicated itself to him during the conversation, and when he had finished talking he picked up the receiver again and rang Magnus Newton who turned out to be attending a legal dinner in London. Newton was not pleased to be called away to the telephone, but when he heard what Hussick had to say he agreed to leave after the loyal toast and before the speech. He was in fact not altogether sorry to miss the speech, which was to be given by a retired Lord of Appeal renowned for his prolixity. The four of them met at eleven o'clock that night in Newton's chambers.

Clarence Newhouse was a blustering red-faced man who wore a Guards tie. Newton listened to him for a couple of minutes and then said, "This is the man who got the information? Then I'd like to have the story from him."

Dimmock had been sitting in a corner, overwhelmed by the occasion. The visit to a barrister's chambers late at night, the pat on the back from the Chief and his warm words about good work, and now this request that he should take the centre of the stage—what a tale he would have to tell the wife to-morrow. He moved forward from his corner seat into the circle of light cast by Newton's desk lamp. As he did so he sneezed.

"You've got a cold," Newton said accusingly. He produced a little inhaler from his jacket and sniffed noisily up each nostril. "Well?"

If there was one thing that Dimmock knew he could do, it was to make a clear and succinct report, and afterwards he felt that on this evening he had really excelled himself. The great man lighted a cigar and offered the box to the rest of them (the Chief took one and lit up, but Dimmock felt that it would have been presumptuous in him to smoke at the same time as the Chief), but his keen piggy little eyes looked steadily at Dimmock even while the mouth puffed smoke from its fat tube. When he had finished Dimmock waited in awe to hear what the experts would say about it. The Chief began to expand on all the trouble that had been taken by the agency, but he was cut short by the solicitor, Mr. Hussick, whose eyebrows seemed to be climbing up into his scalp.

The great man opened his mouth. What would he say?

"Take anything for those colds, do you? Is it on your chest? Or just the nose?"

"Nose. And throat."

"This may help." He wrote something on a piece of paper, pushed it across the desk. "Get it made up. Use it myself."

For a moment Dimmock thought he must be lightheaded, and that he was really in a doctor's surgery. Then Newton continued. "This woman, Russell, she'll give evidence in Court? And the boatyard man, what's his name, Clegg?"

"Clynes," said Mr. Hussick.

"I've got their signed statements." Dimmock drew the papers from his briefcase.

"That was intelligent." Dimmock glowed. Newton's words seemed to be a justification of his whole career.

"All our operatives are intelligent," the Chief said with a jolly laugh. Newton swivelled to direct on him a gaze that was by no means wholly friendly.

"Who's paying you?"

"I'm afraid I can't reveal that." The jolly laugh was slightly uneasy. "Professional ethics."

"Never mind, doesn't matter."

"I believe my employer is—ah—a friend of the accused."

"Didn't know he had any friends." To Dimmock's bewilderment Mr. Hussick and the Chief laughed heartily as though this was a good joke. "We had a firm on to this and they turned up nothing, eh, Hussick." Mr. Hussick nodded. He seemed to find this amusing too. "Must remember you next time. But insist that they put Mr. Dimmock on to it, Hussick, insist on that."

Newton's hand fell like an accolade on to Dimmock's shoulder as he said that they would need him also in Court. That was an exciting prospect, but Dimmock afterwards thought of the hour he had spent in those chambers, rather than the session in Court, as the crowning point of his career. He had the prescription made up, and although it had no effect upon his cold he treasured the piece of paper to the end of his life.

When they had gone Newton and Hussick got down to it. After Clynes and Sarah Russell had given evidence it would be necessary to recall Mrs. Foster, and notification of this must be given to the prosecution. Then there was the matter of serving a subpoena on these two new witnesses. Hussick nodded and smiled, nodded and smiled. Newton's cigar was out before they had finished.

"About Mrs. Foster," he said at the end. "She's still going to be a tough nut. She was in Court to-day. I don't want her there to-morrow."

"I'll see to it."

But there was no need for him to see to it.

SEVENTEEN

"I'll drive." Jenny held out her hand for the keys.

"The hell you will." Lands opened the car door and sat down heavily in the driver's seat.

"You shouldn't drive. The breathalyser. If the police stop us——"

"They won't. Are you getting in or not?"

She got in and sat sideways on the seat with the door half open. She had begun a sentence saying that she was still sober and he was not when he started the car and it shot forward so that she had to slam the door to save herself from falling out. He went out of the drive into the road, ignoring a car which swerved and hooted.

"Let me drive."

He pushed down the accelerator. They were going at sixty. "You know what's wrong with you? You don't like men, you hate them, want to take everything away from them. You're the boss, they dance when you tell them." He muttered something else.

"What?"

"Not going to drive my car," he shouted. "Going to drive my own bloody car." He turned on the radio and the Beatles came shrieking out of it. He hooted a Jaguar in the fast lane, then cut inside it just as the Jaguar moved into the slower lane. Lands tugged at the steering wheel to get back into the fast lane and the car responded. Their tyres screeched, the Jaguar driver yelled something as they passed him. Almost for the first time in her life she was frightened and cried out some words that he did not hear above the sound of the radio. But anger was an emotion that came to her more easily than fear, and as she heard him begin to sing some drunken accompaniment to the music she felt an access of rage against this feeble sot who was unable to carry through the small part given to him in her plan. She cried out that he should stop the car and leaned over trying to wrench the steering wheel away from him.

Mortimer held on to it, and raising his left hand chopped it down hard on hers. The cry she gave was pleasant to him. Did she think that he was not a man? Yet at the same time he wanted to tell her that he was sorry. He turned his head to say so when he heard her cry out, saw that they had strayed into the second lane, and heard the blast of the Jaguar's horn. Again he tugged at the steering, but this time the car over-responded. They went straight through the central barrier into the path of an oncoming lorry.

As they broke the barrier Jenny had time to feel one last quick surge of anger against the absurdity of what was happening. How was it possible to make plans when they were at the mercy of other people? The last thing she saw was Mortimer take his hands off the wheel and put them over his face.

The lorry struck the car head on, turning it over and over in the road. The driver was carrying a load of machine tools, and the lorry suffered nothing worse than a badly damaged radiator. The collision forced open the passenger door of the car and Jenny was thrown out into the road. It was said at the inquest that she had died instantly of a broken neck, but her body went directly in front of an oncoming car in the middle lane, and his wheels passed over it. The steering wheel went through Lands's chest, and he was trapped in the crumpled car. He was still alive when the police arrived, and it seemed to the sergeant that he was trying to say something, but in fact he never spoke. Before they had cut through the pieces of the bodywork that were holding him, he was dead.

EIGHTEEN

Tony stared at Mr. Hussick and repeated the word. "Dead."

"It creates, let's be frank about it, an unusual situation." Mr. Hussick was not a man easily overborne by events, but that late session with Newton and then the news about Mrs. Foster had momentarily quelled even his exuberance.

Tony stared at the short paragraph headed: *Mrs. Foster Dies in Car Crash*, and read it again.

"We would of course have recalled her. And Lands. Now that won't be possible." Mr. Hussick gave a slight cough in deprecation at this statement of the obvious. "But the vital thing is the new evidence. I had a conference with Mr. Newton last night long past the witching hour——"

"What's that?" The young man looked quite dazed. Perhaps it was not surprising.

"Long past midnight. A very late night, and a very early morning. I have somebody now talking to Miss Russell." Jones did not know the name, and he had to explain who she was. "I don't mind telling you that Mr. Newton is much more confident to-day than he was yesterday." He managed a little dance with the eyebrows. Jones nodded.

"The firm involved is called the Second To None Agency. I'm bound to say that they discovered things which we had missed. I take it a friend of yours employed them?" Jones said he didn't know. Altogether, Mr. Hussick was not sorry when the interview was over and he was able, as he said, to leave his client to digest the good news.

Those who were living are now dead. Those words— were they a line from a poem?—remained in Tony's mind after the lawyer had left him. Yesterday he had looked across the Court at the pale face and had felt hatred. Now that he knew he would never see her again the hatred had gone, everything had gone except a series of pictures which ran through his mind like lantern slides, showing their first meeting, the interview at the Villa Majorca, the bedroom scenes when her abandonment to pleasure had appeared complete. When people die those closely linked to them reconstitute their personalities in terms of what they wish to remember, and with her death Jenny became again instantly the woman who had loved him and whose plans were all devised for the fulfilment of their love. The dream of their life together in Caracas was omnipresent, a dream all the sweeter because now it would never know fulfilment in reality. Nothing could take the perfection of the dream away from him.

He had not really thought about the way in which the new evidence had been obtained. It was not until he was on the way to Court and one of the police officers asked how things were going and said that if there was anything he could do for Tony without stepping out of line he'd be glad to do it, that the mystery was suddenly clear to him. "If there's anything I can do——" he remembered those as being the General's very words, and in spite of Tony's reaction he had obviously gone on to do it, he had gone to the enquiry agency. Tears welled in Tony's eyes. He murmured : "He's a good man, a very good man."

"What did you say?"

He shook his head, said there was nothing he wanted done, and wiped away the tears. As the police officers agreed afterwards, he was a bit of a soppy type.

NINETEEN

Sarah Russell wore her best clothes for the occasion, topped by a hat ornamented by red and white cherries. She followed Dimmock, whose evidence was confined to an account of his discoveries and the fact that he had interviewed Sarah. She was intimidated at first by the formality of it all and the fact that the lawyers were dressed so strangely, but the little man asked her such simple questions, about how long she had worked for Mrs. Foster and what kind of work it was, that she soon felt at ease and even began to enjoy herself. After the preliminaries Newton got down to business.

"Now, Mrs. Russell, I want you to cast your mind back to that Friday morning, the morning of the murder. Is there anything you particularly remember about that morning?"

"Something funny happened. I didn't think much of it at the time."

"Yes?"

"There was this bit of carpet in the hall, you see. It was all rucked up because some of the tacks had come out of it, so I thought I'll tack that down. Mr. Foster, he was no good at that kind of thing."

"Yes, I see. So what did you do?"

"I looked for the hammer, it was always kept in the

tool box out in the scullery. But it wasn't there. So I spoke to Mrs. Foster."

"Will you tell us what she said."

"Told me not to bother, she had a headache. And mind you, the day before she'd been saying she must get it done." Sarah looked round with an air of triumph and touched her hair, which she feared was untidy.

"And then what did you do?"

"I thought, what's happened to it, must be somewhere, and eventually I found it. In one of the kitchen drawers, where it had no business to be."

"Will you tell us how you found it?"

"It was wrapped in tissue paper."

These words created some interest. The judge made a note. Hardy listened with a frown. Newton repeated the words and asked if she could remember anything further.

"Yes, I called out to Mrs. Foster and said 'I've found it' and I was just taking off the paper when she came out into the kitchen and told me to leave it alone. She was quite sharp."

"You saw the hammer?"

"Of course I did."

"Did you touch it?"

"No, I was taking off the wrapping when she said that. Said again she had a headache and told me to leave it. So I did."

"Exhibit fifteen, please," Newton said. The hammer was handed to Sarah. "Is that the hammer?"

"That's the one."

"Had you ever known it to be put away like that before?"

"Never."

"Can you tell the Court why you haven't mentioned this previously."

"I didn't think anything more about it. And nobody asked me about anything funny. Not till Mr. Dimmock."

The mention of Dimmock's name launched Newton nicely on to the question of the raincoat. This was the really vital piece of evidence, for Sarah had recognised the fabric as coming from a raincoat that Mrs. Foster had bought a week before her husband's death, and Dimmock had confirmed this with the shop from which it had been purchased. The inference was overwhelming that she had visited the *Daisy Mae* after buying it, although in the witness box she had sworn otherwise. And there was something else, which Newton had been allowed to bring out without objection from Hardy. There were spots on the raincoat, and an urgent forensic examination had revealed that they were blood. The blood group had been identified as AB which was Foster's blood group, although it was Mrs. Foster's blood group too.

In ordinary circumstances this information would have been kept from the prosecution, but the circumstances here were remarkable. When he heard of Mrs. Foster's death Newton thought it his duty to make the situation known to Hardy. There had been a conference that morning at which, slightly to Newton's surprise, Hardy had refused to acknowledge that the new evidence made much difference to the case against Jones. But this was typical of Hardy who, for all his air of languor, was not inclined to drop a case once he had got his teeth into it. Now he rose and looked for a moment silently at Sarah Russell, who returned his look with some belligerence.

"Did you like Mrs. Foster?"

"We never had any argument."

"But did you like her, Mrs. Russell?"

"Didn't like or dislike. She kept herself to herself, didn't talk much."

"You know that she died tragically in a car accident last night, so that she cannot comment on your story?"

"It isn't a story. It's the truth."

228

"I'm sure you are saying what you believe to be true." Hardy smiled at the witness, but the smile came out as ironic rather than friendly. "You say you fixed the date on which this hammer incident occurred as the morning of the murder. How can you be sure?"

"It's not a day I'm likely to forget."

"I suppose not," Hardy said humbly. "And you remember all the other details too. Are you sure the hammer was wrapped in tissue paper?"

"Quite sure."

"It wasn't just lying on it, with the tissue below?"

"I said before it was wrapped round in tissue."

"So you did." Hardy was apologetic. "How did you know it was a hammer?"

"How did I know—I don't understand."

"It's very simple." He spoke as though to a child. "You opened the drawer. There was some tissue paper. What made you think it was a hammer?"

"I didn't—I don't——" She made another false start and the judge told her to take her time. "I suppose I was poking about in the drawer. I don't quite remember."

"You don't remember that. Do you remember if you pulled aside the tissue?"

"I must have, mustn't I? To see the hammer."

"But you don't remember doing it?" Suddenly, sharply, he said, "You did see a hammer, you're sure of that?"

"Oh yes, I'm sure."

"You saw the head of it? Or the handle?"

These are silly questions, she wanted to say, I know I saw the hammer and so do you, but she knew she must not say that. "I'm not quite sure."

"Not quite sure. But you identified the hammer, Mrs. Russell."

"It was the same hammer. I know it was."

"Yet you can't be sure how much of it you saw. Well,

229

we will leave it at that." Hardy smiled at her again, then his voice hardened. "You did forget, though, didn't you?"

She looked at him, confused. "I don't know what you mean."

"You'd been questioned already. And you didn't mention it."

"Nobody asked me about anything funny. Not until I saw Mr. Dimmock."

"Mr. Dimmock, ah yes, we have heard Mr. Dimmock," Hardy said in a voice implying that they wanted to hear no more of him. He went on to establish that she had seen the accused with Mrs. Foster and that there was no sign of friendship between them, that the Fosters had never quarrelled in her hearing, and that Mortimer Lands had seemed on good terms with Mr. Foster. But Hardy did not press this, nor did he ask more than perfunctory questions about the raincoat. His interest was not in demonstrating Mrs. Foster's innocence, but in showing Jones's guilt.

TWENTY

The passage that most struck the wise men in the Court (and there is always a number of wise men in any Court) about Hardy's final speech was that in which he ingeniously combined defence of Mrs. Foster with a demonstration that even if she had lied it gave no assurance at all that Jones was telling the truth.

"Genevieve Foster, as you know, is tragically dead. She cannot be here to answer the matters raised by the last defence witnesses. But what did the points they raised really amount to? That indefatigable investigator Mr. Dimmock discovered that she occasionally dined out with her cousin in a place, it was suggested, that was 'significantly far away.' But what is there significant about this when you remember that both she and Mr. Lands were members of the same golf club? And then, what do you think of Sarah Russell's evidence about the hammer, that hammer which was so curiously wrapped up in tissue paper? Isn't it strange that while she recalls all this so clearly she can't remember why she thought the thing in tissue paper was a hammer at all, or whether she saw the whole of it or just the handle or the head? I am not attacking her sincerity—nobody who heard her would do that—but I suggest that what she saw was the handle of some quite different tool and that when Mrs. Foster said she did not want the carpet tacked down at that moment it was simply for the reason she gave. She had a headache. When we have that good common sense explanation why should we look for something sinister?"

Hardy looked about with an air of mild triumph, and continued more seriously. "And then we come to the raincoat. There are spots of blood on it, and you may have noticed that my learned friend was not very precise about how they may have got there. Let me be as precise as possible. If those spots on the raincoat have any meaning in the case at all Mrs. Foster must have attacked her husband with the hammer while wearing the raincoat. She must also have been wearing gloves, since her prints were not on the hammer. Now you will remember that she was a slim, I might almost say a frail woman. Can you really picture her putting on the raincoat and gloves and then using the hammer to commit this brutal murder? Isn't it far more likely that she made a mistake in saying that she hadn't visited the launch for three weeks before the murder, that she went there for some completely innocent purpose, tore the raincoat and cut her hand at the same time so that some blood spilled on to the raincoat? And that when she noticed this she stuffed it away so that her husband shouldn't notice that the new raincoat was ruined?" Hardy paused. "And mark this. Even if you accept that she took part in her husband's savage murder, it does not follow that Jones is innocent. If her association with him was really an adulterous one, is it not over-whelmingly likely that he was a partner in her husband's murder?"

Now Hardy turned to the prisoner in the dock and appeared to be addressing him directly, using a tone of withering scorn which made him almost visibly shrink. "If you prefer to believe the tale that Jones told, you will acquit him. But can you believe it? Didn't he impress you when he gave evidence as a rather intelligent young man, and also as one who would tell any lie to save his own skin? Listening to his account of the charade in which he says he took part, and which he says utterly deceived him, the dummy wrapped up as a body and the rest of it, ask yourselves: can any man have been as big a fool as that?"

Although Newton had the advantage of the final speech, his task was not an easy one. He had to decide just how far he could go in attacking Genevieve Foster without alienating the jury. In the end, after a long discussion with his junior, he decided to play it low and calm. As he asked the jury to accept the story told by the man in the dock, and recalled just what that story was, Newton did not once look at his client, who felt at times that he was being attacked rather than defended.

"Ladies and gentlemen, you have heard my learned friend Mr. Hardy, and I will take up at once his last words: 'Can any man have been as big a fool' as to act as Jones did. Just look at this question in another way. You must all of you have wondered when you heard my client give evidence why a man should concoct so clumsy

and so discreditable a story in his own defence. I do not
put him before you as a particularly virtuous man, or as a
man whose intentions were anything but wicked. But, as
my learned friend says, he quite obviously does not lack
intelligence. To admit that, in the stress of passion, he
entered into an agreement to murder Eversley Foster, and
then to. leave the country and wait for his criminal partner
in a foreign land—to tell this tale that he knew would
have little chance of belief because it was bound to be
contradicted at every turn—can you believe that a man
of reasonable intelligence would tell such a story unless it
were true?

"For some time this story rested on his own word, and
probably it was a word that few of you would care to
accept. Happily, it is now supported by evidence. You
have heard that Mrs. Foster was sufficiently friendly with
Lands to dine with him sometimes at a place which, in
spite of what has been said to the contrary, was I repeat
significantly far from her home. You have heard what
Sarah Russell had to say about the hammer with which
the crime was committed, and you may feel that there is
no doubt at all that she did see a hammer and not the
'other tool' which has been mentioned. If you accept that
she did see the hammer you will make what you think
right of the strange fact that, once having got Jones's
fingerprints on it Mrs. Foster preserved this hammer in
tissue paper. You have heard the story of the new raincoat,
a small piece of which was found in the motor launch
Daisy Mae. You will remember that Mrs. Foster said at a
time when the matter did not seem important, that she
had not visited the launch for three weeks before the
murder. You have heard that the raincoat had on it those
damning spots of blood and you have heard where it
was found, stuffed away in a junk room."

Newton lowered his voice, his tone became sepulchral.

"It is painful for me to have to say these things. I do not wish to accuse the dead. But the points I have mentioned are some of those I should have questioned Mrs. Foster about. Do you think, can anybody think, that she could have given satisfactory answers?"

There he left the question of Genevieve Foster, and went on to a peroration which certainly did not spare his client.

"I cannot put him before you as anything but a contemptible character, but I ask you to accept his story as true. And if you do accept it the important thing, the vital thing, that you must remember is this. He has told you frankly that he was prepared to enter into a conspiracy by which he would take part in the murder of Foster. That is, of the man he knew as Foster, for in fact he never met the real Eversley Foster. But if you accept his story *he did not take part in it*, he was deceived into thinking that he was taking part in a murder plot when in reality he was the dupe of the real murderer and of her accomplice Lands. If you find that this is really what happened, that Jones agreed to take part in a murder but really participated only in a charade, as my learned friend rightly called it, then I am telling you as a matter of law—and I am sure my lord will make reference to this later on—that he is not guilty of any crime at all, and that you must acquit him. You may think whatever you please of his character, but his character is not in question. I submit to you, members of the jury, that Anthony Jones is completely innocent of the crime of which he is accused."

Had Newton really pitched it too low? That was the general opinion of the wise men. Looking at the jury, at Blue Rinse and Iron Hair and the others, noting slight signs of impatience while they listened to Newton in comparison with the close attention paid to Hardy's bell-like lucidity, they really hadn't much doubt about it.

TWENTY-ONE

This assessment of the jury was quite wrong. Iron Hair had been on his side from the first. He bore a strong resemblance to a nephew of hers who had gone out to Australia and sent a splendid food parcel home to her every Christmas. Blue Rinse and Pretty But Fatuous had been inclined all along to think that Mrs. Foster was too good to be true, and the man resembling Clinker, who was a director in a firm of woollen merchants, thought that Jones looked too intelligent to have behaved so stupidly and by an odd jump in reasoning therefore believed him innocent. Most of the others had thought he was guilty, but they were shaken by the raincoat evidence. They talked about it for an hour and a half, but there was never much doubt about which side the waverers would come down on.

The "Not Guilty" verdict caused little surprise. Hardy congratulated Newton. Clerks tied up the briefs with bits of tape, white for the D.P.P.'s file, pink for all the others. Tony stepped down from the dock and Mr. Hussick came over to him, eyebrows dancing. He shook hands with Mr. Hussick, then with Newton and Newton's junior. Newton spoke a few words and turned away. It was all rather anti-climactic. The only people who seemed really pleased were Bill and Joe, the prison officers.

"You're away then," said Bill. "I knew that was the way it would be. I could feel it in my water. Had to get up to pee in the night, that's a sure sign. Never wrong, the old water."

Tony felt like a departing guest who should thank his hosts for their hospitality, but it turned out that he had to collect various belongings from the cell below the Court.

"What'll it be then?" Bill asked. "Off for a night on the town, a bit of a celebration?"

He shook his head. There was nobody for him to celebrate with. Bill and Joe agreed afterwards that they had never seen a man acquitted on a murder charge take it so quietly.

Standing outside the Old Bailey in summer sunlight he wondered what he should do. He owed his freedom to the General. Should he telephone to thank him, or go down to Leathersley House? A Rolls-Royce car nosed down the road and slowly drew to a halt. The judge's car, perhaps, or would he be trying the next case? A chauffeur got out and opened the rear door. Tony stared at him. The man made a gesture indicating unmistakably that he should step inside.

He got in. The woman already in the car leaned over to kiss him. It was Violet Harrington.

TWENTY-TWO

"Aren't you going to say thank you?" She was wearing a peacock blue dress with short sleeves. Her bare brawny arms touched his.

"Thank you, yes, I didn't realise——"

"When I saw you were in real trouble I thought, I'm going to try to get him out of it even if it does cost money. When a friend's in trouble money doesn't matter."

"This is a different car," he said inanely.

"I'll tell you a little secret. There was a takeover bid for Harrington's companies. A handsome offer. I can afford anything I like now, Tony." She placed a hand on his and he saw that there was a new diamond bracelet round her wrist. She indicated the neck of the chauffeur, who was separated from them by a glass partition. "Including Meakins. I think it's a bore to drive yourself about when you can be driven."

"Where are we going?"

"Home. To Burncourt Grange. Everything's arranged." Her hand on his was hot and faintly moist, but the rings beneath the flesh were hard. "You can leave it all to me now. You don't have to worry about anything."

You don't have to worry about anything. The seat was soft, immensely luxurious. He closed his eyes.

her some she indicated the neck of the bottle in what was extracted from them by a wise and just . . . returning "Wraith, I said ... how to think you, if those whom you can be duly so?"

"What answer you?"

"Here," I said, turning a box and taking Weighing's pretend ... breaking ... the ... box and taking inside, but the grip beneath the chair were there. To re-examine it, ask ... me . . . I've had I kept to converse and lay little?"

Yes, they I became interested and implied . . . That was that, and I turned it towards me, that close his eyes.

PART FOUR

How the Dreams Came True

ONE

They were married within a fortnight. There were no
guests, no reception, not even a notice in *The Times*. "We've
got each other," she said. "We don't need anybody else."
He started to write a letter to Widgey and then tore it up.
She belonged to the past, and he felt such a revulsion
against the past that he could not bear to do anything
that brought it back to him.

We've got each other : but the truth was, as he quickly
realised, that she had him. He was not the squire of the
village but a kept plaything. The servants—there were four
of them, as he had imagined, although only two lived in—
treated him with barely-concealed insolence. No doubt
Meakins had told them about the trial, or they had seen
pictures of him in the papers. Meakins himself, a spare
man with slicked-down hair, had a slightly twisted lip
which made his expression appear to be fixed in a sneer,
and his manner had a familiarity which made it seem
always that he was on the verge of asking some intimate
question, like whether Mrs. Harrington, now Mrs. Jones,
was a good lay.

About this there was in a sense no question. He was
expected to be on duty at night, often in the morning and
occasionally in the afternoon. It might have been like the
paradise promised to believers by Mahomet, but in reality
these encounters made him feel like a stallion condemned
to endless servicing of a single mare. There was also something profoundly unsatisfactory to him about the form of
their love-making. He closed his eyes and thought of Jenny,
but the contrast between her almost angry dominance and

the whimpering eagerness of Violet as her shuddering bulk lay beneath him was so disagreeable that he tried instead to make his mind completely blank.

He would have felt better if there had been any sign that she meant to carry out the promises she had made in the days before their marriage. On the second day after his release he had suggested that they might go abroad. She bit into her breakfast toast and nodded. Her Pekinese eyes were bright.

"I still can't believe this is real. That prison hospital——" He left the sentence unfinished. In retrospect the hospital seemed horrific, whatever it had been like at the time.

"Poor boy." She snapped off another piece of toast, crunched it up. "It was lucky I decided to help, wasn't it?"

"I owe everything to you." The words were true, although they seemed merely dutiful. "I ought to get away. People talk." He was aware already of the servants' attitude.

"Not if we were married."

"You're sure you want——"

"Ever since I first saw you."

"We could go abroad for our honeymoon. To Venice perhaps."

"Don't you like it here?" He said truthfully that it was a wonderful house, but he meant really that it was wonderful to be waited on, to have the cook enquire in the morning about what they would like for dinner, and to order tea by ringing a bell. "Then that's settled."

Within a week of their marriage he knew that he had made a mistake. He should have seen to it that the tickets to Venice were bought before the ceremony, he should have made a firm arrangement about a monthly allowance. He realised too late that he had failed to realise his potential value and had sold himself for nothing. When he spoke of the honeymoon abroad she said that she hated travelling and that just to be with him was honeymoon enough for her. He had spent the last of his own money on an eternity ring, which seemed a nice symbolic touch, and he waited for her to say that they would have a joint bank account which he could use, but she said nothing of the kind. At last he raised the matter at what seemed an appropriate moment, after one of their afternoon sessions.

Her hand, with all the rings on it, including now his eternity ring, stroked his arm. "Smooth. Not much hair on your body, is there? Harrington was a hairy man."

It was not easy, but he said it. "We're husband and wife. I ought to have my own bank account. Or a joint one."

Her hand moved, touched his nipples, then moved down to his stomach. In her brown bulging eyes he saw nothing of what he looked for, but only greed and pleasure. "Kiss me."

He knew that this was not what she meant, but with an effort he did as she wanted. As she lay back afterwards, panting with satisfaction, she said, "Five pounds a week."

He was about to protest, even to strike her. Then he saw that she would enjoy this too, and that protest would be useless.

Within a few weeks he knew that he was trapped in a net from which there was no escape. The Grange was a mile outside the village of Burncourt, and the village itself was in the Dorset countryside five miles from the nearest small town. She had told him that the Rolls was to be driven only by Meakins, but there was another car, an old one, and in this he went out two evenings a week. He spent his allowance on drink and an evening meal. It was very much like life with the General, except that he was paid less money. Violet said nothing about these evenings out, until one night he took the Rolls. Driving it gave him less pleasure than he had expected, because he had a schoolboy's feeling that there would be trouble when he returned. He came back slightly drunk to find her waiting for him.

"I told you that the Rolls was to be driven only by Meakins." He had rehearsed a scene that began something like this, and he should have said now that as her husband he would drive any car he wished. In fact he said nothing. When she held out her hand for the keys he gave them to her. "I have told Meakins to keep the garage locked up in future. There is another thing." She had a glass of brandy in front of her and invited him to have some. He shook his head. She spoke slowly, savouring the words and watching him.

"You were tried and acquitted. But I remember that you admitted that you were ready to plan with that woman to kill her husband. I think I should tell you that I have made a will leaving my money to charities. Not to you. Do you understand me?" Her painted mouth curved in a smile. "Of course it's possible that I might change my mind."

Looking at her fat fingers twisting the stem of the glass as though she might break it, he knew what she felt for him was not love but hatred. She spoke as though she read his thoughts.

"You remember that afternoon in the car? I haven't forgotten. I told you, didn't I, that I usually get what I want."

She put down the glass, got up and walked out. That night he slept in one of the spare bedrooms. In the morning he heard the maid who lived in giggling with the one who came daily, no doubt telling her that husband and wife were occupying separate rooms. He went for a long walk through the woods that were part of the estate, and wondered whether any thought of Violet's death had crossed his mind. Perhaps he could withhold his services, a male Lysistrata? But he knew that his persistence was no match for hers, and that this was a fantasy. He sat on the grass in a clearing, broke up some small twigs and said aloud: "I could leave her, I could just walk out."

Yet he knew that this also was not possible. Something had been destroyed in him by those weeks in the prison hospital. The mainspring of his being had broken, so that he could not seriously contemplate either resisting her or leaving the undoubted comfort in which he lived to face the world again without money. He had no confidence any more in his ability to charm old Generals or to please women, and he shuddered at the thought of selling insurance again. He was imprisoned in this house as effectively as if he were in a cell. Two nights later he went back to her bedroom.

He had given his address to Hussick, and it was a week after this that the letter came. He stared unbelievingly at the cheque and then read the relevant lines of Hussick's letter. ". . . happy to say that we were able to obtain a refund on the air ticket you booked to Caracas . . . cheque for this amount is enclosed . . ." The cheque was for a hundred and forty pounds.

At lunchtime that day he said to Violet, "I shan't be in this afternoon. I'm taking the car. Not the Rolls." She looked at him smiling, and he felt it necessary to say something more. "I thought I'd go to Cerne Abbas. I believe it's very pretty."

"It is." She crunched celery. "You didn't ask if I wanted to come. You're looking very nice." Her smile broadened as she saw his expression. "Don't worry, I shan't. What is it, a girl?"

He was able to make his denial all the more convincing because it was true.

"I wouldn't mind. You can take the Rolls if you like. It might impress her."

You're very sure of me, he thought as he said that he

didn't want the Rolls, you know I'm caught. Her desire to touch him was something he had come to know and hate, and he had to restrain himself from flinching when she patted his shoulder as they got up from the table.

"If you're a good boy, Tony, you won't find I'm unreasonable."

The bitch, he thought as he drove away down the drive, the bitch thinks she's got me but she hasn't. The feeling of elation lasted as he parked the car at the tiny Burncourt Road Station and bought his first class ticket, lasted even half the way to London. It was succeeded by a depression which deepened as the train approached Paddington Station. He had drawn a hundred pounds from the bank and it was in his pocket, but what did it give him but an illusion of freedom? He could stay away from her until the money was spent, but after that what could he do but go back? He looked at himself in the railway carriage glass and was slightly cheered to see that he was still a very good-looking young man. "You can decide what to do when the time comes," he said to this young man. "What you need first of all is a good strong drink."

From Paddington he took a taxi to the Ritz. There he settled down with a vodka-based drink called a gimlet, drank it quickly and ordered another. He could feel the horrors of Burncourt Grange peeling away from him. He had got away and he would stay away, at least for that night. Ought he to telephone Violet and tell her so?

"Tony," a voice said. "It *is* you."

A girl stood beside the table, smiling down at him. She wore dark glasses as she had done long ago. Fiona.

TWO

Fiona. It seemed natural that he should use her assumed name, that she should sit down at the table and let him buy her a drink. She sat there opposite him with her slim legs crossed, wearing the dark glasses, and he knew suddenly that his luck had changed and that he was being given a chance to alter all the decisions that had been made so disastrously in the spring. When he thanked her for writing she simply smiled. She had changed, she was now totally at ease, a quite different figure from the nervous girl who had come into this bar carrying her suitcase.

"Are you still with Carlos?"

"For the moment."

"What does that mean?"

"He's an awful bastard." She raised the glasses briefly and he saw a bruise round her left eye. Then she lowered them again. "However. He's in Bristol opening up a new place. I'm on my own."

"Come with me, Fiona."

"To your flat? At Marble Arch?" She smiled and he smiled back, although impatiently.

"It's important. Don't you see I'm lucky, meeting you means I'm lucky. I want you with me when I play." It was true, he could feel the luck in him. First the money coming from Hussick, then meeting her again, it had to mean that he was lucky.

"To *play*." She wrinkled her nose. "The bank always wins, you said so yourself."

"Not if you're with me."

"You couldn't go to one of Carlos's places. One of his

boys might know you. Anyway I couldn't come with you, he'd slay me."

"There are other places."

"Yes." She contemplated him for a moment. "You're a born sucker, you know that? I want another drink."

He ordered one and then tried to get over to her somehow the seriousness and the importance of it. "For a gambler there's a time when things are right, you understand? I can't tell you how I know it, but this is the time. If I make a real killing I'll never play again, I shall go away, get out of England."

"Alone?"

"It doesn't have to be alone." She merely smiled.

They went to a club she knew in the Edgware Road called the Triple Chance. It was early, and there were only a dozen people in the club, half of them playing blackjack and the rest roulette. He bought chips for the whole of his money. She shook her head when he offered her half of them.

"I never have any luck."

"You've got to take them. Don't you see, we repeat it all, just the way it was."

"You're a nut." But she took the chips and they sat down at the table. The croupier was a brass-haired boy with a broken nose. Tony began to play a modification of the Rational system. Fiona bet on the first dozen and then on the last, with occasional bets on red and black. After half an hour he had won a little, she had lost half her chips. The time was eight o'clock.

"When do we knock off work? I'm hungry."

"We've got to stay here."

"Like hell *we* have." She pushed the rest of her chips towards him. He was alarmed.

"Don't leave me, Fiona. Please. Give me another half hour."

"All right, but I'll tell you something. You're not going to get very lucky playing that way. If you finish fifty pounds up you'll be doing well."

What she said was true. The Rational system is designed to give a regular but small profit. If he wanted to win a lot of money he would have to abandon systematic play. He began to bet á cheval, and put five pounds on the numbers 3 and 4. Number 3 came up at odds of eighteen to one. He repeated the bet and put another five pound chip between numbers 13 and 14. Number 13 came up. He enlarged the bet to include all numbers with 3 in them. In five minutes he had won five hundred pounds. His mind was quite blank. He could not have said why he pushed all the chips on to a carre of the numbers, 13, 14, 15, 16, which would pay out at nine to one.

The brass-haired croupier shook his head. "Two-fifty limit."

Fiona spoke fiercely to the croupier, pointing to a bald man sitting next to her. "He's been betting over that."

"On pair and impair, madam. That's different." His stare at her was mocking, an insult. Tony felt incapable of speech.

"If you've got a limit like that, you should put it up."

"It's on the wall, madam. Behind you."

Tony began to take back some of his chips. "It doesn't matter. Don't break my concentration."

"To hell with that. It does matter. Where's the manager?"

"Do you want the manager, sir?" the croupier asked Tony.

He was about to say that he didn't, when the manager appeared. He was a willowy man with a long face. He wore a purple dinner jacket and a lilac dress shirt, and he smoked a black cigarette in a white holder. His voice had the drawl of an Oxford aesthete in the Twenties. "Something the matter, Bob?"

Bob told him what was the matter. He said languidly to Tony "Very happy to accommodate you."

Did he want to bet five hundred, the whole of his money? He no longer knew. His hand moved uncertainly towards the chips and it was Fiona who gripped it. The broken nosed boy spun the wheel.

The ball rolled about and came to a stop. "Sixteen," the croupier said. "Red. Even." His glance met that of the Oxford aesthete, who removed his black cigarette from the holder and stubbed it out. The chips, black, red and white were pushed across the table.

"Leave it," Fiona said fiercely. "Leave it. *Now*."

He got up from the table.

THREE

Because he had known that he would win, that he must win, he was able to take it all coolly. And the same coolness marked his further actions, for he knew exactly what had to be done next. For three-quarters of an hour they drove about London in a taxi, looking for the place that he knew must exist. She sat with him in the taxi, over-whelmed. "Five thousand pounds," she repeated over and over again. "You've won five thousand pounds."

"Four thousand nine hundred. I had a hundred to start with."

In the end they had to drive out to London Airport. It was Thursday night. He made a reservation for two on the Saturday morning K.L.M. flight to Caracas. Because it was late they gave him a reservation slip instead of the tickets, and he paid the money.

She turned down the corners of her mouth when she heard where they were going.

"Caracas. I'm not even sure where it is."

"Venezuela. Perfect climate. You've got a passport?"

"Yes. Carlos made me get one, said I might need it sometime."

"Get a smallpox inoculation to-morrow. It's compulsory."

She giggled and then was serious. "You won't be able to take all that money out."

He had not forgotten what Jenny said, and now he was able to improve on it. "I'm going to buy one of those dummy books that people use for cigars. I shall put the money in that and post it to myself at the Grand Hotel, Caracas. We'll be there when it arrives. It's a million to one against its being opened."

"We shall want some——"

"I shall take two-fifty with me." On the way back to London he said, "You do want to come."

"Yes. I've had Carlos. And you know that day, when you found out I wasn't Fiona Mallory. I wanted to stay. Your face then, if you could have seen it." She began to laugh and he laughed too. It was almost the first time in his life that he had laughed at himself. "We'll make a good partnership," she said, and he knew she was right.

Her flat was in Hill Street. When they arrived he handed the driver a ten pound note and told him to keep the change. It was a wonderful feeling.

The flat was interior decorator's Regency, with everything possible done in stripes. She poured drinks from a cocktail cabinet done in differently striped woods. "To Caracas. Do you know something? Hours ago I was hungry. I'll make bacon and eggs."

"I don't want bacon and eggs."

She giggled. "In the bedroom the ceiling's white stars in a blue sky. You look up at it."

"Or you do."

In the bedroom she took off his jacket, felt inside it for the wallet, spread the money on the bed and started to kiss it. "Doesn't it make you feel good?"

He pushed her back. "Come on."

"I'm keeping these glasses on."

"It's the first time I've made love to a girl in dark glasses."

Five minutes later they heard voices in the sitting-room. She had scrambled off the bed, but they were both still naked when the door opened. Carlos Cotton stood in the doorway. He was wearing a dark blue pin stripe suit and a sober tie. He stood staring at them. Then he said "Get dressed," and closed the door.

There were two other men with Cotton in the living-room when they entered it, and Tony had seen them both before. One was the bruiser named Lefty. The other was the small dark man who had stubbed out a cigarette on his hand. Cotton had a glass in his hand.

"I won't ask you to have a drink, I see you've helped yourselves." He spoke to Fiona. "It's a fine night and I decided to drive back. Just as well. Take off those glasses."

She took them off. Her bruised eye was half-closed. The other eye was wild, frightened.

"I like to see who I'm talking to." He turned to Tony, his manner calm, his voice quiet. "You've given me a lot of trouble." Tony did not know what to say. "And now you've had one on me, friend. You'd better go."

Cotton was letting him go. He could hardly believe it. He moved towards the door and then turned. "Fiona."

"You get out. I shall be all right." Her good eye rolled despairingly at him. He thought, once I get out I can call the police. Cotton spoke again in his mock-cultured voice.

"Lefty and Milky will see you safely away. We call him Milky because he drinks a lot of milk. That's sensible, isn't it?"

He had begun to say that it was when the two men closed on him. Lefty quickly jerked his arm up behind his back so that he cried out with pain, but he managed to turn.

"Fiona, I'm not going to leave you." He felt the absurdity of the words as they were uttered.

"Don't be a bloody fool." She was staring at Cotton, she did not even look at him.

Lefty gave him a push. They were outside the flat and in the lift before the hold on his arm was relaxed. "Now we can be nice and friendly," the big man said in his hoarse whisper.

In the flat Fiona said, "Carlos. Please."

"Get packed." She stared at him. "Nothing's going to happen to you. Just get packed and go. I thought you had class. I don't like tramps."

"You don't like tramps." She laughed. "That's good. You're a tramp yourself. Do you think you fool anybody with the way you talk?"

"Get out before I change my mind."

He followed her into the bedroom and stood watching. When she had finished she turned with her hand to her mouth. "Carlos, what are they going to do to him?"

"Nothing. He wasn't here. Right?"

"He wasn't here," she repeated. Her teeth were chattering. When she got outside she began to cry.

FOUR

At the entrance to the apartment block Tony pointed towards Shepherd Market. "I'm going that way."

"Why, so are we," Lefty said. "Just nice for a stroll, isn't it, Milky?"

"That's right." Milky had a clear tenor voice.

There are street lights, Tony thought, it's as bright as day, they can't do anything to me here.

His arm was suddenly jerked behind his back again and now they had turned into a narrow passage between houses, big black walls reared up on either side. They're going to hurt me, he thought unbelievingly, and he put his hand into his jacket to get out the money, to tell them that he would pay them if they left him alone. He thought of that scene in the lavatories with Bradbury, of white delicate Jenny, and of the other dark alley from which he had escaped. I shall escape from this too, he thought, it's my lucky night. But the gesture he made towards his wallet had been wrongly interpreted. The karate chop across his neck was decisive. His run of luck had ended.

Milky put on a pair of gloves. He took the money from the wallet, an unexpected bonus, but left everything else. Later they gave the money to Carlos and it was split three ways. A couple of weeks afterwards Carlos met a girl named Eleonora Mainwaring, and she moved in with him. She was the daughter of a baronet and, as he said frequently, had genuine class.

It was early morning before a passer-by noticed the body. The dead man's identity was quickly established, and so was the fact that he had won a great deal of money in a gambling club. He was obviously the victim of a gang who had followed him around. The police thought it likely that the girl with him, who never came forward, was a finger for the gang but they were never able to prove this. The other contents of Jones's wallet were littered round the body. It had rained during the night and everything was sodden. A wet piece of paper which had fluttered away to the other side of the passage remained unnoticed. In due course a road sweeper picked it up, found it illegible, and pushed it down a drain. It was the air reservation for Caracas.